THE FU

TURNBACK
Time

Annette G. Anders

Copyright TURN BACK TIME © 2020 by Annette G. Anders.

Email: Author@AnnetteGAnders.com

First Edition

ISBN: 978-1-7350261-1-4 (E-book)
ISBN: 978-1-7350261-0-7 (Paperback)

To those I love.
Forever in my heart.

When I had to leave you,
I believed
We would meet again.

When I saw time passing by,
I felt the loss of you.

When I could spend the day without you,
I was afraid of meeting you again.

(author unknown)

CHAPTER 1

David—July 2015

He heard her before he saw her.

Hoping to avoid the oppressive midday heat, David walked under the shelter of old trees in Independence National Historic Park, sipping his iced tea—and winced.

Her off-key singing insulted his ears, although he knew not everyone was gifted with an angelic voice. Yet he had tremendous respect for people who didn't let this little misfortune keep them from doing something they enjoyed.

At the next missed note, he winced again and checked out his surroundings, oblivious to the condensation from his cold drink running down his fingers.

A slender brunette in a red sundress sat on one of the benches under a canopy of lush green trees. Her upper body swayed rhythmically.

Are those wretched sounds coming from her?

She dug through her oversized purse—what women carried around in their bags would forever remain a mystery to him—and pulled out a book, still crooning about ghosts in the neighborhood.

He knew because of firsthand experience how important privacy and personal space were—but couldn't stop himself.

His vocal cords responded to the challenge, his feet developed a mind of their own, and he approached her bench, singing along much more harmoniously. He leaned closer to her and intoned just one word.

"Ghostbusters."

She dropped the book and whipped off her enormous sunglasses. The biggest brown eyes he'd ever seen glared at him. "You... You scared me!"

He guessed her to be around his sister's age, which made her a few years younger than his own thirty-two. Her high cheekbones were free of makeup, and he admired her natural look.

David swallowed several times. His voice deserted him. Man, she was beautiful in her fury.

"Sorry, I didn't mean to startle you." He picked up the book and held it out to her.

"Then why did you do it?" She snatched back the book and dusted it off.

Think, Danvers, and fast. "Would you believe me if I said it was an impulse?" *Not great, but honesty is always a good start.*

She still stared at him as if he had two heads or his nose was crooked. He was tempted to touch his face just to make sure everything was in its proper place.

"Why don't you follow your impulse somewhere else?" Her fingers fluttered between them.

Whoa, did she just dismiss him with a flick of her hand? Well, he couldn't blame her. But he enjoyed the situation too much to just walk away.

"Mind if I sit down?" he asked.

Without waiting for her reply, he moved her Frappuccino and settled on the bench, pretending to take in the surrounding of the park. The golden weathervane on top of Carpenter's Hall swayed in a light breeze, and he looked around for the heirloom roses with their intoxicating smell, but his eyes kept circling back to her.

"I'm curious; why did you sing about ghosts on this beautiful day? Halloween is more than three months away."

She stuck her sunglasses on top of her head and pointed to her right. He looked where she pointed, across the lawn, and saw a black-caped young woman with white face paint and a shaved head swinging an old-fashioned lantern and talking to a group of people.

"I don't know why I'm explaining myself to you, but I overheard the woman advertising ghost tours," she said.

He turned his attention back to her. She seemed a little calmer. At least she was no longer clutching the poor book as if she wanted to smack him over the head with it. *Which you would have deserved, Danvers.*

"What are you reading?"

"Oh." She showed him the cover. "The book is called *Miracle at Philadelphia.*"

"Never heard of it. What is it about?"

"It's an account of the constitutional convention in the summer of 1787."

"Sounds like heavy reading." David mostly listened to audiobooks, and he preferred legal thrillers or mysteries, but he wasn't about to admit it.

"True, but it gives me a different perspective about time and place. To me, it's a way to take me back in time, to let me experience history. By reading this, I'm right there with these brilliant men, in a summer as hot as ours this year. And when I'm walking through our beautiful city, I imagine them next to me, arguing or tossing ideas around." She wiped a bead of sweat off her forehead before slurping her iced coffee. "I just think books are a wonderful way to connect the past and the present."

She sounded more relaxed when she talked about books, and David wanted to hear more of her warm voice and watch her eyes light up when she got excited. He was intrigued, and wanted to get to know her.

4

"Can I buy you lunch?" he blurted out without thinking.

Are you serious, Danvers? What's wrong with you? He mentally slapped his forehead. First, he scared the living daylights out of her, and now he was asking her to have lunch?

"To make up for startling you earlier," he hastened to add.

He could almost see the wheels turning in her pretty head while she considered his invitation. She'd be a lousy poker player—but a cute one—and he was disappointed when she didn't agree right away. *Who do you think you are, man?*

But the million-dollar question was... Had he lost his damn mind? He hadn't asked a woman out in years, and he alone knew the reason why.

So why her?

CHAPTER 2

Stella—July 2015

Stella gave her book another quick shake before slipping it in her purse, then hoisted her bag on her shoulder. "By the way, I'm Stella."

"I'm David. Nice to meet you, Stella." He bowed and tipped an invisible hat.

Stella bit the inside of her cheek to suppress a grin. *Is this guy for real?*

They fell in step and walked past Carpenter's Hall, crossed Chestnut Street, and entered a sunny courtyard planted with trees and perennials.

He pointed to a low building with a long glass front. "Ah, now I know where we are. Last time I came in from the other end of the yard. I have to come back later to buy a birthday gift for my sister."

She didn't even think before she offered, "We can go in now, since we're here."

"Are you sure?"

"Yup." Inside the little gift shop, she said, "I'll check out the postcards. Take your time." She skimmed through a few cards with quotes until she read, "The person who deserves most pity is a lonesome one on a rainy day who doesn't know how to read." Stella was tempted to buy it and use as a bookmark, but decided against it.

Being a library curator, she agreed one hundred percent with the popular Ben Franklin saying. How empty would the world be without books?

Letting David poke around by himself gave her the perfect opportunity to take a closer look at him.

He was a little taller than her brother, maybe 6'4". His black, curly hair was closely cropped, and the stubble of a five o'clock shadow covered his chin, even though it was only noon. There was something familiar about him, but she knew they'd never met. *Must be one of those 'I've seen you before' faces.*

His black polo shirt showed well-toned arms and hinted at an athletic body, and the way his jeans hugged his hips... *Stop ogling, Stella!*

"Stella," he beckoned her over to a display of glass vases and matching bowls. "Do you think I should get the blue or the green?"

"Without knowing anything about your sister, it's difficult for me to choose. What's her taste in tableware?"

David looked sheepish. "I'm a guy and don't pay attention. As long as a glass is clean, I'm good." *Luca would've said the same*, Stella thought of her brother.

"What's her furniture like?"

He scratched his chin, then said, "Lots of black and white."

"Then I'd go with clear glass. Your sister can dress it up with colorful flowers and fresh fruit or candy in the bowl."

"Great! Give me a few more minutes to pay and get it wrapped."

She walked back to the postcards but glanced to him. It was hard to believe that she'd accepted a total stranger's invitation to lunch. Yes, he startled her in the park. But his voice was so melodious, and as soon as her heart rate came down, she wanted to hear more of it. And the twinkle in his dark brown eyes told her he was only teasing her.

Her best friend, Naomi, often accused her of being too trusting, but Stella disagreed. She believed in the good in people and listened to her gut feeling.

Another thing Naomi often told her was to take off her thinking cap and to have a little fun. Which is exactly what she just did!

Hours later, Stella stood dithering in front of her closet. Naomi bought them tickets to the touring Broadway production of *The Phantom of The Opera* as a birthday gift, and Stella couldn't decide what to wear. Images of her handsome lunch companion kept popping up in her head—as they had all afternoon, together with snippets of their conversation.

He had asked lots questions about her, and she told him about growing up in Philadelphia, then about living in Boston while attending college and grad school, and about moving back only a few months ago for her dream job as curator at the Library Company of Philadelphia. She was almost embarrassed at how much she rattled on about working at America's first successful lending library and oldest cultural institution.

What did she find out about him? He said he was from Chicago and traveled a lot for work. But whenever she asked for more details, he managed to reroute the conversation back to her.

She narrowed down her dress choices to three, then decided on her new emerald green maxi-dress. At the last minute, she added a lightweight sweater in case the air-conditioning was set to arctic temperatures.

After getting dressed, she went to the kitchen and munched on a few crackers with cheese, since she and Naomi were going out to eat later.

While she ate, her thoughts circled back to David again. Stella was surprised how at ease she was with him, as if they'd known each other for a long time. To any passerby, they might have looked like old friends catching up. But it didn't explain why some people stopped and stared. A few even took photos, which she thought was very rude, but he didn't seem bothered. Sometimes he even smiled at them, but mostly he focused on her.

When they parted ways, he said, "Thank you for a wonderful time, Stella."

There was no hugging, no cheek kissing, no handshaking. A smile, a nod, and a wave was all.

Washing down the last crumbs of a cracker with a sip of water, she regretted one thing. She should've mustered the courage to ask for his phone number. She had felt a connection she couldn't describe.

But it was too late; she'd never see him again.

CHAPTER 3

STELLA—JULY 2015

S tella and Naomi still sat in their seats at the Kimmel Center. The performance was over, the curtains remained closed, and the audience was leaving the theater. All lights in the auditorium were lit at their brightest, a stark contrast to the darkened room of a few minutes ago.

Back to reality...

"Do you need a tissue?" Naomi asked and handed her a small package.

"N-no...Yes... I'm such a mess. Here I am *again*, feeling sorry for the Phantom. He loves Christine so much, but he just...let her...walk away." Stella hiccupped. Sometimes it was embarrassing, how easily she cried.

"I'll always be Team Phantom, never Team Raoul." She dabbed her eyes, then blew her nose in rather unladylike fashion.

"I know. And you'd rewrite half the book if you could." Naomi hugged Stella. "Come on, let's go to Betty's. I'm starving! Ooh, I can almost taste my first sip of a River-horse."

"I don't know how you can drink that stuff." She shuddered at the thought of draft beer and tucked the playbill inside her purse. "But I'm sure they have a glass of pinot noir with my name on it! And wait until I tell you what happened to me today."

"Let me guess. You went on another one of your creepy tours. Aren't you getting tired of listening to high school kids making up stories about weird sightings?" Naomi asked as they headed up the aisle and out of the building.

"I told you, I haven't gone on even one ghost tour yet. Maybe in October. And maybe I'll make you come with me."

"I don't think so. Then what *did* you do for fun?"

"I'm not telling... You have to wait until we're at the restaurant." She knew Naomi wasn't good at waiting and would try to wheedle it out of her on the way. Making her wait was part of the fun.

Once out of the theater, they turned left, and spotted a crowd gathered at the side exit, holding up pieces of paper or snapping photos.

"Look, some actors are giving autographs. I want one." Naomi hauled on her arm. "Come on, hurry, or they're gone!"

"I thought you were hungry and thirsty," Stella said. Wasn't it just typical of her friend to change plans on a whim? "I don't need an autograph. I want a glass of wine and something to eat!"

"Don't be such a pooper and stop whining. Come on, where's your precious playbill? Remember..." Naomi almost sang it, "...it's the *Phantom!*"

Deciding it was easier to give in than to argue, Stella groped in her purse. She'd just hold paper and pen in front of whichever actor was closest to her.

"Stella?"

The voice! She looked up—into a familiar pair of eyes.

"What are you...?" she stammered. Someone shoved a piece of paper into David's hand, which he signed and returned with a half-smile.

"Why...who...?" She still couldn't get a coherent sentence out.

David covered the front of his face, leaving only his left eye and cheekbone visible and said in a dramatic voice, "I go by many names. Some call me...Erik."

A woman squeezed past her and leaned closer to him. "Can you do it again so my friend can take a photo?" He repeated the gesture.

Now I know why he wasn't too bothered when people snapped his photo at lunch. How could she not have made the connection? *Maybe because the mask covers most of his face in all the billboards?*

Somewhere in the crowd, another woman announced for all to hear, "I'm so glad they found someone who gives the role the classical elements it deserves. Not just some actor who took a few voice lessons."

Stella recalled an interview in which the composer said he had a non-operatic voice in mind for the phantom when he wrote the musical. But she had appreciated David's rich, baritone voice and dynamic star performance tonight. With a voice like his, he should be singing on the biggest stages in the world.

He still stood close to her, giving autographs and posing for photos, then waved to the crowd and said, "Sorry, we're done for tonight. Thank you all for coming."

The theatergoers scattered in all directions, many humming tunes from the musical.

"Look, I've got two autographs," Naomi said in a peppy voice and elbowed Stella. "Are you ready to go?"

"Wait a second, Nam," she turned to David, "Do you... umm...want to join us for drinks and something to eat?"

Goose bumps battled with the heat spreading through her belly when he rested his hand on her lower back and said close to her ear, "How could I say no to you?"

CHAPTER 4

⇌∘⟨⟩∘⇌

Stella—July 2018

Stella groped for the tissue box on the side table.

Empty, of course.

"Why is it always empty when you need one?" she muttered and wiped away the tears rolling down her cheeks with her hand. She leaned back in the soft leather chair and read the last sentences of her cherished book. The ending always got to her.

And, now, what do they mean to do with that skeleton? Surely they will not bury it in the common grave!... I say that the place of the skeleton of the Opera ghost is in the archives of the National Academy of Music. It is no ordinary skeleton.

Following her tradition, she wrote the current date on the back of the final page, where it joined entries from previous years. July 2015, July 2016, July 2017.

She held the book close to her heart and remembered David's voice when he gave it to her, "When you read this book, it's like turning back time to when we met. Remember our dreams and let them guide us into our future."

She had believed in their dreams and in their future.

Until he blindsided her last year with his letter.

After reading it countless times, shocked and hurt beyond words, she had shoved it in the book. The two belonged together, since they marked their beginning and their end.

Now, with shaking hands, she unfolded the single sheet of paper again and read a few sentences. For the last time—as she had already promised herself so many times.

July 2017

I've been in Budapest for a few weeks now...makes me think about us...We've been together for two years now...I don't have the right to ask you to wait for me any longer...

And the one when he shoved her off the cliff—and out of his life.

I have to let you go.

She didn't need to read more; she had the letter memorized. Stella replaced it in its envelope, then slid it back in the book.

What's wrong with me? Why do I do this to myself? She only re-opened old wounds which were barely starting to heal. She had lost count of how many times her family and friends encouraged her to move on. With little to no success. David still held her heart hostage.

What would it take to free herself from his hold on her heart and soul?

How much longer would she torture herself with what-ifs and whys? And when would she accept that not every story had a happy ending?

There was only one thing she regretted. She should've demanded an explanation.

Stella caressed the cover with her fingertips. The way she used to caress his body...

She jumped out of the chair. *Enough!* It was time to move forward. There had to be a way for her to be happy without David.

Determined to start a new phase of her life, her first step should be letting go of the book. Maybe the smart thing would be to throw it away. Or ritually burn it in the fireplace.

No. Burning it would amount to sacrilege. Books had always been an important part of her life. Even as a little girl, she had cherished the feeling of them and loved the sound of flipping through the pages.

Her mother used to take her to the library every week, and Stella never tired of the musty smell of hundreds of books. While her brother, Luca, usually asked for a new baseball bat or a fancier skateboard, her birthday and Christmas wish lists were for new books. While her friends were trying on clothes or costume jewelry at tag sales, she was hunting for book treasures.

Old books tell more than one story.

She liked to imagine the previous owner's life, and whether the book had played a special role in it. Did other children sit in a corner of their closet as she did, hoping to go on adventures with Pippi Longstocking or fight the evil White Witch?

Stella paced up and down the living room.

"What am I going to do with you if I can't throw you out?" she said, her nose still stuffy thanks to her cryfest, and tapped her fingers on the dark red cover. Yes!

Taking two steps at a time, she ran to the bedrooms on the second floor. Yanking open the closet doors in the smaller of the two rooms, she reached for the plastic bin hiding in the corner and pulled it out.

Before she could change her mind, she opened the lid, put the book at the bottom, rearranged the rest of the items on top, and replaced the lid with a resolute *click*.

There. It could rest with everything else she didn't have the heart to part with—yet. Maybe someday everything would be consigned to a ceremonial fire.

Her eyes fell on the silver and gold bracelet on her left wrist, the tiny crystals sparkling in the star charms. Stella reached for the clasp, then dropped her hand.

No, I'm not parting with you as well. One step at a time.

The ticking of the wall clock in the hall reminded her to check the time. *Oops!*

Today was Storytime-with-Stella at the Family Center, where she volunteered every Wednesday afternoon. The children would be the perfect distraction after her trip down memory lane and pity party.

After splashing water on her blotchy face in the bathroom, she hurried down the stairs and picked up the book she planned to read to the four- and five-year-old kids. She couldn't wait to see their reaction to the book about a pigeon who wants a puppy.

Stella silenced her cell phone and tossed it in her purse. The world wouldn't come to an end if she couldn't be reached for a few hours.

She grabbed her keys and was on her way to the Family Center.

The next two hours went by in a blur. While she read to the kids and afterward kept them busy with coloring a picture or doing a simple craft project, the exhausted-looking moms were enjoying free coffee or tea, getting advice from the counselors if needed, or sometimes just putting their feet up for a moment.

As expected, most of the children shared their hopes for a puppy or a new toy in not-so-hushed voices while they doodled inside and outside the lines with earnest expressions.

Manny, a serious five-year-old, showed her his drawing and said, "Look, Miss Stella, I remembered the book you read last week. About the boy with a monster under his bed."

She saw he had not only colored the pigeon and drawn a puppy, he also added a pair of eyes in a corner of the page. She pointed to them. "You must've liked the book if you're still thinking about it. Do you think he only imagined the monster?"

"Maybe... I don't know." He thought for a moment, wrinkled his forehead, and puffed out his chest. "I'm not afraid of monsters and ghosts, Miss Stella. They aren't real. Nobody believes in them!" He paused and scrunched his face again. "But it would be fun to have one to play with when I'm supposed to sleep. That's why I added the eyes."

Moments like this reminded her why she enjoyed this age group so much. The way they still got lost in the imaginary world of books warmed her heart.

On her way home, she enjoyed the summer afternoon while she walked past the old cemetery of St. Peter's Episcopal Church.

She paused a moment to gaze at the Osage orange trees in the churchyard. They were said to have grown here since 1804, after Lewis and Clark sent the first seeds to Thomas Jefferson. The original trees were long gone, but a lot of time and effort went into taking saplings from the current trees and growing new ones. The trees were so enormous their roots lifted nearby gravestones and markers.

Stella's mind went back to her mini ritual of burying her book. Would it ever see the light again? She shook her head. It was time to let the ghosts of the past go, to shove them under the bed, like Manny's imaginary monster friend.

Turning the corner of her street, she saw Naomi sitting on the stone steps in front of her home, picking at the abundant weeds growing in the flowerpots on both sides of the stairs.

"What brings you here in the middle of the afternoon?" she called out when she was closer.

"Let me in and I'll tell you! And hello to you, too." Naomi pushed to her feet and picked up a small gift bag. She dangled it in front of Stella's face. "I have a sur-priiiise for you."

Stella unlocked the front door and let Naomi step inside.

Even after living here for three years, she often marveled at the beautiful townhouse. Luca and his best friend, Revan, took advantage of the low real estate prices right after the Great Recession and bought two adjacent fixer-uppers after they graduated from college. They removed most of the first-floor walls between the two homes and converted the space into an airy, open living area with dark gray tile floors and white walls with built-in bookshelves. Framed black-and-white prints of photos taken by Revan on his many travels as a documentary photographer adorned the walls.

When Stella announced her intention to leave Boston and move back home with a brand-new PhD in Library and Information Science, Luca suggested she stay with them until she made her own living arrangements. Which suited her, because living with her parents again at twenty-seven didn't hold much appeal. Shortly after she moved in, Luca accepted a position at a news agency in New York and relocated, and she took over his two bedrooms. She paid him minimal rent and enjoyed living in a house she wouldn't be able to afford otherwise.

She walked to the gray and white modern kitchen and held up a paper box. "I must've sensed you were coming, because I stopped at the deli on my way home. Would you like coffee with your raspberry turnovers?" Knowing the answer, she stuck a pod into the coffee machine and arranged the treats on a platter.

Naomi sat on one of the barstools at the long glass and steel kitchen island and reached for one of the freshly baked triangles sprinkled with coarse sugar. "Ooh, they're still a little warm. Yummy."

After taking her first bite, she narrowed her eyes and asked, "Why don't you answer your cell phone? Where is it?"

"Oh, darn it! I silenced it before I went to Storytime and forgot to turn it back on." Stella got it out of her purse. Yup, three missed calls, all from Naomi.

The decadent aroma of fresh coffee wafted in the air, and Stella set the first cup in front of her best friend before making her own.

"What's so important that you left work and waited here for me? You know I'm at the Family Center on Wednesdays. You could've called me there."

"And risk the wrath of Mighty Anna? She's the perfect office manager for that place. I mean, she's nice, but she's getting bossy when it comes to the kids and her schedules. Or maybe she just doesn't like me." Naomi waved the thought away like a pesky fly and took a deep breath. "Anyhow, wanna know my surprise?"

"Sure, I can see you're almost bursting."

"You and I are going to France, missy," Naomi swished her finger back and forth between them, then finished her raspberry turnover.

CHAPTER 5

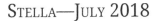

STELLA—JULY 2018

"We're doing what?" Stella dropped the spoon she was using to stir her coffee, and it clattered to the tile floor and slid under the fridge.

"As you know, Mom and I were supposed to go on a business trip to France," Naomi started.

"How could I forget?" Stella parodied Naomi. "Going on a four-day trip to Normandy, Brittany, and a few of the Loire Valley castles. Meals complete with delicious French wines included. Pretty much all paid for by the trip operator." She switched back to her own voice. "Maybe you mentioned it once or twice. It sounds like a wonderful trip. I wish I could go."

"I just told you! You're coming with me," Naomi said with a smirk. She opened the gift bag and handed Stella a travel guide for France. "I happen to know you have the next two weeks off with no plans." Stella didn't correct her. She had planned to visit Luca for a few days.

"I hope your passport is valid."

"It is, but..."

"Here's the thing. Well, it's two things. Gram fell yesterday and sprained her ankle badly. Mom doesn't feel comfortable leaving her alone for a week, especially because Aunt Mary is in New York visiting Jo. So she thought you might wanna take her place and go with me." Naomi took another turnover and beamed at her.

Stella shook her head and closed her eyes for a moment. An unexpected trip to France was hard to top! What a wonderful surprise after her earlier emotional roller-coaster ride.

Maybe it was the result of her Bury-the-Book-in-the-Bin ceremony. Had she freed a genie? If she got one free wish, what would it be? Easy—she'd want to see David one more time.

She snorted. Yeah, fat chance.

"What's so funny?" Naomi asked and licked sugar off her fingers.

"Ugh, I had a crappy day earlier."

"Which brings me to the second reason why I came this afternoon. I'd be a lousy friend if I didn't cheer you up on the blackest day of your year." Naomi squeezed her hand, then said, "So, do you have to clear our trip with anybody? The Mighty Anna, maybe?"

"No, I know Anna will cover for me, and Luca won't mind if I cancel our plans. He's done it to me a few times. What do we need to do next?" She rubbed her hands together. Never in a million years would she have dreamed of something like this happening. She was so lucky to have Naomi as her best friend.

"Our plane leaves Friday evening, so we'll have to hustle to put your travel information into the system. I'll call the airline as soon as I'm back at the office and transfer Mom's ticket into your name. I contacted them already and explained the circumstances."

"Sounds great. Let me know what I owe you."

"If there's a fee, Mom covers it, since she's the one who's dropping out. She has insurances for everything. Anyway, we'll have two days in Paris on our own, and meet with the group on Monday morning. The days in Paris aren't included in the tour. We need to pay for meals and sightseeing, but Mom covered the hotel."

"That's very generous of your mom. I'll have to think of a way to thank her."

"Oh, shush, she wouldn't hear of it. She wants us to have a good time."

For the next half hour, they chatted about what kind of clothes to pack and googled the weather forecast. Should they bring euros, or exchange money in France? Would they have the opportunity to dress up in the evenings?

After Naomi left, Stella ran upstairs and pulled out her suitcase. A week-long vacation was exactly what she needed. Her memories wouldn't be able to follow her there.

CHAPTER 6

─◦◦⟋⟍◦◦─

STELLA—JULY 2018

"Who comes up with those weird names for nail polish?" Naomi turned a small bottle of indeterminable color upside down and squinted. "It's called 'After Dark.' Is this green, black, brown, or purple? It should be called 'Mudslide in a Bottle.'"

"Have them put it on one nail and decide if you like it." Stella picked up a bottle of dark pink nail polish. "This is pretty...it looks like cherry blossoms. 'Shower with Flowers.' The name's kinda cute."

The owner of the nail salon waved them over and they settled into the massive massage chairs, sliding their feet into the heavenly-smelling warm water.

Naomi sighed. "This is one of my favorite moments! And the foot massage."

"I guess I like everything about pedis. Okay, are you ready to party?" Stella held up two cold mini bottles of champagne, then filled the two glasses she had stashed in an insulated lunch bag. "To friendship, to fun, to new journeys! To us!"

"To us! Speaking of journeys," Naomi said after taking a sip, "We're all set for our flight. The plane departs at 9:15, and we need to be there three hours earlier."

"Perfect. What do I owe you?" Stella relished the sensation of tiny bubbles exploding on her tongue and watched the spectacle as they floated around in her glass.

Naomi waved the comment away. "I told you the trip is all covered. In Paris, we can take turns paying for meals and sightseeing, or we'll square up afterward. Mom said she'd drive us to the airport, and we'll pick you up at 5:30."

"I'll be ready. Since I'm packing my suitcase tonight, I only have to water my plants and take the garbage out. I think Rev is coming home on Sunday or Monday, and I want to stock the fridge with some prepacked cheese and cold cuts for him. But knowing him, he'll just go to the deli to grab something to eat."

She noticed Naomi's eyes lighting up at the mention of Revan's name. She knew her friend had a huge crush on him for many years, but Rev either didn't notice or deliberately ignored it. Stella wished there was something she could do.

The thought almost made her burst out laughing. What a ludicrous idea. She hadn't fought for her own relationship with David last year, so playing Cupid in her friend's love life would only end in disaster.

"Do we have to change planes somewhere? What time will we be in Paris?" She tried to redirect her thoughts to their trip.

"No, it's a nonstop flight. We'll arrive at Charles de Gaulle airport at 10:30 on Saturday morning. I notified the hotel about checking in early, and I hope they'll have our room ready. And then," Naomi took another sip, "we'll explore Paris! *Paris nous voilà!*"

"Paris what? My high school French is very rusty. You'll have to translate for me, but don't show off all the time, okay?" She chuckled.

"Don't you worry. You don't need to say a word! Just look all innocent and smile like an angel, and all the Frenchmen will melt at your feet."

"Stop it." Stella swatted Naomi's arm. But she was only half joking—she did wish Naomi would leave the topic alone.

On her way home the next day, Stella picked up an arrangement of peonies and roses for Naomi's mom as a thank-you for letting her go on the trip and for driving them to the airport.

With just a few minutes to spare before she would be picked up, she went through her checklist. Windows and doors locked, plants watered, coffee machine unplugged, suitcase and carry-on by the door, book and iPhone charger in purse, passport—check, check, check.

She was ready for a change of scenery!

By 7 pm, they sat in comfortable club chairs in the business class lounge, snacking on appetizers from the complimentary buffet and sipping champagne.

Stella noticed several men looking at Naomi, who seemed oblivious to their stares. Being 5'9" and having a toned body, Naomi could pass for a model right out of *Women's Health* magazine. Her looks often seemed to invite men to assume she was arm candy, but nothing could be farther from the truth, and she knew it hurt Naomi when men treated her like a brainless dummy with great boobs. It was no surprise when she dropped the jerks like hot potatoes after a few dates.

"Yoo-hoo…Earth to Stella… Didn't your mom teach you it's rude to stare at other people? Even if it's just me?"

Stella grimaced. "I'm sorry, Nam. I guess I spaced out thinking how comfortable you look in this environment. And then I thought about how different you and I are in some respects, and how we complement each other in others. Like Yin and Yang."

"Ouch, you're hurting my brain... Please don't go all Tao on me," Naomi said and cupped her right hand around her ear. "Wait...what? I think Confucius is telling me I need another drink. How about you?"

"Don't play dumb. I know you know Taoism and Confucianism aren't the same. But whoever whispered in your ear was right! You go get us a refill, and I'll watch our bags."

When Naomi came back with two more flutes of champagne and another plate of finger food to share, she said in a mock-serious voice, "Okay, spill it. Where is this Yin/Yang shit coming from?"

When Stella didn't answer, Naomi waved a finger in front of her eyes. Left, right, left, right. It was an annoying newer habit. "Are you overthinking things again? Are you clinging to the past again? Didn't I tell you to let go and have fun?"

"I can't change who I am. And take your finger out of my face. I'll always be more serious than you are, but it doesn't mean I can't have fun. Fun for me is reading a great book or discussing something I discovered in the archives at work."

"Oh, boy... The last book I read front to back was in college. Why spend weeks with a book when the story can be told in a two-hour movie? And if I don't like the movie, I'll press the stop button." Naomi pushed an imagined button in front of her.

"Don't pretend to be so shallow. I know you're not. It's fine with me if you prefer to watch movies and would rather read travel magazines and archaeology reports in *The New Yorker* or *National Geographic*." She leaned closer. "I also know you're fine-combing through those magazines trying to find Rev's name. It's all about motivation. And, like all of us, you're afraid to get your feelings hurt."

"Was your last bedside reading a book about analyzing your friends? It sounds to me as if you really need a break. And of course, for someone to whisk you far away from memories of the Troubadour." Naomi even had the nerve to hold her hand in front of her face exactly the way David did three years ago.

Stella laughed. "You're terrible. I wish I could find out what he thinks of your nickname for him."

CHAPTER 7

STELLA—JULY 2018

"I'm sorry, Miss Winters, but your room is not ready yet. The guests before you couldn't vacate the room at checkout time." Pierre, the twenty-something front desk employee, looked from Naomi to Stella and back again.

"May I offer you something to drink in our courtyard while you wait? Your luggage will be safe in the storage room and will be taken to your room as soon as house-keeping has finished cleaning." He printed two vouchers and handed them to Naomi with an apologetic smile.

"Please let us know when they're done," Naomi muttered.

Stella could see Naomi wasn't happy, but it wasn't the man's fault, so she said, "Thanks for helping us, Pierre."

"Are you coming, Stella?" Naomi was already halfway to tall glass doors opposite the check-in desk.

Outside, Stella counted six small groupings of bistro tables under huge yellow umbrellas, and three outdoor sectionals with colorful cushions tossed into the corners. There were no other guests, and she was surprised how quiet it was. The only sounds were of a small backyard water fountain and the muffled traffic on the other side of the tall buildings.

"Look at those palm trees!" She couldn't believe it. "In Paris? I think I'll have breakfast, lunch, and dinner here."

As soon as they plopped down in one of the sectionals, a waiter came to take their order.

"Just a coffee, please," Stella said.

"Two cafés crème, please," Naomi clarified. After the waiter left, she explained, "You have to ask for café crème or café Americano, otherwise you'll get an espresso in a cup no larger than a thimble, but so strong you won't sleep for the next eight days."

When Pierre informed them their room was ready twenty minutes later, Naomi jumped up, but Stella was reluctant to leave. It was just too peaceful, and she was tired. She didn't get much sleep on the plane. Between reading, the anticipation of their trip, and the ever-present humming of the airplane, she barely managed a couple of hours of shut-eye.

Their room was on the top floor. A low wall separating two double beds almost gave it the illusion of two bedrooms.

There was also a sitting area with two deep chairs, a coffee table, and a small but luxurious bathroom.

She opened a glass door and saw the narrowest balcony she had ever seen, no more than two feet wide, but easily eight feet long. Two chairs and a rickety table were squeezed onto it.

"I changed my mind," Stella said. "You'll find me on this balcony in the mornings with coffee and a croissant, and in the courtyard the rest of the day, until it's time to have a glass of wine on our balcony in the evening. Over the rooftops of Paris, just like in a movie."

"Not happening. We're here to see something, not to hide from the world. Let's take turns in the bathroom, freshen up, and let the fun begin."

"I read in *The New York Times* not long ago that part of the joy of exploring Paris is getting lost and wandering about. I'm not so sure I agree," Stella unzipped her suitcase and opted for shorts, a sleeveless blouse, and slip-on canvas shoes for their afternoon excursion.

"Where's your adventurous spirit? But I think we're going to be fine. You can't take the girl scout out of this lady." Naomi thumbed her own chest.

"Which is exactly what I'm afraid of. I remember you got lost more than once on hikes and field trips in school!"

Naomi pulled up a map on her phone, then read the street signs again. "Ah, this way," she said, nodding to the right. It hadn't taken them long to get lost in the spiderweb of Montmartre's cobblestone streets.

"I can't imagine anybody walking through this quirky arrondissement and not falling in love with it," Stella gushed as she peeked into the window of one of the many charming stores lining the streets.

L'Objet Qui Parle, The Talking Object. *What an interesting name.*

"Look at the mish-mash this store's selling," she called to Naomi. "I wanna go in and browse."

"If we continue at this rate, we'll never make it to the top of the hill." Naomi joined her at the storefront. "I'm hungry. Want to check out this *patisserie*?" Naomi pointed to a small café at the corner of the street. It wasn't very wide, with barely enough space on both sides of the door to put up signs to advertise the daily specials, and no more than twenty feet long. Three tiny sets of chairs and tables were squeezed hazardously on the sidewalk, which was just wide enough for one adult to walk on it. She couldn't imagine anyone with long legs, like David, sitting there and being comfortable.

"Now you mention it, I am hungry. And I want to buy a bottle of water. It's hotter than I expected."

After refueling their energy levels with *ratatouille* on toasted sourdough bread with basil and garlic, they continued their uphill climb. Five minutes later they rounded a corner, and Stella gasped.

"This is un...be...lie...va...ble!" She reached for Naomi's arm and squeezed it hard.

Basking in bright sunlight, the Sacré-Cœur Basilica rose into the azure sky. Built of white stone, the majestic landmark had watched over Paris from the highest point in the city since 1891, and now greeted them in all her perfection.

Stella felt tears pooling in her eyes and didn't even try to stop them from trickling down her face, knowing it would be futile. She sat down on one of the many benches.

I wish David could see this with me. He always hoped we could visit Paris together.

But David would never see this with her; he made it crystal clear. She shook off the unwelcome thought.

After taking pictures of the church, the views, and each other, they continued strolling through the idyllic streets, absorbing the flair and the symphony of languages. It was impossible to count them. *This is what a meeting at the United Nations must sound like.*

"Do you know what *Montmartre* means?" Naomi interrupted her musings and peeked through iron gates into a private backyard. A small dog jumped up and down, barking at the prying intruder.

"No."

"Mount of Martyrs."

"Kind of gloomy. Do you know why?"

"It has something to do with pilgrimages." Naomi didn't elaborate further.

The charming hamlet, a village perched atop the vast city, was a giant beehive of activity. They stopped to watch artists painting amazingly skillful portraits of tourists, sellers offering fresh fruits and mouthwatering juice, and there were little shops everywhere, as well as a small working vineyard on the slopes of Butte Montmartre.

Stella liked how many of the houses were covered with dark green ivy or purple wisteria. To her, it was very humbling to walk where artists like Edgar Degas or Pablo Picasso painted, where Alexandre Dumas wrote some of his novels, Jacques Offenbach composed masterpieces—in short, where those geniuses lived and loved. Or suffered, if their inspiration left them, when their muse abandoned them. Maybe the name of the hill was fitting.

She said with reverence, "Can you imagine what these buildings have seen and heard in their lifetimes, and what secrets they still keep?"

"Maybe it's better not to know," Naomi chuckled.

Reaching the bottom of the hill, Stella looked over her shoulder, hoping to catch one last glimpse of the Basilica of Our Lady of the Sacred Heart. There she stood, tall and proud, watching and protecting them.

"Have you ever seen anything more beautiful?" she breathed, and a feeling of contentment settled around her heart.

Meandering back to their hotel, they passed the famous windmill of the Moulin Rouge—and came face-to-face with another side of Paris. Gone was the fairy-tale world of artists, replaced by the harsh reality of greedy salesmen offering their worthless trinkets, desperate men and women using drugs in plain view, and homeless people sleeping on benches, their meager belongings squeezed into a few plastic bags.

"This is so depressing," Naomi said in a hushed voice. "And how must those people feel, being watched by nosy sightseers? Look at those morons on the bus taking pictures of them!"

"I can't even imagine," Stella replied. It was disgusting how many gawkers held up their cell phones and snapped photos of the less fortunate ones. "Let's keep walking. I have no desire to linger here."

CHAPTER 8

Stella—July 2018

"Looks like Pierre's recommendation is a good one," Naomi said after they were seated at an outdoor table in a small restaurant. "Did you see the other guests' food? I'm almost drooling."

"No, I don't stare at people's plates," Stella said and pulled her feet out of her shoes. "Ouch, my feet hurt from all the walking. They need a good soaking before I go to bed."

"Guess what I brought? I never travel without my emergency stash of bath salts. Naomi to the rescue!" With a quick fist pump, she added, "You better be prepared for more walking. We'd never be able to see all of Paris, even if we had a whole week, but I think we'll manage to hit quite a few more highlights tomorrow. I've put an itinerary together and will tell you at breakfast."

"Why not now, while we're sitting here?" Stella stretched her legs out under their table.

"Because I want to surprise you."

"Then I better be patient and wait. By the way, I don't think I have thanked you enough for asking me to come along. This is already amazing."

"Yes, you did. Things just fell into place. Now, shush!" Naomi waved it off and rolled her eyes. "Where did our waiter disappear to? I'm thirsty."

"Give him a minute. The restaurant is packed."

Naomi looked around, taking in the hectic coming and going of cars, tour buses, cyclists, and pedestrians. "I count six busy streets merging at this intersection."

"The French seem to love their traffic circles. I noticed them on the way from the airport."

"I've read Place de Clichy," Naomi pointed at the roundabout, "is one of only a few places in Paris where four arrondissements—the 8th, 9th, 17th, and 18th—meet at a single point. And look, all drivers know how to enter the traffic circle and go around the bronze statue in the center of it without causing accidents. Oops! I spoke too soon. A Peugeot almost took out a tour guide."

"How do you know he's a tour guide?" Stella chortled.

"Hint, hint…see the umbrella he's holding up? And all the little ducklings wearing name tags and headphones who are following him?"

"Are we expected to wear name tags on our tour?"

"I don't think so, since our group is small. There are only representatives of six or seven agencies and their guests." Naomi made air quotes when she said guests. "It won't take long to memorize everyone's name. And by the end of the first day, we'll have figured out who we want to hang out with at meals, and—even more important—who to avoid. There are always a few fellow travelers too chatty or nosy for their own good."

"Says the one who's talking to every stranger," Stella laughed.

"True, but I prefer to be the one asking questions instead of being interrogated by some snoop."

"At least you don't deny it."

"Nope, you know me too well," Naomi admitted.

The waiter arrived with two glasses of champagne on his tray and set them in front of them. They looked at each other, confused and surprised.

"Thank you, but we didn't order those," Naomi told him.

"The two gentlemen at the bar are sending their regards," he pointed to two men in their thirties. Both were wearing dark business suits with ties hanging around their necks. The men winked and raised their own drinks in the international gesture to say "Cheers." Naomi and Stella tried to suppress giggles and raised their glasses, mouthing "*Merci*."

"Do you think they expect an invitation to our table?" Stella whispered.

"I hope not...since they'll be disappointed."

"Maybe they'll get the message if we don't pay them much attention. Stop looking over there." She pulled out her cell phone. "Oh, I have an idea. Let's take a selfie and send it home. Luca asked me to let him know when we landed in Paris, but I forgot. He can forward it to my parents. And then I don't wanna hear anything from anybody until we're back in Philly."

"Sounds good. Mom asked me to send a short note, too. Seeing your phone reminds me of something. Did you add an International Pass to your cell phone plan? Otherwise the roaming fees will kill you."

"I never cancelled the plan after we went to Niagara Falls."

"Good." Naomi got up. "Now move over, I'll sit next to you. Then we have the guys in the background, and we can tell Luca and Rev how we made *friends* on our first night in Paris."

"Why would they care, and why send a photo to Rev?" Stella held up her phone. "Ugh, I hate selfies, maybe the waiter can take it."

"Why send a photo to Revan? Easy. I'd like to see his reaction to the guy on the right." Naomi stopped the waiter and asked him for the favor.

"Why?" Stella smiled for the photo, then sipped the champagne. "Mm, this is delicious. I could get used to having a glass every day before dinner."

Naomi went back to her own chair. "Have you never noticed how Revan is always trying to show off his chest hair? He'd be envious of the guy behind us. Rev is such a down-to-earth guy, but sometimes he can be pretty vain."

She leaned over the table and whispered, "Take a look next time he takes off his shirt."

Stella scanned through the photos and sent one to Luca. "Listen, I've known Rev since he and Luca were in middle school, and I have no desire to eyeball him the way you do."

Naomi fluttered with her hand and shook her head, "Speaking of Luca..."

"Not another discussion about chest hair, please. He's my brother."

"Did he say anything about Jo?" Naomi went on.

"What's Luca got to do with Jo? She's your cousin." She made it a point to look at the menu. Her friend was like a bloodhound when she thought she was hot on the trail of something. "I'll have the linguine with salmon. And you?"

"Sounds good, I'll have the same."

After they ordered, Naomi continued, "Jo mentioned she and Luca went out for drinks a few times. She used to text me almost daily, but she's been quiet. It makes me suspicious."

"Maybe she's busy with her job. Isn't she trying to build up her client base as a personal trainer? And she's teaching yoga a few times a week. It's a lot. New York City's a tough place to establish a clientele."

"Mark my words. I can smell it! Something's going on. She's 'I'm in love' quiet." Naomi tapped the side of her nose. "Ask Luca."

"I'm not about to ask Luca. If they had drinks, great. Having a beer with a friend doesn't mean anything. We accepted the champagne from those two Casanovas, and we're not doing anything with them. By the way, look over. They found someone else to hang out with. Good, we're off the hook."

"I think I'll ask Revan. I'm sure men talk about their latest conquests with their best friends," Naomi went on.

"Now Jo is Luca's conquest? You're terrible," Stella choked out. "Nam, they've known each other as long as you and I have been friends. They happen to live in the same city. Leave 'em alone."

"I can't. Because she's my cousin, and since I'm five days older than she is, it's my responsibility to look out for her."

Naomi could come across as bossy, but she meant well, and protected those she loved. "I think she can do it for herself," Stella said.

After the waiter served their food and they both ordered a glass of wine, Naomi asked, "What did you think of the Wall of Love? *Le mur des je t'aime.*"

"I think it's very romantic. Four hundred square feet of blue lava tiles with 'I love you' written on it in more than three hundred different languages. With all the rose bushes planted in front of it, it's like a garden dedicated to love."

Naomi gave Stella a thoughtful look and said, "Do you believe there's only one person out there who's meant just for you?" She made air quotes. "Your soul mate."

"Yes." *At least I used to think so.* "And you?"

"Well, I guess it depends on how you define soul mate," Naomi propped her chin in the palm of her hand. "If you say it's someone you're predestined to be with, then I'd say no. If it's someone who understands you, who gets under your skin like no other person, someone you can't walk away from without being in physical pain, then maybe."

"So, does it mean you believe in soul mates or not?" Stella repeated her question.

"I don't know."

CHAPTER 9

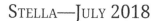

STELLA—JULY 2018

"I can't believe we're up this early. At least we're getting first dibs on the breakfast buffet," Stella said, and filled her plate with fresh fruit, some scrambled eggs, and toasted slices of fresh baguette before helping herself to coffee from a large urn. It looked and smelled like regular coffee, so she added sugar and skim milk to her cup.

"How did you sleep last night?" Naomi chose two fresh croissants with butter and jam and asked the waiter for a café au lait. "After our foot-soaks, I didn't hear a peep out of you."

"I was out as soon as my head hit the pillow. I couldn't even keep my eyes open long enough to read more than a page. How 'bout you?"

"Same. I didn't even manage to say my prayers," Naomi said, straight-faced, and bit into her first croissant.

Stella burst out laughing. Naomi was many things, but not the praying-before-bed type. "The last time you prayed was when you thought the guy on your Napa vineyard tour knocked you up. When was that? Five years ago?" Stella chewed on a small chunk of pineapple.

Naomi shivered and grimaced. "Ugh, not one of my proudest moments. Let's not talk about it."

"So. What're we doing today? You made it sound like a big secret last night."

"Yup. Today, you have to follow my lead."

"Okay...As long as you have more bath salts."

"I sure do! And the first item on our list is taking the subway to..." Naomi paused for effect. "No, I'm not gonna tell you."

"Then don't. But is it safe to travel by subway in Paris?"

"As safe as in any other big city. Millions of people take it every day. Stop worrying."

Less than an hour later they emerged from the dark tunnels of the subway system and stepped into the bright sunlight of the gorgeous Sunday morning.

"I don't see many tourists. It looks as if it's just locals walking their dogs and enjoying a cup of coffee." Stella looked around while they walked toward tall buildings with a wide terrace between them.

"Not for long. The first tour buses will be here soon." Naomi pulled her to a stop and said, "Close your eyes."

"Why?"

"Just do it. I promise you won't regret it," Naomi took her elbow. "I'll guide you."

After a few cautious shuffling steps, Naomi said, "Open your eyes!"

"Wow!" Despite the already hot day, Stella had goose bumps and rubbed her arms.

For the second time in two days, Paris lay at their feet. And right in front of them, the Eiffel Tower stretched high into the blue sky.

"It looks as if I can just reach out and touch it."

When they reached the end of the open stone platform, she said, "But it's much farther away than it seems at first. All the way on the other side of the Seine."

"Yeah, it's a good twenty- to thirty-minute walk from here," Naomi confirmed, then pointed to the buildings around them. "Here's a bit of background about where we are. We're standing on the terrace of the Palais de Chaillot. The wings to our left and right are part of the palace too. The huge park between us and the Eiffel Tower is called the Trocadéro Gardens."

"Why is the building called Palais de Chaillot, but the subway station and the park are called Trocadéro?"

"This used to be the site of a village called Chaillot. The hill of Chaillot was first arranged for the 1867 World's Fair. For the 1878 World's Fair, the Palais du Trocadéro was built as a concert hall and to hold meetings of international organizations." Naomi took a breath and continued, "For the World's Fair of 1937, the old Palais du Trocadéro was partly demolished and rebuilt, and the Palais de Chaillot now stands in its place."

"Wasn't the Eiffel Tower also built for the World's Fair?"

"Yes, but for the 1889 Fair. I guess they loved their fairs in those days."

"Interesting... When did you learn about all this?" Stella asked.

"Well, since I'm working in the travel business, I'm expected to know a few things. But everything I just recited with such eloquence," Naomi smirked, "will be forgotten in a few days. My brain only retains this kind of information short term. But it sounded professional, didn't it?"

"No doubt! Now let's go through the pretty park and over to the other side of the river."

Thirty minutes later, standing under the impressive iron structure of the Eiffel Tower, Stella gasped. "Look at the size of each of the four legs. The tower looked enormous when we were over there," she pointed back to the Trocadéro, "but now I feel smaller than an ant. Are we going up?"

"I thought we'd skip it this weekend, because we had some grand views of the city already. Maybe next weekend? My plan was to go on a one-hour boat tour on the Seine, then let one of the hop-on hop-off buses drive us around."

"Perfect. Where do we need to go to get on the boat?" Stella rubbed her hands.

"Don't tell me you're cold? It has to be at least eighty degrees."

"No, I just can't believe I'm really here. It's surreal. And thrilling!"

"Then let's go. We've lots to do today." Naomi pointed in the general direction and led the way.

They bought combination tickets, which were valid for both the boat and the sightseeing bus and were soon seated on one of the medium-sized, one-level boats.

"How far is this cruise taking us?" Stella asked.

"This one takes us past the Notre-Dame cathedral," Naomi explained. "Each way is about half an hour. We could get off the boat where it turns around, but it makes more sense if we stay for the round-trip and then get on the bus at the Eiffel Tower stop."

"Makes no difference to me—I'll follow your lead."

"Do you want to get the audio guide?" Naomi asked.

"No, I want to just look around, take lots of pictures, and read later about the buildings we pass."

"Me too. I can't stand those germ-infested audio guides. They give me the creeps," Naomi shuddered.

For the next hour they kept their conversation to a minimum, enjoying the views and pointing out landmarks to each other.

By the time they got off the boat it was close to lunchtime, so they found a little cafeteria-style restaurant near the quay and bought sandwiches and bottled water.

"It was the right decision to skip the Eiffel Tower in favor of taking the boat tour. It's so relaxing to be on the water and to let the scenery float by," Stella said.

"And a different perspective, too. I like how we passed under all the bridges. Did you see those beach-like areas on the sides of the river?"

"Let's google what they are." Stella pulled out her phone, and, after a quick search, read aloud, "It's called Paris Plages. Every July and August, roads along the banks of the Seine are closed off and artificial sand beaches are created, including palm trees, swimming pools, lawn chairs and umbrellas. Also, various activities are held there, including concerts and sports events."

"It's a neat idea! Wouldn't it be something for American cities to copy?"

"You're right, but I doubt it'll happen anytime soon. Well, we have the Schuylkill River Trail at home," Stella said, "but that's boring compared to this beach scene."

"You can't even compare the two. But—different topic—did you see all the brides this morning? I think there were at least four or five wedding parties posing for pictures between the Trocadéro and the Eiffel Tower."

"And I noticed a few couples who got engaged."

Naomi hummed the first notes of the *Wedding March*, then said, "I've told you before, and I'll say it again. I find the whole 'getting down on your knee' nonsense stupid. If—and it's a big if—I ever get married, I wanna pick out my own ring to make sure I get the one I like, and not the hand-me-down from grumpy old great-aunt Hilda. Then I'd go to the nearest Justice of the Peace and say my 'I do,' after which I'd jump on my lucky new husband's motorcycle and we'd take off on our honeymoon."

"A motorcycle?" Stella almost choked on a bite of her sandwich.

"Well, I guess a convertible would do in a pinch."

"So, first you say you're not sure you want to get married, and now you're telling me the details of your dream wedding. Which one is it?"

"I guess if the right man came along, I could be persuaded to give it a try. But I don't see one on the horizon, so don't go buy your bridesmaid dress yet." Naomi raised her water bottle and grinned at Stella. "Here's an idea. Why don't you get married first, and I'll see how it goes? If it goes well, I might think about it. Maybe."

"Well, since husband pickings are slim to nonexistent for both of us," Stella looked at her left-hand ring finger, then at Naomi and said, "maybe we'll move in together, have twenty cats, and our tombstones will say *They lived a purrfect life.*"

"I'd rather marry the next guy I meet than live with twenty cats. One would be one too many for me." Naomi put her half-empty water bottle in her purse and said, "Let's go, missy. Break's over. Off to the bus."

After securing seats on the upper level of the double-decker bus, Stella said, "So, where are we off to? Let's look at the map."

"Right now we're on the red line, but we can change buses here," her friend pointed to a stop, "and switch to the blue line. But I don't think we have enough time if we want to visit the Louvre later. Okay with you?"

"Sure."

A young woman rattled off her well-practiced speech: "*Bonjour* and welcome aboard. My name is Monique, and Pascal is our driver. Please allow me to go over a few safety reminders I'm sure you've all heard before, but I was told to refresh your memory." A few people laughed and Monique instructed them to stay seated, keeping their hands inside the bus, holding on to their cell phones, and watching out for low-hanging branches.

"If you want to get off at any of our stops, please let me know," Monique finished her routine. "Pascal, we're ready to roll."

The driver pulled into traffic, and Stella and Naomi listened to Monique and relaxed while they rode along a large public park behind the Eiffel Tower. When the bus approached an enormous building, Monique explained, "To your left is the Hôtel national des Invalides, a complex of buildings all relating to the military history of France." She went into details about the history of Les Invalides, but Stella wasn't interested in French military history and instead took photos and soaked in the sights.

"I can't get over the sheer size of all the buildings," she said as they drove past the Grand Palais des Champs-Élysées. "No wonder it took centuries to build everything."

"Right," Naomi chuckled, "and it probably didn't help when whatever one general or king started, the next one didn't like and changed half of it."

After a while, Stella yawned. "Monique lost me. Between the slow pace of the bus, the heat, and all those French names, I'm tired. I guess jet lag is catching up with me."

Naomi consulted the map. "Why don't we get off the bus soon? The Louvre is only two more stops away. It's not too far to walk."

"Sounds great. Maybe we can grab some coffee and ice cream, too."

"Oh, now you're talking! I see two scoops of chocolate ice cream on a waffle cone. Or one scoop of chocolate, and one of coffee flavor? Choices, choices... I'll have to think about it."

Their bus circled around the Place de la Concorde, its obelisk and two fountains, and stopped for a brief moment to allow them a glance down the tree-lined Champs-Élysées.

From their seats on the bus, Stella overlooked the busy street life surrounding them. Throngs of tourists aside—and she was one of them—Paris was a lively city. She watched people talking animatedly in the middle of sidewalks and families sitting in small bistros scattered everywhere, laughing and having fun.

And couples. They were everywhere. Holding hands, kissing, showing the world they were in love.

Keep rubbing it in, she thought when Monique said, "Our next stop is Palais Garnier, also known as Opéra Garnier or the Paris Opera."

She froze. Instantly, beads of sweat formed on her forehead and trickled down the back of her neck. Her hands were clammy.

Monique continued, "It's one of, if not *the* most famous opera house in the world. Due to in no small part to...?"

When a few people called out the answer, Monique nodded and said, "*Le Fantôme de l'Opéra.* Gaston Leroux used this opera house as the setting for his novel."

Stella felt Naomi watching her, but she couldn't turn to face her. Her eyes were glued to the masonry walls of the building and she crumpled up the tour map.

She came to France to escape memories centered around this book, this musical, this phantom! This opera house!

Yes, of course she knew it was in this city, and she had hoped to see it one day. But not on this trip. Why was life so cruel?

Stella didn't know if she wanted to laugh or to cry, and the sound she made was a combination of both. She covered her mouth with one hand and reached for Naomi's hand with the other.

"I have to get off the bus. Please, Naomi! I have to get off." She grabbed her purse and water bottle. "Now."

CHAPTER 10

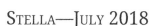

STELLA—JULY 2018

"Stella, for crying out loud, we'll get off, I promise. But we need to wait until we reach the bus stop. I can see it coming up." Naomi gripped her hand.

A few minutes later, which felt to Stella like hours, they stood on the sidewalk, and she said, "I'm going in there. There's no way I can just walk away without going inside."

"What good is it doing you? Why torture yourself?"

"I don't know. I truly don't know! But if I don't go in, I'll regret it forever." She looked around. Where could she cross the busy street?

"Do you want me to come with you?"

"No—but thank you. I have to do this by myself. Maybe then I can shut the door on this chapter of my life."

"Okay, here's an idea," Naomi said. "I'll do some shopping at Galeries Lafayette, which is not far from here."

"What do you want to buy?"

"Lingerie, of course! A little something in black lace. Or blue?"

"What? Are you serious? Don't you have enough of the stuff?"

"What better place than Paris to buy something truly sexy? And who knows? It might come in handy during this trip. Always gotta be prepared for an emergency, the old Girl Scout motto."

Naomi had the nerve to give her the Girl Scout salute, then looked up and down the street. "There's a café over there. Can you read the name?"

"It says La Brioche. Let's meet there in two hours." She checked the time. "Okay, it's almost one o'clock now."

"See you at 3 pm sharp, and don't get lost in there. No trying to find the underground lake!" Naomi teased.

Stella hugged her friend, then walked to the next crosswalk. Once she was safely on the other side, she took her time walking around the building.

In a haze, she reached the front, noticing people sitting on the wide steps. She was so utterly unprepared, she didn't even know if the theater was open to visitors on Sundays.

The thought of being part of a large group right now horrified her. She really needed to get through this all by herself, and hoped it was possible to visit without taking a guided tour.

Stella noticed people disappearing through the tall stone arches and decided it must be open.

To calm herself, she studied the facade, recognizing major architectural styles, but skimming over countless sculptures and busts—stopping at the golden capital letters above her head. ACADÉMIE NATIONALE DE MUSIQUE.

She whispered, "I say that the place of the skeleton of the Opera ghost is in the archives of the National Academy of Music."

She shook her head. She didn't want to uncover skeletons. She didn't want to disturb ghosts. She only wanted to find peace.

Peace of heart and mind.

Her heart hammered.

Stella tried to tell herself, *It's only a building. Walk in, look around, walk out*, but her nerves weren't so easily persuaded.

She counted the marble steps in front of the large doors as she climbed them—*ten, eleven, twelve*—and sat down at the top. *Time to google must-see tips.*

What do I want to really see? Stella scrolled through the suggestions. *Of course! The auditorium.*

And there was a Library-Museum, known as Bibliothèque-Musée de l'Opéra National de Paris, housing several permanent exhibitions. Exactly what she was interested in. A library-museum was almost like home turf, and it calmed her.

She startled a couple next to her when she jumped up and exclaimed, "Let's do it!"

Time to be spontaneous.

The foyer was a feast for the eyes, and Stella could only stare at the grandeur. She was greeted by marble in various colors and shades, bronze statues and sculptures, sparkling mosaics, and gold-leaf flourishes everywhere.

As soon as she bought her ticket, she was on her way to the enormous double white marble staircase with its red and green marble balustrade, and from there to the foyers and the many floors of the magnificent theater. This was so much more than a theater.

This building was a shrine. A shrine dedicated to art, music, passion—and to the past.

Stella imagined the swishing of petticoats and silk or cotton dresses of the women who walked here since its inauguration in 1875. She could almost hear the playful laughter and flirting, the tinkling of lead-crystal glasses bubbling with champagne, and the confident, maybe possessive voices of husbands and lovers. These walls must have seen their share of scandal and shame.

As if she was pulled by invisible strings, she climbed stairs and followed hallways—until she entered the horseshoe-shaped auditorium and halted.

And saw red! Red and gold galore!

Red upholstered velvet seats, red curtains, red carpet, golden columns, golden balustrades, golden ceiling.

She craned her neck, looking straight up. And what she saw took her breath away.

A bronze and crystal chandelier hung from the ceiling; a ceiling painted with such vibrant colors there was no doubt in her mind whose art it was.

She admired Marc Chagall's work and made it a point to see it in person wherever she was. His distinct use of bright, lively colors, and his almost poetic, figurative style, spoke to her, and made his work easy to recognize. His figures floated in the air, untethered and free.

She continued to gaze up at the ceiling, hunting for the small images and references Chagall was famous for, then decided to do more research about this amazing work of art later. Or maybe they sold a book about it at the gift shop. She'd have to stop there on her way out.

A nearby English-speaking tour guide told his group, "This ceiling was inaugurated in September 1964. The twelve panels, plus the central panel, are Chagall's interpretation of scenes from opera and ballet."

Someone asked, "Is this the chandelier that plays a part in the musical?"

The guide explained, "Yes. In 1896, two of its heavy counterweights broke off and fell through the ceiling during a performance, causing one death and several injuries. This is the accident that inspired Gaston Leroux to write his novel."

Stella checked the time and saw she only had a little over thirty minutes left before meeting Naomi.

Hmm. Not enough time for the Library-Museum. Instead, she decided to look at some of the costumes and stage props exhibited everywhere while making her way to the exit.

Unfortunately, it also meant she didn't have time to find out if the underground lake was real or invented by Leroux for his novel. The Phantom's lair, where he hid from the world, where he plotted his schemes, and where he found love—and lost it again. Stella's eyes misted just thinking about the Phantom's solitary life, and she blinked a few times to stop the tears.

Standing with her back to the stage, she studied the five tiers of galleries and private boxes. She didn't think she'd enjoy being in one of them, where all the people in regular seats could watch her.

Turning to leave the auditorium, she saw people entering one of the boxes on the middle level. Two men were deep in conversation, with one of them pointing to the stage.

Then a third man entered the box.

Their eyes met across the theater.

Stella's heart hammered. She couldn't breathe.

She shook her head and closed her eyes.

When she looked up again, she saw only two men.

CHAPTER 11

DAVID—JULY 2018

D avid followed his agent Aaron and Jerome, the Musical Director of the Opera House, through numerous hallways and staircases and had lost all sense of direction. They had finished touring the backstage and dressing rooms, when Jerome said, "Let me show you one more thing."

He led them through carpeted foyers until he stopped in front of three wooden doors, where he inserted a key in the middle one and said to David, "It's not loge 5. But I'd be happy to show it to you later."

David smirked and replied, "No, thank you. I know better than to enter the resident ghost's personal loge."

Jerome opened the door, swept his arm in a wide arc, saying, "David, you're looking at Europe's largest stage, built to accommodate up to four hundred fifty artists, and our auditorium has a capacity of two thousand seats."

David stepped into the private box. He didn't see the stage.

His glance fell on a woman turning to leave the auditorium. She looked up and their eyes met.

Stella!

Stella?

The blood rushing through his ears was louder than any orchestra warm-up. His heart raced. He swallowed. Swallowed again. His mouth was dry.

Her eyes, her face, her voice had haunted him for the past twelve months.

He had to go to her.

He had to talk to her.

David raised a hand toward Aaron and, without a word, ran out of the private box.

Damn... Which is the shortest way to the auditorium?

He hurried to the central staircase, running down two steps at a time, ignoring the people gaping at him or pointing fingers.

Breathing hard, he raced into the auditorium, scanning every box and aisle and seat, every corner and exit, and then the stage. Thank God he was close enough to see most of the backstage area—on the slight possibility she had ventured there.

He couldn't draw a complete breath. The air had been sucked out of him. Loosening his tie and gasping for air, David crouched down in front of the stage, oblivious to the curious stares.

She was gone.

Again, he swept the auditorium from left to right. This *was* where he saw her, only a few moments ago.

She had disappeared—like Cinderella, but without leaving a glass slipper behind.

He cradled his head in his hands and stared at the carpet between his feet.

This can't be real. Was his mind playing tricks on him? Had his conscience chosen this moment for payback? Well, the timing sucked.

And he'd better come up with a believable explanation for his strange actions—fast.

Aaron would understand. He might still give him an earful, but he had represented him for a few years now, and knew him well enough to know this wasn't David's usual behavior.

But Jerome was a different case. David was here to negotiate a contract. He was expected to be professional, not act like a toddler chasing after a puppy.

Too late. All he could do was apologize and be honest. But to be honest with a stranger about something so personal, he'd have to be honest with himself first.

He was a total asshole last year, which he wouldn't share with Jerome. The only person who needed to hear his confession wasn't here anymore. And what were the chances of running into her here, of all places?

But he knew it was Stella. She wasn't a figment of his imagination.

Call her, his conscience told him. It was the only thing he could do. Finding Stella in Paris would be impossible. Where would he even start looking? Was she staying at a hotel or with a friend, maybe in a private home? And worse, was she here with somebody?

In the flash of a second when he saw Stella, she was alone. *Don't go there, Danvers. None of your damn business anymore. You waived that privilege with your stupid letter.*

There it was again, the nagging voice of his conscience. He wanted to yell, *Shut up! Where were you when I needed you, before I made the biggest mistake of my life?*

He still couldn't manage to take a full breath, and his heart beat a fast and furious staccato. He tried to open the top button of his shirt, but his fingers didn't cooperate.

David pulled out his iPhone, praying she hadn't changed her number. Seeing her picture assigned to her contact, he thought, *Oh, baby, how can I fix this?*

He pressed "call" before he changed his mind. His hands were shaking so hard he almost dropped his phone.

Ten agonizing rings later, he heard, "You've reached Stella." The sound of her voice almost crushed him.

He was about to reply when she said, "I can't take your call right now. Please leave a message and I'll get back to you as soon as possible. Unless you're trying to sell me something, then don't bother. Bye."

Voice mail... he hated voice mail. But he had no choice. This was his one chance to get in touch with her while they were both in the same city. The city where he'd always imagined taking her for a romantic getaway.

"Stella, hi, it's me." His voice shook. "Listen...umm...I don't know if...umm...my eyes played tricks on me, but I swear...I swear I saw you a few minutes ago...umm...at the Paris Opera House. You know, the one on rue...oh, what the hell, I don't know what street it's on. You know me and directions."

This was why he hated answering machines. It was impossible to say a few consecutive words without babbling and getting tangled up in word salad. "Can we...umm... meet? Can I take you out to dinner tonight? Please, call me back. I..."

Beep...

Her voice mail cut him off. David stared at his phone and disconnected. All he could do now was hope. And wait...

If he hadn't waited too long already.

CHAPTER 12

STELLA—JULY 2018

S tella squinted at the private box. It wasn't possible. It must have been a hallucination. For a moment she thought she'd seen David. She wanted to call to the two men, "Excuse me, but did I just imagine seeing the jerk who broke my heart?"

Maybe she was dehydrated?

No—she knew it was him.

The last time she saw him in person was May of last year. He visited her for her birthday and told her he was going to Budapest for six months.

She had no idea where he lived right now, in fact had stopped following him on social media after he broke up with her.

He could be anywhere. He's a nomad. He has no roots.

She didn't know how she found her way out of the building. Time and place no longer existed. A cold, dark cloud engulfed her, leaving her disoriented.

She had no recollection of walking out into the warm sunshine. She didn't know how her feet knew where to take her, and she didn't see Naomi waiting for her at one of the tables at the brasserie.

She didn't look back at the Opera House.

She didn't feel arms coming around her, holding her tight.

She didn't hear Naomi say, "What happened to you? You're white as a sheet!"

Before Stella could answer, she heard music coming from her phone, deep in her purse. The unmistakable trombone and organ music which still meant everything to her.

A chill crept through her bones, and she shivered.

It was real.

He was real. And here in Paris.

CHAPTER 13

Stella—July 2018

"I'm so going to wring his scrawny neck!" Naomi hissed. The water bottle crinkled as she crushed it one-handed.

"His neck isn't scrawny, so I don't think you'd be able to get your hands around it," Stella hiccupped. It was almost pathetic how grateful she was for Naomi's support.

Hearing David's ringtone was too much, and she sat in the little brasserie crying her eyes out. Had she done the right thing by running away? Part of her wanted to go back and confront him, and part of her wanted to pretend they hadn't come face-to-face out of the blue.

She pushed away the café au lait in front of her and reached for the more potent beverage Naomi ordered as soon as Stella burst into tears. The cognac tasted of fruit and wood and left a trail of fire down her throat. She gasped at the burn, then welcomed the powerful sensation.

Naomi pointed to Stella's purse. "What are you going to do about his phone call? I wonder if he left you a voice mail."

"I don't know. I'm not sure if I want to hear his voice." She shuddered. "Seeing him was hard enough. And you should've seen the shocked look on his face." She shook her head. "But I guess I at least owe him the courtesy of listening to what he has to say."

"Oh, no-no-no! You don't owe him a damn thing!" Naomi shook her head at Stella. "If I were you, I'd tell him in very specific language where he can shove his message. Which you should've done last year."

Stella ignored her friend's rant and reached for her phone. *Might as well get it over with.* She put it on speaker and held it up. "Can we...umm...meet? Can I take you out to dinner tonight? Please, call me back. I..." Hearing his familiar voice was painful, and she shored herself up with another sip of her cognac.

"Dinner? He wants to take you out to a freakin' *dinner*?" Naomi was furious. "Who does he think he is?" She took a breath and pointed a finger at Stella. "I know what we'll do! I'll go with you to the dinner. And I will have a few choice words with The Undesirable, and when he goes to the bathroom, I'll drop a few jalapeño seeds into his drink.

They should give him a helluva sore throat for at least a day or two." Naomi made a throat-clearing sound.

"You wouldn't hurt a fly, so I suspect he's safe from your assault." Stella tried not to laugh and tossed her phone back into her purse. "I'm not going to do anything right now. Let's go to the Louvre. It's been our plan all along, and I won't let his reappearance mess up any more of our day."

"Are you gonna accept his dinner invitation?" Naomi finished her own cognac.

"I can't think about it right now. Let's talk about something different. What did you buy?"

"I can model for you tonight," Naomi held up a small shopping bag and double-winked at her.

"I think I'm the wrong audience." Knowing Naomi, she'd parade in front of her anyway, whether she wanted to see it or not.

"I'm pooped. Whose harebrained idea was it to walk from the Louvre to the Arc de Triomphe instead of taking the subway?" Naomi announced hours later while she flopped down on her bed.

"Yours," Stella said and shook off her sandals. "You wanted to stroll along the Champs-Elysées."

"Don't remind me. Now...how about chilling for a couple hours before we go to dinner?"

"Sounds good to me. And I still have to reply to David."

"You don't *have* to do anything."

"Yes, I do. It wouldn't be nice to leave him hanging without an answer."

"Nice? Did you just say *nice*? We're way past the 'nice' phase," Naomi's voice rose. "But I admire you for having the strength to be the bigger person. I don't think I could do it."

"Don't sell yourself short, Nam."

Naomi got up and said, "You know what? I'm going to go sit in the courtyard for a while. Want to come?"

"I'll soak my feet and reply to David, then I'll join you for a drink. Ask Pierre about another restaurant recommendation. The Italian place last night was good, but I don't want to run into those two guys again."

While she pampered her feet and let the lavender-scented bath salt relax her, she listened to David's voice mail again. It was cut off after he said "I..." at the end. What else did he want to say?

It didn't matter. At home, knowing he was thousands of miles away, it was easier to ignore her messed-up feelings. She could lie to herself for as long as she wanted, but she still loved him. And she knew she'd never find closure without talking to him one last time.

And besides, she'd scolded herself dozens of times in the past year for not confronting him about his letter. This was her chance.

But not today. It needed to be on her terms, when she was prepared, not blindsided.

She knew how much he disliked emails or text messages. He always said they were impersonal and too easy to misunderstand, and he preferred to talk in person. He considered FaceTime an acceptable compromise. *Too bad if he doesn't like me texting him. There are a few things I don't like either.*

It took her almost fifteen minutes to compose a brief message, but in the end, she thought she nailed it.

> David, I didn't expect to see you here in Paris. I can't meet you for dinner tonight. Naomi and I are leaving early tomorrow morning. We'll return on Thursday before flying home on Saturday. I'll be in touch when I'm back. Maybe we can talk then. Stella.

There! It was none of his business why she was in Paris and where she was going next.

As soon as she sent the message, she wanted to take it back. She should've asked how long he was staying. What if he had left Paris by the time she got back?

She shook her head. Second-guessing herself was exactly what Naomi always told her not to do.

Stella dried off her feet and went downstairs. She found Naomi standing at the bar, laughing with a tall man around their age.

"Stella," Naomi called when she saw her approaching, "there you are! Did you get everything done?"

"Yeah, I sent a message saying I don't have time today and will be in touch when we're back."

Naomi gave her an encouraging smile, then introduced her, "This is Kai. He's from Germany. Where exactly did you say?"

"Hamburg. Also known as Gateway to the World. Hi, Stella. Nice to meet you," Kai said.

"I've heard it's a beautiful city," she said and thought, *I can think of a more suitable nickname. Gateway to Hell.*

"Naomi told me you both live in Philadelphia. I was there last year. Rented a Harley and rode from Boston to Miami. Fun trip. Three weeks up and down the East Coast." His English was tinged with a German accent.

"Kai just told me he's riding his motorcycle everywhere. Reminds me of Rev," Naomi said to Stella.

"Who is Rev?" Kai asked. "Boyfriend?" He looked from Stella's to Naomi's ring fingers. "Husband?"

"He's a very good friend," Naomi said.

Stella turned to the bartender and ordered a glass of wine, then asked Kai, "What brings you to Paris?"

"It's my summer vacation, and I'm planning to spend three to four weeks in France. Bee and I got here two days ago, and we're probably staying another day or two."

"Bee?" Naomi asked.

"My bike! She needs a name if I'm riding her, and 'Beemer' sounds too male for my taste." He raised one eyebrow and grinned.

Naomi almost spit out her drink and reached for a napkin.

What a stupid comment. Stella tried not to roll her eyes and asked, "Where are you going next?"

"Not sure, but I think the D-Day beaches are calling me."

"Oh, maybe we'll run into each other there," Naomi said. "We're leaving for Normandy tomorrow, too. Wouldn't it be fun to bump into each other somewhere?"

He laughed and put his beer on the counter. "Why not... Ladies, please excuse me for a moment. Will you still be here when I come back?"

"Sure, Stella just ordered her drink," Naomi said, taking a sip of her own wine.

As soon as they were alone, Naomi said, "Should we ask Kai if he wants to join us for dinner?"

"Why not? He seems nice." She didn't really care, but his presence would make it less likely the conversation would turn to David.

When Naomi asked Kai about his dinner plans, he replied, "Sorry, I can't. I'm meeting a group of people for a night tour of the catacombs."

"The catacombs?"

"There are over three hundred kilometers of old tunnels and caves beneath Paris. You can take a tour and visit a small section during the day," his voice dropped, "but there are always cataphiles around willing to take people down there after dark."

Naomi cocked her head. "How far is three hundred kilometers in miles? I can never get it sorted out. And what's in the tunnels? Why do people want to see them?"

"It's a little less than two hundred miles. All kinds of crazy things are happening down there. I heard about caves set up as bars for parties, I heard about a mushroom-growing business, a movie theater, and some people just get a bang out of spending the weekend in the tunnels."

"Why would people want to go underground overnight?" Stella asked.

"It adds a new kick to it. There was something on the news last week about a new tunnel or cave being found. The department overseeing the tunnels announced they're closing the catacombs for the time being. I can't wait to meet the guys and go down myself."

"You just said they are closed," Stella said.

"Yeah, our tour's not really an official one, which makes it more fun." He finished his beer. "But I get it's not for everybody. The underground tunnels were used to bury people in the seventeenth and eighteenth centuries, when Paris ran out of space for cemeteries. The bodies were just carted away and dumped there so they didn't stink up the city. It's morbid, but also exciting, don't you think?"

Stella said, "No, not really. Pretty creepy if you ask me."

Naomi said at the same time, "If I had known about them, I might've gone on one of the tours."

Stella shuddered. "Wouldn't surprise me, but not with me."

"Well, ladies," Kai got up, "I better get going if I want to find the meeting place. Enjoy the rest of your time in France." He looked at Naomi and winked, "I'll look out for you in Normandy!"

When Naomi excused herself and went to the bathroom, Stella used the solitary moment to check her phone. *No reply from David. He's obviously not too upset about my refusal to meet him.* For a moment, she was lost in thought and rotated the phone in her hands.

"I hope you're not checking for messages from The Undesirable. By the way, did you hear anything from Luca or Revan? Wasn't Rev coming home today?" Naomi peeked over Stella's shoulder.

"He said Sunday or Monday, and with him you never know. It could be any day. But I haven't heard from Luca, which surprises me a little."

"Well, you got what you wanted. You said you don't want to hear from anybody while we're here." Naomi reminded her.

"True! Did you hear anything new about your grandma?"

"Gram's making Mom wait on her hand and foot. Knowing Mom, it won't last long," Naomi said. "Let's go, dinner's calling."

CHAPTER 14

STELLA—JULY 2018

"Rise and shine, sleepyhead," Naomi's cheery voice blasted out Stella's eardrums, even from her side of the room. "Let's hurry so we can grab a cup of coffee and something to eat before we leave."

Stella was exhausted, and being rushed didn't improve her mood.

She wasn't a morning person, and preferred to have a cup of coffee in solitary silence before she started her day. Naomi, on the other hand, was an early bird and had no problem chatting away as soon as she opened her eyes. Most of the time she didn't even require a response. An occasional grunt or "Uh-huh" was enough.

"What happened to you? You look awful!" Naomi peeked over the half wall between their beds. "What's up with the red, puffy eyes?"

"Thanks a bunch!" Stella snapped. "If you need to know... I watched movies most of the night."

"Let me guess," Naomi said while she pulled clothes out of her suitcase and headed toward the bathroom. "*Mamma Mia*?"

Stella covered her face with a pillow. *Please!! Only ten more minutes...*

"I hope it wasn't *Moonstruck*! I don't know why you keep watching that old flick. It was filmed before we were even born."

Stella could feel a headache coming on. She didn't want to have this conversation right now. She needed coffee! "Why do I have to defend the movies I watch?"

"So, did you watch one or both?" Naomi was in pit bull-mode.

"Both. I just told you I couldn't sleep."

"Did you even try to? Maybe we need to get you a sleep mask like the one Audrey Hepburn wears in *Breakfast at Tiffany's*."

"Can we please not talk about it right now? Go get ready." Stella got out of bed and stowed her tablet and charger in her carry-on.

"Yup, but we'll talk later." Not waiting for an answer, Naomi closed the bathroom door, and Stella heard her turn the shower on. She let out a sigh of relief and picked out her clothes for the day, then looked around for stray personal items and shoved them in her suitcase.

What Naomi didn't know was, not only had she watched two movies, she had also pulled up videos on YouTube. "One of Us" still played in her head. The beautiful, timeless music of ABBA always spoke to her.

"Which is why I watch those movies when I'm feeling down!" She looked in the mirror and said, "Because the music helps me through tough times."

"Are you done talking to yourself?" Naomi interrupted her thoughts.

"Wow, you're done? Did you speed-shower?"

"Yes. I told you I wanna have breakfast. The bathroom's all yours! I'll blow-dry my hair here."

Naomi plugged in the hairdryer but didn't turn it on. She said, "And I put my eye cream next to your cosmetic bag. Use it! I know it covers up oopsies from the previous night."

"When was the last time you cried yourself to sleep?" Stella laughed.

"It's been a while, but I might've had a few late nights with little sleep and needed to look presentable in the morning."

Stella gave Naomi a tight hug. "You're the best."

"I'll remind you again after we have our little chat."

Forty-five minutes later, Pierre came to their table and said, "Excuse me, there is a gentleman at the front desk asking for you. He says he's from Merveille Tours."

"Thank you, Pierre, and please tell him we'll be there in two minutes," Naomi replied.

On their way out, Stella stopped at the breakfast buffet. "Wait, I'll get a coffee-to-go. Do you want one?"

"Yes, good idea."

The man who waited for them was in his mid-fifties and wore a baseball hat saying *France 2018* over his graying hair.

Naomi held out her hand to him. "Hi, I'm Naomi Winters, and this is Stella Harrison. You're from Merveille Tours?"

"Yes, I am. My name is François Moyenne, and I'm your driver. Allow me to take your luggage to the bus while you are checking out." He spoke English with a strong French accent.

"Thank you, François," Naomi said.

Pierre offered, "Give me a moment to show Monsieur Moyenne your bags."

Outside their hotel, a woman waited for them in front of a minibus. She was impeccably dressed in a dark gray, above knee-length wrap dress accentuating her petite figure, and wore her black hair in a shaggy pixie. Stella guessed her to be in her forties, and the youthful haircut looked great on her. "*Bonjour*, please step in."

All the seats in the front of the bus were occupied, but Stella didn't mind sitting in the back, where they had four seats to themselves. As soon as they sat, she looked around, counting fourteen guests, including her and Naomi.

After the woman joined them on the bus, she said, "Good morning, everybody. My name is Caroline Gulliver, and I am excited to be your guide on this tour to some of the most romantic locations in France. On behalf of Merveille Tours de Luxe, François and I welcome you aboard! I know you haven't all met yet, but instead of calling out names on the bus, I suggest we do it at lunchtime, when we can sit around a table and look at each other."

A few people nodded, and Caroline continued, "While François is trying to get us through the rush hour traffic, I'll give you a short overview of the next few hours, and then I'll hand out information packages with more details about the next four days, including our hotels and schedules.

"As you all know, Merveille Tours has established a reputation as one of the leading travel providers for deluxe weekend and destination getaways in France. We are planning to add luxury honeymoon packages starting next year. The travel agencies you represent are our most valued business partners on the East Coast of the United States, and we're excited to have you with us on this maiden voyage. It is our way of thanking you for your patronage and support. We need your continued help in selling our travel packages, and we're hoping your feedback about the hotels and locations we visit will help us choose the best ones for our customers. You are our guinea pigs, so to speak."

Her comment was greeted by some good-natured laughter.

"According to our research, France is among the top ten honeymoon destinations worldwide. Twenty-five percent of marriages are destination weddings. Eighty percent of the couples who have a destination wedding have been married before. People are willing to spend more money on weddings than ever before, especially those taking the step for the second or third time. We want to be there with those newlyweds and make sure they have a memorable beginning of their happily-ever-after."

Stella leaned close to Naomi's ear and said, "Excuse me, you brought me on a *honeymoon* tour?" It took a lot of effort not to shout the word.

"Well, it *is* also a tour of Normandy, Brittany and some Loire Valley castles. Who cares about the spousal nirvana nonsense?" Naomi didn't look at her but focused on the couple two rows in front of them, holding hands and sharing a secret smile.

"Me, for example," Stella hissed. "I hope we don't have to taste test wedding cakes for the next four days?"

"Oh, shush. We'll have fun."

Caroline continued, "The highlights of this tour are the coastal towns of Honfleur, Arromanches, Saint-Malo, and Mont Saint-Michel, and we'll end with a few of the Loire Valley castles.

"But we're adding short stops en route to experience the hidden gems, the idyllic corners so often overlooked in the rush from one major tourist spot to the next."

She paused when the driver said something in French to her, then went on, "Because our focus is on romantic getaways, we will not be spending time visiting the D-Day beaches or World War II memorials. Which doesn't mean we will ignore history altogether, because the reminders will be right in front of us. If our customers are interested in spending their honeymoon climbing around bunkers or artillery holes, we're going to make it possible for them, too. The customer is king, and the king rules!"

More laughter followed the worn-out statement, but Stella noticed a few group members nodding. Their businesses only continued to flourish if they were able to satisfy their customers' whims and needs—or dreams.

"*Alors*, we're on our way to our first stop, Rouen. In medieval times, it was one of Europe's largest and most prosperous cities, and the second-largest city in France after Paris. It was also where Joan of Arc was burned at the stake in 1431.

"During World War II, about fifty percent of Rouen was destroyed, but most of the historic center survived undamaged, so we'll be able to stroll through the beautiful old streets on a ninety-minute walking tour."

Caroline picked up a stack of folders stuffed with brochures. "Here are your tour packages, one for each group. They also include general information about Wi-Fi access at the hotels and on this bus, a link to download our itinerary to your phones, and my personal mobile number.

We're planning to stay together on our excursions, but it doesn't hurt to have the details saved somewhere."

She walked through their compact bus and gave each pair of guests a folder. "François has a cooler with bottled water, juice, and some fresh fruit behind his seat, and there is also a box of fresh pastries. Please help yourselves at any time. We will make sure to keep them stocked every day. Today's lunch will be around one o'clock in Honfleur."

When Naomi accepted their package, Caroline said, "I have to ask, is your mother's name Lisa?"

"Yes, do you know her?"

"We met a few years ago on a tour through England and Scotland. We didn't stay in touch, and I was looking forward to seeing her when I noticed her name on the guest list. As soon as I saw you, you reminded me of her."

"She had to drop out last minute due to an emergency with my grandmother. I'm sure she would've enjoyed seeing you, too!"

"Please give her my regards."

"I'd be happy to."

Stella said to Naomi, "I'll have a look at the folder later. I need to rest a little."

But instead of closing her eyes, she gazed out the window. The low murmur of voices on their bus and the countryside flying by lulled Stella into a meditative state. Thoughts of David had kept her awake last night—plus checking her cell phone every five minutes.

Why didn't he acknowledge her text message? How long was he going to be in Paris? What was he doing in Paris? The same questions whirled in an endless merry-go-round in her head.

Stella reached for her bracelet and touched the charms. She hadn't removed this bracelet for even a moment since he gave it to her with the first charm.

It was her talisman.

She remembered when David gave it to her…three years ago.

CHAPTER 15

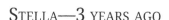

STELLA—3 YEARS AGO

"I can't believe you didn't tell me you and David have been hanging out the past two weeks." Naomi put down the glass of wine she'd been holding. She dropped her feet on an ottoman and pouted.

"I just did." Stella leaned back in her chair. Naomi was so nosy, which made it lots of fun to tease her.

"You know what I mean. And I want *all* the details."

"Well, at the end of our dinner at Betty's, when you went to the bathroom, David asked me for my phone number and called me the next day. We met for lunch again and went for a long walk."

"Okay, the short version will do. Thanks."

Stella grinned, "Make up your mind, Nam. Anyhow, when David heard I'm working only minutes away from the theater where he performs, he suggested meeting for a sandwich or a hot dog from a food truck during my lunch break."

"Aw, how sweet." Naomi rolled her eyes. Then narrowed them at Stella. "And that's *all* you're doing?"

"We sit in a park. We talk. We just like being together, I guess. It feels right." Was it possible to fall in love with someone after only a few days?

"Hello?? And?? Anything else? Eating a hot dog in the park? I'd have a hard time containing my excitement."

Stella didn't want to talk about her feelings for David. Not even with Naomi, who could usually read her like an open book. Stella wanted to savor her happiness and protect their delicate relationship.

"Have you slept with him?"

Leave it to Naomi to get right to the point. "No, but why do you want to know?"

"I don't want you to make a mistake. Which includes sex with guys from out of town. Remember when you dated what's-his-name in high school? Who dropped you for the Swedish exchange student?"

"You're right. Josh was a jerk, but I'm not seventeen anymore. David and I are taking it slow. I'm not about to report about my sex life to you or to anybody else."

"I tell you about mine."

"True, but you volunteer the info. I don't ask for it," Stella said.

"Has David met Luca and Revan?" Another one of Naomi's habits; changing the subject when she didn't like a comment. It could be annoying, but sometimes Stella wished she could do it, too.

"Not yet. But I want to invite him over for dinner when both guys are in town next week. David doesn't have a show on Wednesday. Can you come? Around six?"

"Of course I'll be there," Naomi beamed. "Nothing can keep me away from witnessing such an epic meeting."

"Why? What do you expect to happen?"

"You're bringing home a boyfriend. To meet your brother and your... What shall we call Rev? Your 'otha' brotha'?"

Stella rolled her eyes at Naomi's fake Boston accent and sighed. "Oh, come on! It's not as if David is meeting my parents and asking for my hand in marriage. Meeting in restaurants and parks is so impersonal, and I live right here. It's what friends do."

"Yeah, keep telling yourself you're only friends. But I'm happy for you! He seems like a nice guy. At Betty's, he only had eyes for you. I just want you to be careful. What're you going to do when he leaves?"

"I'm trying not to think about it too much. We're taking it day by day," Stella muttered.

But she had a feeling it wouldn't be easy to let him go. With David she experienced a closeness, a bond, she'd never experienced with any other man.

The next Wednesday, Stella cleaned the house like a maniac. When Revan was around, he often left T-shirts lying around and coffee mugs or whiskey glasses sitting on the coffee tables. She wanted the house to look inviting and welcoming when David came for his first visit.

She made a large pan of lasagna with fresh garlic bread and planned to serve it with a tossed salad. It was almost six, and she was in a state of high anticipation.

When she told Luca about David, he gave her a long look and said, "He must be someone really special. I don't remember meeting many of your boyfriends."

"Well, maybe it's because you don't live here anymore," Stella countered. But she agreed with Luca. David was special.

And it had been a while since she had a boyfriend. In Boston, she'd been lucky if she found time to have dinner with friends. There was no room for a relationship.

She checked the time on her phone again. Would David like how she lived? Would he like Luca and Revan—and vice versa? What if they didn't get along?

She glanced to where Revan and Luca sat in front of the cold fireplace, each holding a glass of whiskey. Stella couldn't hear what they were talking about, but she loved the low rumble of their voices and occasional laughter.

She wiped down the kitchen counter and hummed along to "Don't Ask Me Why" playing softly in the background.

"Cinderella, any good reason why we're being forced to listen to Billy Joel and your lovely humming?" Rev called from his chair.

"Because I want to know all the songs before David and I go to the concert in Chicago."

"Chicago? Why not Baltimore or DC? It would be a little closer to home," Luca said.

"David's going to visit his parents for a few days at the end of August, and he asked me to meet him there."

"Wait a minute! We haven't met the man yet. You're not going anywhere!" Rev announced and jumped out of his chair, almost sloshing his sacred whiskey.

"What's wrong with you guys? Why is everybody acting like I'm a child? I don't need your permission! And don't call me Cinderella." Stella snapped, then added in a more normal voice, "Not in front of David. It's embarrassing." She glared at Revan, then focused on Luca. "Are you just going to sit there and say nothing?"

"I don't have to say anything. Revan has it under control." Luca smirked.

The doorbell rang and kept her from giving her brother an earful. Those two could be such morons. *No wonder they're best friends.* And worst of all, they really believed they were in the right. *Not happening, busters. I make my own decisions.*

Stella ran and opened the door before either of the jerks got there first.

David held out a bouquet of yellow roses. "Hello, beautiful lady."

She took the flowers and put an arm around his neck to pull him close. His kiss was tender and sweet.

"Unlock those lips for a second and let a thirsty woman in," Naomi hollered from the other side of the street.

David said to Stella, "You look amazing. I love this color on you." She blushed and vowed to buy more clothes in shades of green.

"Shutterbug... pour me one of whatever you have," Naomi called out as soon as she entered the house and hugged Luca and Revan. "And give those two turtledoves a moment to say hello. After all, they haven't seen each other for a few hours."

"How many times have I told you not to call me Shutterbug?" Revan's grumpy demand came from the bar, where he was fixing Naomi's drink.

Stella said, "Maybe I should apologize in advance for this trio of knuckleheads. But..." she waved her hand at them, "contrary to first impressions, they can be nice—if they want to. Why don't you go talk to the guys? I'll get a vase for these roses."

"Nothing wrong with friendly banter. You should hear me and my sister."

He greeted Naomi with a kiss on the cheek, and she grinned at him. "Hello, David, nice seeing you again. I hear you've been around."

Next, he looked at Luca and said, "You must be Luca. I can see a resemblance to your sister."

"I'm not sure why she called me a knucklehead. I haven't said a word," Luca replied with a laugh, shaking David's hand. "Good to meet you."

Stella called, "You were doing a great imitation of a knucklehead a few minutes ago."

David turned to Rev, who handed Naomi her drink. "And you're Revan. Pleasure to meet you all."

He reached into the paper bag nestled into the crook of his arm. "I don't know what we're having for dinner, so I hope this works." He pulled out two bottles of pinot noir and put them on the mantle. "And some Woodford Reserve Double Oaked Bourbon for later." He handed the bottle directly to Revan. "I hear you're a whiskey connoisseur."

"David, my man, excellent choice!" Revan grinned and shook David's hand again. "I was in Kentucky last year and visited this distillery. Great place. I have some very fond memories of the day."

Naomi looked at him and said, "Did you meet one of your *acquaintances* there?"

"Nugget, let me remind you of something. A gentleman never tells." Rev winked at Naomi, who stormed off into the kitchen, where she asked Stella, "Anything I can help you with?"

"No, thank you. We're eating at seven, so I thought maybe we can all sit outside until then." Stella pushed the vase around the kitchen island until she found the perfect spot. Did he know yellow roses symbolized friend-ship or a platonic relationship? Was he trying to tell her something?

When she looked to David, he held a glass of whiskey on the rocks in his hand, and the three men were in a deep discussion about one of Revan's photos on the wall. He fit right in, and it thrilled her. After pouring herself a glass of red wine, she beckoned Naomi to follow her outside.

The next hours flew by in harmony. David and Revan exchanged stories about their travels, and when Naomi announced Luca and David's discussion about politics had taken up enough time, the conversation turned to the subject of book-to-movie or stage adaptations.

Luca and Revan were good guys, and Stella loved them, so their approval of David was important to her. She knew Naomi liked him, too.

A few days later, she also introduced him to her parents. They weren't inclined to be starstruck, but they had both heard of him and knew how successful he was. When Stella listened to them interacting as if they'd known each other for a long time, hearing him tell stories about his family and background, she began to wish David could stay forever.

It was then when Stella realized she'd fallen in love with David. When she allowed a glimmer of hope to settle into her heart. Perhaps they could have a future.

They spent as much time together as possible. And, every night, David came over after the show.

One evening, a week before his time in Philadelphia was over, he pulled her close and walked his fingers up and down her naked arm. "I'd like for us to stay in touch."

"I'm hoping the same. But what do you suggest?"

"I'm planning to swing by here whenever I have a few days off between cities, but it's not always possible. And we have the weekend in Chicago. We'll go to the concert, I'll show you where I grew up, and I can't wait to introduce you to my parents and sister."

"You make it sound so...official." She trailed her hand over his chest and his abs, relishing his reaction to her touch.

"I enjoyed meeting your parents when they came for a show and we had dinner afterward. And Sabrina has been bugging me to meet you ever since I told her you helped me pick out her birthday gift." He continued to caress her arm.

"Okay, now I can't wait to go to Chicago." She shivered when his fingers grazed her breasts, and David pulled her closer.

"We've got to make this work, babe. But please, if you ever feel like I'm neglecting you, let me know. Promise to tell me if you think I'm not giving you enough time and attention." His dark eyes bored into hers. Did she see fear lurking in those depths?

"I know how demanding your job is. Our relationship is still new, but we agreed to do our best to make it work, even if we can't be together all the time. So I'm not sure what else you mean."

"I... I've seen too many long-distance relationships fail. They aren't easy to maintain when one person is always on the road. But I love you, Stella. You have to believe me!" David's kiss, full of passion and longing, took Stella's breath away. They didn't need to say anything more, instead letting their bodies speak, and she gave a part of her soul to him.

On their last evening together, they cuddled on the sofa in Stella's living room. It was getting late, but neither cared. Their last few moments together were more important than anything else.

David's reached over to where his jacket hung over the back of the sofa, and took out a special edition of *The Phantom of the Opera*.

"When you read this book, it's like turning back time to when we met. I want you to remember our dreams and let them guide us into our future."

Her voice quavered when she said, "I will."

Then David pulled out a rectangular box wrapped in silver paper. Stella gasped when she opened it. In it was a gold and silver bracelet with a single star charm.

"I want to give you the moon and the stars, Stella. You're my North Star, and wherever I am, I'll look at the night sky and wish I could be with you. Think of me when you wear this."

He sang to her, "Think of me... Remember me..."

All Stella could do was cling to him while tears spilled down her cheeks.

CHAPTER 16

—◇○◁⁓▷○◇—

STELLA—JULY 2018

T he bus rumbled over a pothole and jolted Stella. She wiped away a tear. *Darn, David... I hate what you did to me!*

She touched the bracelet. For two years he sent her a new charm from every city where he performed. Little silver, gold, or two-tone mementos. Her favorite one had clear crystals arranged in a curve resembling the waning moon, with light blue stars and clear dots filling a dark blue sky.

His wish had come true... She thought of him whenever she wore the bracelet. And she wore it every day.

Naomi bumped her shoulder and said in a low voice, "We're in Rouen. Better wake up."

"I'm not sleeping. I'm reflecting."

"Ah, Stella code for 'thinking about David.' While you've been reflecting," she made air quotes, "I've been getting acquainted with our fellow travelers."

Now Stella grinned and said, "Which means you've made up stories about every one of them."

Naomi loved to people-watch, and the histories she invented for them were quite often not too far off. "I'm sure you'll fill me in later!"

"Sure will, my friend. You know once a thought's in my head, it has to come out of my mouth."

Their bus pulled into the drop-off area near a large town square. After everybody gathered in a semicircle around her, Caroline said, "We have arrived at the place du Vieux-Marché, the Old Market Square. Our tour begins at the Joan of Arc Church, which is behind us, then we'll walk toward the Notre-Dame Cathedral, follow rue Saint-Romain, and end our walk at the Plague Cemetery, where François will pick us up again."

"A cemetery sounds very romantic," a man remarked. He was portly and unkempt, with grayish three-day stubble creeping over his double chin and down to his shirt front. Stella guessed him to be around sixty. The way his beady eyes wandered over the female travelers made her feel uncomfortable. *Like a predator picking out his next victim.* Stella couldn't wait to hear Naomi's thoughts about him.

Caroline nodded and smiled. "You are correct. The plague wasn't romantic at all. But I'm taking you there because of the buildings and their history. Over the next few days, I will show you romance can be found in unexpected places, which will give your customers something special to remember."

She pointed behind her. "Take this square, for instance. This is the Joan of Arc church and was built in the 1970s. What does it look like to you?"

"An overturned boat," a young woman said.

"Yes. The Vikings left their mark all along the coasts of France, and this church honors Normandy's Nordic roots and heritage. But the roof also symbolizes the flaming pyre on which Joan of Arc died. To me, it's a good example of the present remembering the past.

"In a few minutes, we'll go inside and look at the gorgeous sixteenth-century stained glass windows, which were saved from another church destroyed during World War II.

"But while we admire this building, keep in mind this spot also has seen more than its share of death. What's now a lively square with cafés, small stores, and market stands, was Rouen's place of public executions during the Middle Ages and later." Caroline walked toward a tall aluminum cross with flower beds surrounding it. "This marks the spot where the guillotine stood during the French Revolution and cut short eight hundred lives."

"More uplifting stuff, eh?" remarked the unkempt man. "When are you showing us the best hidden spots to steal a kiss?" he winked at the blonde who'd been sitting with him.

Stella overheard her say, "I don't think so," while she took a step away from the guy.

Stella gave Caroline bonus points for staying calm when she said, "We don't want to take the magic out of discovering these places for yourselves, so I suggest saving juvenile games for after our official program ends each day—if the need is warranted." The last remark had a bit of a bite to it.

Naomi whispered to Stella, "What an asshole! I pity the poor woman who's with him. She doesn't seem to like him very much. Can't wait to find out what their story is."

Stella whispered back, "What? You haven't made it up yet?"

"Oh, I have a few scenarios in mind, but I hope I'm wrong."

"We'll take ten minutes for you to look around on your own or use the public restrooms over there," Caroline pointed to the other side of the church entrance, "and then let's meet here again."

After visiting the church, the group moved on to follow old cobblestone streets lined on both sides with half-timbered houses.

Caroline explained, "These colorful houses were built on waterproof stone bases, some with heavily decorated oak jetties. Jettying means that an upper floor extended beyond the dimensions of the floor below. It gave the owners more living space without having to pay more taxes, which were calculated based only on the footprint of the house, not the number of rooms or floors. But having wooden structures standing so close together increased the danger of fires spreading between the buildings, and jettied houses were no longer built after the sixteenth century."

They approached a building with a large arch spanning the street and an enormous clock embedded in the middle, its face showing a golden sun and the blue night sky with stars surrounding it.

"This is the Gros-Horloge, the Great Clock, an astronomical clock dating back to the fourteenth century," Caroline said. "The clock's mechanism is from 1389 and the oldest in France."

Stella held her bracelet in front of Naomi. "Of course we have to come across a star clock at our first stop."

"You'll always come across something with stars or the moon, and it doesn't always have a connection to David. Let it go."

"Easier said than done," she muttered.

Caroline kept the group going, but Stella didn't listen to her explanations about building styles, or which fire destroyed what and when. It was an inevitable part of history and repeated itself time and again.

"Is everybody ready for the ossuary of Saint-Maclou, the Plague Cemetery?" Caroline asked and explained while they walked on, "In 1348, the Black Plague killed seventy-five percent of Rouen's citizens. When the disease returned in the sixteenth century, sixty percent of the parish succumbed. The cemetery of the Church of Saint-Maclou wasn't big enough, so the bodies were buried in communal graves in this courtyard."

They entered an atrium with more half-timbered houses on all four sides. The center of the courtyard was welcoming and cool, with trees and benches where people took shelter from the hot summer sun.

Caroline gave them time to look around before she said, "Getting back to our purpose, which is finding romantic locations, I agree this isn't the first place you'd think of. But we are seeing more themed weddings, and I believe some couples won't be opposed to having their pictures taken in front of a medieval treasure."

Making their way out of the former graveyard, Naomi rubbed her arms, "All those carvings of skulls and bones on the buildings gave me the willies. It was spooky. I don't think I'd like to spend even one minute of my honeymoon there."

Stella hooked arms with her. "Where's your famous adventurous spirit?"

Back on the bus, Caroline described their next stop. "Honfleur is one of the most romantic port towns along this coast. Impressionists in the nineteenth century were drawn there because of the striking light conditions. And it wasn't destroyed by bombs in World War II, making it an even more popular location for artists and tourists.

"Once there, we'll first stop at the Côte de Grâce lookout, where you will have a breathtaking view of Honfleur and the Seine estuary. Afterward, François will take us to the

Vieux Bassin, the Old Port, where we'll have an authentic Norman lunch before we explore the old streets."

"I hope they serve beer with lunch. All this walking makes me thirsty," came the voice of the unpleasant man. "I could do with a nice, cold can of Bud."

Again, Caroline proved to be a professional and didn't allow the man to bait her.

When they reached the viewing point, Naomi said, "The scenery isn't quite as breathtaking as Caroline described it. That huge bridge and the freight cranes in the harbor are spoiling the view. But," she pointed behind them, "let's go check out this chapel."

Together they walked to an ancient building made of brown stone. It looked kind of squashed, as if someone once sat down on it.

"The poor thing. It succumbed to the weight of the world," Stella said.

As soon as they stepped inside, Naomi exclaimed, "Flapping sails!"

Stella reached for a brochure. "The Chapel of Notre Dame de Grâce was built in the early 1600s and is dedicated to sailors and seamen. I guess it explains the boats and images of ships everywhere. Look," she pointed to a glass window, "even there. I think I've seen enough in here."

As they strolled back to the bus, bells starting ringing. Stella stopped walking and turned around.

"Naomi, look. All the bells are visible behind weathered beams. I wonder why it's next to the church? Aren't bell towers always the highest part of the building?"

Caroline approached them, "The bells would be too heavy for the old church and required a more solid foundation. They are called the pilgrimage bells. Missionaries and other travelers who were leaving for the New World came here to pray for a safe crossing. Isn't their sound one of the loveliest you've ever heard? I want to bring every couple who books one of our tours to this spot and let them find peace and tranquility."

Tranquility, Stella thought. *Exactly what I'm looking for.*

After a simple but delicious meal of fresh seafood, sitting around a long table, Caroline said, "I think this is a good moment for everyone to introduce themselves."

One by one, each shared a little bit of their background. Besides François, Caroline, Stella, and Naomi, they also heard from Karen and Jenna, sisters whose family owned a travel agency with several offices in different cities.

Andrew and Sarah were the couple who didn't seem to be able to stop holding hands and gazing at each other. Stella wanted to get to know them better.

Susan and Lynn were friends who owned a travel agency together. Both were married and had families, but enjoyed going on promotional trips together. Susan said, "Because it's part of our business," and Lynn added, "And it gives us some girl time!"

Steve and Linda were a married couple in their sixties.

John and Michael were a couple in their mid- to late thirties. They were so fit, tanned and outdoorsy-looking, Stella never would've guessed they were running a travel agency.

And lastly, there was Harry and Julia. The unpleasant guy and the younger woman. When it was their turn to introduce themselves, he informed the group, "I'm Harry. My wife, Emily, owns our travel agency, and I'm a silent partner, but she couldn't come on this trip. Our oldest son crossed paths with a truck not long ago and now he needs surgery."

Stella noticed Julia was shaking her head, and even opened her mouth to say something, but closed it again.

Harry went on in his squeaky voice, "I told her to let him deal with it by himself. But poor Emily is too soft and thinks the kids still need her fretting over them, so she told me to go on this trip in her place. Lucky Julia, here," he patted her hand, which she snatched back and moved as far away as she could without falling off the wooden bench, "is my wife's friend and her accountant. When Em dropped out, we didn't want Julia to miss out, too. And she had something else to do in France. What are you here for again?" He looked at her but rattled on without waiting, "It's not important, eh?"

"Poor Emily should have let Lucky Julia go by herself," Naomi whispered to Stella. "He reminds me of someone, I just can't place him yet."

"And is this what you thought their story would be?"

"Not quite, but I would like to ask her why she agreed to come. She clearly doesn't like him."

"Well, he said she had other business in France. And maybe she hoped being part of a group would keep him from acting like an asshole."

"Assholes don't change." Naomi said, and grimaced. "I know one thing for sure, though. I don't like him."

CHAPTER 17

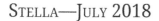

STELLA—JULY 2018

"All right, are you tired yet?" Caroline asked once they were on the bus again.

There were a few "yes's" and a few more "no's," and Caroline said. "Having just seen the dreamy town of Honfleur, can you imagine your couples spending a day or two here? Having their photos taken with the harbor in the background? The red and orange sunshades, the shimmering water and the white boats in the port?"

"Marriage is so overrated." Harry piped up, but no one reacted.

"I'm going to tell you a story." Caroline ignored him, too, and looked at the rest of the group.

"In the 1700s, an old watchmaker's daughter married her sweetheart on the beach in Honfleur. The day after the wedding, friends gathered to help the bride and groom with the cleanup, and later they all took a boat out to a sandbank in the Seine.

"It was low tide, and they danced and had a grand time, not even noticing the rapidly rising water around them. By the time they realized their boat had been swept away, it had gone too far for them to reach it.

"The water continued to rise, and the currents were treacherous. Folks on land heard their desperate cries for help, and boats were sent to save the stranded partiers. The winds picked up, the waters got even rougher, and the rescuers had to watch in shock when an enormous wave crashed over the group on the sandbank and pulled them all under. Nobody survived, and the bride and groom were found on the beach the next day with their arms still around each other."

Stella liked Caroline's voice when she recited old stories, and the way she brought them to life. Her native French combined with a British accent and her proper pronunciations were like special effects in an audiobook.

"Do you know who wrote the story? It's so heartbreaking," Stella said.

"Yes, Jacob Venedey, a German publicist and politician, published it in his travel diaries in 1838. The story, called *The Death-Wedding of Honfleur*, was told to him by an old sailor who was a young child when the tragic event happened.

"Now, back to some practicalities. We have ninety minutes before we reach Arromanches-les-Bains, where we will stay tonight. Arromanches played an important role in the Normandy landings, when Port Winston, an artificial port named after Winston Churchill, was installed almost overnight. Within days the Allies disembarked over three hundred thousand troops and more than fifty thousand vehicles there."

"I thought we weren't doing World War II stuff," Harry interrupted.

"As I said this morning," Caroline glared at him, "we're not focusing on it, but we can't quite ignore it either. Remnants of the artificial harbor are still visible, and at low tide you can walk out to those huge cement blocks. We need to be aware of them, to avoid unpleasant exchanges with our customers in case they expect only sandy beaches and are bothered by it."

"I think Harry needs to get lost somewhere," Naomi muttered to Stella.

"Can't you just ignore him?" Stella whispered.

"No, he's the kind of stupid I can't tolerate. He's going to *severely* test my patience."

"Since when do you have patience?"

Harry looked over at them and winked.

"Ugh," Stella groaned. "I changed my mind. You're right. He *is* going to be annoying."

Their hotel in Arromanches was covered with gray shingles which appeared to have withstood many storms. As they rounded the corner, Stella saw an inviting-looking terrace wrapped around two sides of the hotel, and she could imagine them sitting there later, sheltered from the wind by tall glass panes, sipping a glass of wine, watching the sunset.

"I don't know how François managed to drive the bus through those tiny streets without losing his rearview mirrors. And ours is only a minibus. Imagine one of the large coach buses we saw outside of town," Naomi said. "I was starting to hold my breath, hoping it would help us squeeze through those alleys."

"He must've done it a few times, but I agree," Stella said.

Caroline called for the group's attention. "After checking in, you're free to spend the rest of the afternoon on your own. I'm sure you'll enjoy this picturesque little town, so explore it at your own pace.

"We'll meet at the hotel restaurant at 7:30 for dinner. If anybody is interested in a short side trip to Bayeux, let me know. It's not on our itinerary, but François doesn't mind taking you there. The city was fortunate and avoided destruction following D-Day, and the eleventh-century, world-renowned Bayeux Tapestry alone is worth a visit."

Without hesitating, Andrew and Sarah, as well as Steve and Linda, said they wanted to go and agreed to leave with François within a few minutes.

"I'm going to check out the beach life and work on my tan," Harry announced while he rubbed his round belly.

"Thanks for the warning," Naomi snarked. "Now I know where I *won't* go."

"JuJu, wanna join me? Did you bring your bikini?" he gave Julia one of his creepy winks.

"Harry, it's tempting, but I think I'll catch up with Emily and see how things are going at home," Julia said from the check-in desk, barely bothering to conceal her disgust. Stella wondered how long it would be before she exploded.

"Ah, your loss, ha ha. Tell Em I said hi. I'm sure she's missing me," Harry said and went to the elevator.

Stella said to Naomi, "The wife's probably ecstatic to be rid of him. Too bad her friend has him nipping at her heels. I hope Julia's still willing to be friends with her when she gets back home."

Their room was small, but comfortable and clean, and the bathroom was well stocked with guest amenities. Stella picked up one of the complimentary soaps and held it to her nose. A potent but not overpowering lavender scent greeted her. She decided there were more than enough soaps and called, "I'm going to snag one of the soaps. There are plenty."

"Did you see the sachets on our pillows? A note says they're a welcome gift."

"I love it." Stella remembered how David's mother put lavender sachets in the bath cabinet where she kept guest towels. Maybe Stella would do it at home, too.

"Okay, I'm in," Naomi announced from her bed.

"In where?" Stella had wandered to the balcony, where she took in the view over the bay. It was low tide, and people were walking around the cement blocks Caroline mentioned earlier. They didn't bother her, but she could see where they'd be in the way when couples posed for romantic wedding photos.

"The hotel's Wi-Fi," Naomi jumped off the bed. "And now I'm ready for some ice cream. I never got my two scoops yesterday, so I'll have three today."

"Since it was my fault we got distracted, I'll pay for your treat today."

"It was The Troub's fault." Naomi reached for her purse. "Let's walk around first and work up an appetite."

Strolling through the old, winding streets, they took pictures of cozy houses and the colorful hollyhocks growing in abundance in every garden. They stopped to enjoy the heavy scent of dark red roses climbing up wooden trellises and watch dozens of butterflies flutter from flower to flower. They peeked into a small church squeezed in between two houses and climbed up a hill to an overlook with a magnificent view of the vast English Channel and the picturesque town.

After buying their ice cream, they rested on a large rock on the beach.

Stella dug her feet into the sand and wiggled her toes. "You know what?" she said while she watched gentle waves rolling in from the open water. "I've decided to make a deal with you."

"Oh, I like this opening." Naomi swiped a speck of chocolate ice cream off her nose. She tried to keep her three scoops on the sugar cone, but the ice cream kept running down the sides of the cone.

"From now till the end of this trip, I won't talk about David. Seeing the beauty all around us and listening to Caroline's story of the death-wedding, I've decided you're right, and I need to focus on the future."

Naomi caught some of her ice cream with her tongue before it reached her fingers.

"I still love David, and know in my heart I always will, and it won't be easy to ignore those feelings. But it kills me to wait for the impossible to happen. Then, when we're back in Paris, if he's still there, I'll hear what he has to say. I need closure."

Naomi frowned at her. "I hope you decide to say a few things to him, too. Like, 'Fuck you.'" She licked more of her ice cream. "So, what's our deal if you break your promise?"

"If I don't keep my end of the deal, I'll let you set me up with a blind date at home."

"YESSS!" Naomi pumped a fist in the air—and her ice cream went flying over her head and landed with a *splat* in front of a few happy seagulls. "Oops..." She giggled.

"You know what, Stella? I know it won't be easy to push your feelings for David aside. But a relationship can't be one-sided. Give yourself a chance to move on. And, in case you're wondering, I believe it's possible to be in love with more than one person."

"I can't make myself fall in love with someone else. But I'll try not to compare every man with David. I can't promise you more."

"It's a start. And it's the last time we mention his name, right?" Naomi said with a stern look.

Stella nodded, "Okay."

After dinner Stella and Naomi sipped a local red wine and watched the sunset from the terrace.

The fiery sphere dipped behind the edge of the water, and soon the first stars appeared in the darkening sky.

The sound of waves lapping against the tall stone walls below them, and the laughter of couples and families walking along the promenade, were the perfect background noise to help Stella relax. After a moment, she imagined herself walking along this beach with a little boy holding her hand. And a little girl jumping up and down next to David, singing a song for him or chattering up a storm.

No! Stop it!

There wouldn't be any children holding David's hand. At least not hers! David wasn't part of her future. This was really getting ridiculous. She had promised Naomi—and herself—to let the past go.

She sat up straight and took a fortifying sip of her wine. Two tables away the sisters, Karen and Jenna, sat with Susan, Lynn, and Julia. They were showing each other some of the souvenirs they must've bought earlier—T-shirts, shot glasses, postcards.

"Should we buy something for everybody at home?" she asked.

"We can look in Saint-Malo tomorrow. And maybe we find something with a pirate theme for Rev," Naomi suggested. "Like an eye patch or a bandanna. Arrr."

"What would he do with them?"

"What he does with everything else. Try it on, make fun of it, then leave it on the next chair and forget about it."

"I wonder if he found his coffee mugs you moved around when you were over last week. Don't think I didn't notice, my friend."

"Ha, I forgot about them... I know he hates it when anyone touches his mugs." Naomi rolled her eyes. "Come on, they *are* just coffee mugs. But he treats them like they're sacred."

"You know they're special because Dinah gave them to him."

"Yeah, yeah. It's so cute how much he adores his little sister."

"Did you just call Revan cute?" Stella snickered. "Don't let him hear you. It doesn't go with the image he strives for. The tough guy and fearless adventurer..."

"Ladies, can I interest you in a nightcap?" a familiar voice drifted over to them.

Harry approached the table where the five women sat. He swayed and had to hold on to the backs of chairs. Then transferred his two-handed grip to Julia's shoulders.

Naomi sucked in a breath and her eyes opened wide.

Julia stood up, forcing his hands to drop off her shoulders, and hissed through gritted teeth, "Do. Not. Touch. Me!"

"He did not just...!" Stella gasped.

"Yes ma'am, he did. And he better not come near me with his wandering hands, or he can kiss his family jewels goodbye," Naomi growled.

A half hour later, when they left the restaurant and walked past the inside bar area, the wall-mounted TV showed a reporter standing in front of a police barricade.

"What does the chyron say?"

"Someone took three people hostage in the Paris catacombs. The authorities aren't releasing details yet." Naomi translated while she continued to read.

"Didn't Kai go there? What's up with those catacombs?"

"Yeah, but he went yesterday. It sounds as if this happened sometime this morning."

Stella shrugged it off. "Okay. I'm sure it'll be all over the internet tomorrow, and Caroline can fill us in. It's not really our problem."

CHAPTER 18

DAVID—JULY 2018

On Monday morning, David breakfasted in his hotel room while looking out over the Tuileries Garden. He turned his phone over and read Stella's message again.

> I'll be in touch when I'm back. Maybe we can talk then. Stella.

She had slipped through his fingers...

Throughout Sunday night, he replayed the auditorium scene in his mind while the bright neon green numbers on his digital alarm clock relentlessly ticked off the passage of time. Stella was out there somewhere—so close, but not close enough.

She must have left the auditorium while he was barreling down the stairs at breakneck speed. He must have missed her by seconds. Why didn't she wait for him? She must've known he'd want to see her.

Wrong, you dumbass! You said in your letter you 'had to let her go.' Why would she think you'd want to talk to her now?

Chasing her through Paris was impossible. By the time he managed to leave the voice message on her phone, she could've been anywhere.

He remembered a board game he used to play with his parents and sister on family game nights. One player was a criminal, Mr. X, and the other players were Scotland Yard detectives. They chased Mr. X through London by either taxi, bus, subway, or boat. Mr. X had to reveal his kind of transportation and his current location every five turns. But he also had a few black tokens. They were frustrating, because when he used them, he didn't have to disclose his mode of transportation, and was harder to track.

Right now Stella was in possession of a whole bag of black tokens, and David was empty-handed.

He ran his fingers through his hair, then read her message again.

> I'll be in touch when I'm back.

He clung to those words like a lifeline.

He hadn't planned to stay the whole week. He was here on a two-day audition for the lead role in *Don Giovanni*, and was supposed to return to London Thursday.

Aaron told him Jerome was impressed with his portfolio, but they still had to follow strict procedures to secure the contract for this highly coveted role. To work with this conductor, who had the reputation of being the wunderkind of the century, was a once-in-a-lifetime opportunity.

And David might have sabotaged his chances without singing even one note, courtesy of yesterday's display of wackiness.

When he finally returned to the private box, Aaron was there waiting for him, but they agreed to let things settle a bit before discussing it. Aaron was not only his agent and manager, David considered him one of his few close friends.

One thing was crystal clear to him. He would stay in Paris and wait for Stella. An understudy could fill in for him in London for a few more days.

He loved his work, and took his career seriously, but it had morphed into a very demanding, egotistical lover. It took a lot more than it gave. The balance was off.

He had known the price for this success going in, hadn't been able to spend every holiday at home, and had been okay with it.

And relationships? After the fiasco with an ex-girlfriend several years ago, it was easier to concentrate on his work. Which he was okay with, too.

But then he met Stella and fell head over heels in love with her, and—within only a few weeks—allowed himself to dream of something more.

David pulled Stella's picture out of his wallet. She'd been sitting on the rim of Buckingham Fountain, her hand making circles in the water while she smiled at him.

Just recalling the moment made his heart squeeze.

He inhaled through his nose, exhaled through his mouth. Time to reply to her message. She'd be wondering what was taking him so long. In fact, knowing her, she'd probably been checking her phone every five minutes throughout the night. It was disrespectful of him to keep her waiting.

Being disrespectful didn't stop you last year.

David put her photo on the table and started typing.

Stella, I'm here until Wednesday for an audition, but I'll change my ticket and stay until Saturday. I need to see and talk to you. Please call me as soon as you're back in the city. D.

After he read the message again, he deleted it. It sounded too impersonal. He'd write to her later.

He needed to be composed, calm, and in control for his audition in a few hours, and right now he was neither. Being outdoors usually helped him relax and ground himself, and the park across the street would have to do.

He finished his eggs, toast, fruit and tea—none of which he could taste—and left the hotel. Not even 9 am, but both sides of the boulevard were packed with idling tour buses, and herds of tourist groups with their stupid little umbrellas stood around gaping at every statue they could possibly find.

Man, you're in a great mood. Better snap out of it—fast!

David found an unoccupied bench under a copse of trees close to one of the many fountains and water basins. As it so often did, the sound of the splashing water took David back to his childhood and afternoons spent in Grant Park.

When he was no more than ten or eleven years old, his mother once found him near Buckingham Fountain. He wasn't supposed to go there alone, but when he left his house, he hadn't paid attention to where he was going until he found himself in the park.

His mom sat down next to him and wiped away his tears. "Honey, you scared me. What are you doing here all by yourself?"

"You're telling us all the time to go to a quiet place to think when something bothers us. When I'm here, the water washes my pain away."

"I meant a quiet place at home, and you know it. But what kind of pain are you talking about?"

He struggled how to tell her about what had happened. "Mom, some kids at school are making fun of me because I like to sing. They say I should play sports instead of doing music. I hate them." He smacked the water.

"Honey, hate is a strong word. We have to be very careful with it." She dried his eyes with one of her soft, lavender-scented handkerchiefs.

"But I don't like them. They're mean. And at least I'm not telling them they stink at soccer or tennis."

"I'm glad you don't, and I'm proud of you for being the better person. Sometimes people say hurtful things because they don't know what else to say."

"But they don't say those things to Sabrina. And she likes to sing and dance."

"Yes, she does. But we live in a world where some talents are tied to a certain image. Classical singing or ballet dancing are seen by many as a female prerogative."

"What's a pregotive?"

"A prerogative? It means a right or a privilege reserved for a certain group of people."

"That's stupid."

"Please don't use that word either. But you're right. It's very wrong. And artists like Luciano Pavarotti, Fred Astaire, Mikhail Baryshnikov, and many more have exceptional talent and have proven those people wrong."

His mom pulled him into her arms then, even though he was a big boy and too old to be hugged in public. He didn't care. His mom and dad made him feel safe. "What does Dad tell you at least once a week?"

"He wants to be able to hit a ball like Frank Thomas."

"Well, yeah," his mother laughed, "but what else?"

"Oh, to find something I enjoy and follow my dreams."

"And is singing something you enjoy doing?"

"Yes. I want to be a famous singer when I grow up."

"Then do it."

The voice of a tour guide brought David back to the present. Sitting in this park right now, twenty-five years after his conversation with his mother, he could still feel her arms around him.

His parents were the best role models he could imagine. They showed their children how crucial it is to fight for what's right, and to never accept prejudice and hateful behavior.

What would his mother say if she knew how he had ended his relationship with Stella? He only told his family they weren't seeing each other anymore. His parents expressed their regret but said nothing more. His sister, on the other hand, called him some things which would make a sailor blush.

David checked the time. Ten o'clock. He took a deep breath. Still plenty of time. His eyes were on the fountain in front of him, but he didn't see the glittering drops of water shooting up in the air and collecting in the basin.

He thought about the demands of his career.

In the fall of 2016, after being on the road for Broadway tours for six years, he won the contract for the lead role of *The Phantom* in a permanent stage production in Hamburg, Germany, an opportunity he'd be crazy to refuse. His career was well established in the United States, and he was used to seeing his own masked face on billboards or magazine covers.

Being onstage in Europe would skyrocket his international fame. The little boy who was harassed by classmates stood on the biggest stages worldwide and sang his heart out.

He told Stella about the opportunity while he was in Philadelphia for a week and hadn't yet accepted the offer.

"Are we going to see each other while you're in Germany? How long do you have to be there?" she asked. "Flying to Europe isn't as easy as flying within the States."

"The contract is for six months, and I don't know what'll happen afterward," he answered.

"I don't want to stand in your way or hold you back," she looked up at him and he could see it wasn't easy for her to say.

"I have no right to ask you to decline such an incredible offer. You've worked too hard to get where you are. Just as I worked too hard to get my degrees and my job. I can't imagine leaving the Library Company any more than you can imagine not performing onstage six out of seven days a week."

"I love you more than anything, Stella." David fought back tears. "You have no idea what it means to me to have you support me this way, to have you encourage me to accept the contract."

"If you turned it down, you'd regret it for the rest of your life. Six months will fly by. Our love is strong enough to survive this. I believe in us, and I'll wait here for you."

He left for Hamburg in December 2016, and for the next six months they didn't see each other in person.

In May of 2017 he signed a contract to perform in Budapest for six months. He flew to the States for an eight-day visit and told Stella. When she asked him, "And what are your plans after Budapest?" his honest answer was, "I don't know."

But not long after he arrived in Budapest, he began to ask himself if it was fair to Stella to keep her waiting. How many more times would he have to tell her "I don't know?"

He was constantly on the move. She had her roots firmly planted in Philadelphia, like those old trees in the parks she loved so much. And what could he offer her? A life racing from city to city, from hotel to hotel.

He loved Stella with his whole heart. But the fear of losing her was starting to plant tiny seeds of uncertainty in him.

And a few weeks later, in July 2017, he wrote her a letter.

Just thinking about the atrocious thing made him feel sick to his stomach. He couldn't take it back—no matter how much he'd wanted to every blasted day since he dropped it in the mailbox.

He was a coward last year, and he still hated himself for it. It wasn't who his parents raised him to be, and who he prided himself on being. How could he encourage children to believe in themselves when he hadn't been able to trust his own feelings?

But the greatest shock hit him when he noticed how much his life mirrored the fictional Phantom's life. And just like the desolate man who longed for Christine to ease his sorrow and pain, he knew Stella held the key to his happiness.

If he didn't find a way to set things right with her, he'd not only lose all self-respect, but the woman he loved more than anything would be forever gone from his life.

Seeing Stella yesterday—for a split second from afar—showed him it was time to face his ghosts and fight his fears.

CHAPTER 19

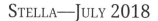

STELLA—JULY 2018

After a full night of sleep, Stella and Naomi were awake in time to watch the sunrise over Arromanches from their room. They saw a few people on their morning stroll and a delivery van dropping off fresh produce at a restaurant. Seagulls circled over the beach, squawking to each other, and swooping down at astonishing speed to pick up anything edible.

Still up on their balcony, Stella spotted the couple who was so clearly in love. Naomi had dubbed them "the honeymooners." They cuddled together on a massive rock, the woman nestled in the man's arms, her head resting on his shoulder. Stella couldn't see their faces, but their body language told her they were content and cherishing the moment.

"You know what?" she said, "this honeymoon tour *is* a great idea. When Caroline rattled off all the statistics about marriages, second marriages, money spent on destination weddings and so on, I thought it was over the top. But I've been thinking about it. When a couple gets married in their mid-twenties, they have loads of college debt and maybe their parents pay for a short honeymoon. But older couples have achieved something in life, maybe had to deal with some setbacks, and can appreciate their second chance at happiness so much more."

"You're right, the average younger couple doesn't look for a trip like this. We sell so many trips to Vegas or Florida, I started to ask myself if there's nothing else out there," Naomi said and put her phone away.

"And granted, not everybody can afford this kind of trip, which is where Caroline's numbers come into play, but I want to find a way to offer this to more customers. There could be two different packages, the more affordable one, and the luxury one."

Stella continued to watch the town waking up. Store owners raising the steel roll-up gates and bringing out racks of postcards and T-shirts. "You know, Caroline is wonderful. I'm fascinated by her stories. They add a nice touch to the tour."

Naomi threw a few personal items into her carry-on. "I don't think she's a random tour guide. Remember how she said she met Mom a few years ago in England? Mom told me later about a woman who had just gotten out of a bitter divorce. I bet it was Caroline. But she's wearing some nice bling on her ring finger, so maybe she found her Prince Charming along the way and it gave her the idea for honeymoon tours."

"Who knows? In any case, I'm ready for breakfast. How 'bout you?"

"Always ready."

Entering the restaurant, Stella saw the honeymooners sitting at a table for four. She elbowed Naomi and tilted her head in the direction of their table.

"Good morning! Mind if we sit with you?" she asked.

"Not at all. Please, join us," the woman said and pointed to the empty chairs. "I have to admit, I couldn't keep up with the names yesterday, so I'll just introduce myself again. I'm Sarah, and this is my husband, Andrew." Sarah beamed at him and reached for his hand.

"I'd rather introduce myself each day anew if we can avoid wearing name tags. They make me feel like a kinder-gartener in the first week of school. I'm Naomi."

"And I'm Stella."

After they sat down and helped themselves to coffee from the thermal carafe, Naomi lowered her voice and asked, "Okay, you have to excuse my question, but how long have you been married?"

Stella couldn't believe Naomi's bluntness.

Andrew winked at Sarah and said, "I told you people would pick up on it right away."

"Two weeks," Sarah said, her eyes locked on Andrew's. "I still can't believe it."

"Me neither, love," Andrew squeezed her hand.

How sweet; is he blushing? Stella felt as if they were intruding, and almost wanted to get up to sit at another table. But Andrew must have sensed it, because he said, "Sorry, we don't want to make you uncomfortable. It took us a long, long time, with many roadblocks, to get where we are today. But what counts is the now, and we intend to enjoy every second of it."

"Enough about us. Now we'll eat," Sarah commanded with a chuckle, "before all those yummy-smelling fresh, hot rolls and croissants are gone."

"You're speaking my language, Sarah," Naomi pushed her chair back. "Chocolate croissant number one, here I come."

During breakfast, Andrew and Sarah shared a little bit about themselves. They were from Baltimore, where Sarah owned a travel agency specializing in culinary tours, and Andrew worked as a laryngologist at Johns Hopkins Hospital.

"Say it again?" Naomi asked. "Is there an English term?"

"I'm an ear, nose and throat surgeon, and specialize in voice disorders and injuries."

"Thank you, but that sounds almost as complicated. At least now I know which body parts we're talking about."

Caroline clapped her hands and called out, "Let's get going, group. François is waiting for us. Fifteen minutes till departure."

Once they had boarded the bus, Caroline said, "We start today in Saint-Malo. The packages I handed out yesterday contain brochures about the mystical town. Maybe you had a chance to look at them last night, but if not, then you have two hours till we get there."

Of course, Harry had to call attention to himself. "What, we had homework? Shucks... Oops, I forgot my folder at the hotel. Julia, gimme yours."

"I don't have one, Harry. We were given one to share, and you took it. I was only able to download some of the information on my cell phone during the bus ride."

Without looking at Harry, Caroline reached for two on the seat next to her and handed one to him and one to Julia.

"'preciate it, hon!"

A throat-clearing sound came from Steve. It was only 8:30 on their second day, but Harry seemed to try everyone's patience.

"Caroline, do you know what's happening in the Paris catacombs?" Steve's wife, Linda, asked after a while.

"I can only tell you what I read in the newspaper this morning. Someone entered the catacombs illegally yesterday morning and took three hostages. The names are still being withheld. And so far none of the usual terrorist groups have stepped up to claim responsibility.

The authorities have been quiet. There's supposed to be a press conference later."

"Please keep us informed if you hear anything new," Steve said. "You just don't know when and where someone will blow a fuse these days."

Caroline said, "I'll certainly let you know as soon as there's a new development."

After they arrived in Saint-Malo, François dropped them off at a sheltered harbor, where Stella saw small and medium-sized boats bobbing on the water. She waved to a couple of boaters drinking coffee and tossing breadcrumbs to the hovering seagulls.

On one side of the harbor stood a massive stone wall which must have sheltered the town for centuries. It was a stark contrast to the picturesque coastal town of Arromanches. Instead of admiring rose hips and hollyhocks, they faced a fortress.

Caroline led them through a stone gate. "This is La Grand' Porte, the Great Gate. It's one of the two oldest gates of Saint-Malo and was built in the fifteenth century. The two round towers were added in the sixteenth century as reinforcement." She pointed to the impenetrable walls. "The ramparts encircle the whole town. The loop is about two kilometers long, that's a little over one mile, and you can leave or rejoin it at several locations. We'll walk part of it together, but feel free to follow it all the way on your own later and enjoy the views over the bay, the rocky shore, and peek into small backyards."

"How old is Saint-Malo?" Stella asked.

"Saint-Malo dates back to a monastic settlement founded in the sixth century. The city wall was built during the twelfth century, mainly to protect the city from pirates and other invaders. Like other regions of France, it has tried to maintain its independence throughout history and saw its share of fighting. Its unofficial motto is, *Ni Français, ni Breton, Malouin suis*, which translates to 'Neither French, nor Breton, but Malouin.'"

"You said pirates. Any famous ones?" Steve asked.

"I believe most have more national than international fame. They weren't called pirates, though. They were known as privateers, or corsairs. And, apparently, it was a very profitable business for many residents of Saint-Malo."

John looked around. "The houses don't look as old as the wall."

"Good observation. Between 1940 and 1944, German forces occupied Saint-Malo. In 1944, the Allies bombarded it and destroyed most of the town.

"When the Nazis retreated, they set fire to the old buildings. What the bombs didn't destroy, the fire did. Only 182 of the original 865 buildings within the walls survived, and all were damaged to different degrees. When the library burned down, thirty thousand old books and manuscripts were reduced to ashes. But the ramparts are authentic. They survived both the bombings and the fire."

"How terrible. Imagine the treasures lost," Stella mumbled.

"Saint-Malo was painstakingly rebuilt, stone for stone, over a period of twelve years between 1948 to 1960," Caroline added.

"Okay! It's 11 o'clock and we have four hours here. Because the tide is low, we're beginning with a walk to Fort National, which was built in 1689 to protect the port of Saint-Malo. If you prefer to spend an hour or two on your own, we'll meet for lunch at a quaint bistro with an adjoining cheese and butter shop at 1:30." She handed out business cards. "Here is the address."

Stella thought she heard a mumbled comment about brats and krauts, but decided it was best to disregard Harry's babblings. She would've loved to ignore the man completely, but since they were part of the same tour, it didn't seem possible.

Everyone except Harry decided to stay with Caroline, and together they walked through one of the many gates leading to the wide beach.

Stella looked over her shoulder toward the town and said, "Imagine how it must've looked when tall ships approached after having spent weeks and months out on the water. It's so impressive."

"The sea is pretty rough here, too. This area has the highest tides in Europe, over forty-three feet. At low tide, you can see endless ocean floor, but when the water moves in, it comes fast and furious," Caroline said.

After returning to the town, they walked on the ramparts before Caroline guided them through narrow streets, when a blue facade caught Stella's attention. Tall white letters announced La Maison du Beurre and the scent of cheese combined with garlic and spices teased her appetite.

She heard Naomi's stomach rumble in agreement, and they both giggled.

Like the day before, the group was seated at one long table. Stella admired the harmony of the bistro's interior, with its combination of modern black tables and chairs, sand-washed walls, and exposed wooden beams.

"I'm going to gain ten pounds this week," Naomi said. "But every ounce is so worth it. This fresh baguette, with the cheeses—I think I'm in food heaven. Now if only there'd be a small piece of chocolate for dessert."

"I agree a hundred percent," Sarah said. "This bistro will go on my must-visit list of recommendations for my culinary tours."

"I'm so glad you like it. And you're lucky because they make candy here as well. Try their caramels," Caroline said. She leaned back in her chair, took a sip of water, and asked, "Who is interested in a Breton lai while we're waiting for our food?"

Stella raised her hand. "Me! Even though I don't know what it is. I just hope it's not some complicated folk dance."

"No, don't worry. It's a form of medieval romantic short story," Caroline explained before she started, "Not much is known about the woman who wrote it, not even her real name. She lived around 1200 and said about herself in a poem, 'Marie is my name, and I am from France.'"

Caroline rested her forearms on the table and looked around. With all eyes on her, she began, "There were two knights who lived near Saint-Malo in adjoining houses, separated by a tall, dark wall. One knight was married, the other wasn't. The wife and the unmarried knight took a liking to each other. They never met in person, but every night, when the husband was asleep, they sat by their windows and talked to each other, sometimes exchanging small gifts.

"Over time, the husband grew suspicious and asked what she was doing at the window night after night. She replied she listened to the nightingale sing. He was enraged, and had his servant capture the bird, killed it in front of her eyes and threw its lifeless body at her.

"Saddened, she embroidered a silk cloth in gold-threaded writing and wrapped the dead bird in it, and to let her lover know she couldn't continue meeting him anymore, sent him the nightingale. He preserved the bird in a small container which he decorated in jewels, and always carried it with him."

"Not the typical love story, but so romantic," Stella said and saw she wasn't the only one dabbing her eyes.

"Marie de France's work depicted women as having to make many sacrifices in the name of love, and often as being virtually imprisoned by their husbands," Caroline added.

"At least the husband didn't kill his wife, only the poor bird," Lynn said. "I wonder what made a young woman write such a story more than eight hundred years ago."

CHAPTER 20

Stella—July 2018

"Our drive to Mont Saint-Michel will take about one hour. Once we arrive there, we'll check into our hotel first, then tour the island together," Caroline announced after they were on the bus again.

"How much time will we spend on the island?" Susan asked. "The itinerary says we'll go to the abbey, then have dinner afterward."

"Yes, I've scheduled two hours to tour the monastery."

"Will we be able to walk around the island? What's the tide schedule?" Lynn wanted to know.

"We should be in luck and have a low tide late this afternoon. If you're interested in walking around the bottom of the island, we can adjust our schedule. In fact, I encourage you to take advantage of the low tide. Not every visitor has the chance to experience seeing it from the bay. Most tourists spend only a few hours here and can't afford to wait for the water to recede."

Two hours later they followed the half-mile-long footbridge connecting the mainland with the majestic island surrounded by marsh grass and sand. The abbey and monastery sat high atop the mount, with a small medieval town at its feet. Soon the grass and beach would be covered by salt water.

Stella stopped walking and grabbed Naomi's arm. "This looks as if time stood still, don't you think?"

"Yeah, if you can ignore all the tourists," Naomi snorted.

"I think everything we've seen so far is amazing, but this is beyond words. I read that only fifty people or so live in the village year-round, but more than three million visitors come through each year." Stella took some photos before they hurried to catch up with the group.

"Mont Saint-Michel's history goes back more than a thousand years," Caroline told them as they got closer to the large stone gate at the bottom of the hill. "It was a popular destination for pilgrims until the Reformation in the sixteenth century. After the French Revolution in the eighteenth century it was turned into a prison. Only since the 1920s has Christian worship been practiced here again."

Climbing up the twisted, steep and narrow cobblestone streets, they often had to walk in a single line. A boy with a British accent asked his father in an awe-inspired voice, "Is this where Harry Potter lives?" and Stella silently agreed with him. She wouldn't have been surprised to see a few Hogwarts students glancing out of second-floor windows of the ancient houses lining the alleys.

After touring the abbey, Caroline said, "We have a little bit of time before our dinner at La Mère Poulard, which is just over there." They stood on a small square at the bottom of the hill, and she pointed to a building across from them. It was made of smooth granite like all the other buildings around it, and had dark red, almost maroon awnings and painted wooden trim. "The tide is still far enough out to walk around the island, or you can explore the village on your own. I'll be happy to give you a few ideas of what's worth checking out. We'll meet here again at a quarter to seven."

Stella and Naomi took advantage of the low tide. Halfway around the island, Naomi stopped and looked up.

"Holy cow. It's impossible to climb up there. What did Caroline say how high the mount is?"

"She said the abbey sits two hundred sixty feet above sea level," Stella recalled, taking in the jagged granite with bushes and low trees covering parts of it.

Continuing to walk over the seaweed-covered sandy beach, they arrived at a small chapel sitting on a rocky outcropping. Built of ancient stone, with watermarks and algae at the base of its four walls, it faced the sea. They climbed the rough stone steps and peeked through a slit of a window, then looked out over the expanse of the bay. In the distance, they saw water glittering in the early evening sunlight.

"You've found a true treasure," Caroline's voice startled them. She sat on a large rock. "This is the chapelle Saint-Aubert, and not many people venture far enough around the island to discover it."

"What do you know about it?" Stella asked, hoping Caroline had another story for them.

"There are many legends surrounding this place. One claims the rock on which the chapel sits was pushed down from the top of the island by a child. I don't know...but have you heard the story about Aubert, Bishop of Avranches, the founder of this abbey?"

Stella and Naomi both shook their heads.

"Well, it is said the archangel Michael appeared to Aubert three times in dreams and asked him to build a sanctuary bearing his name. The first two times Aubert ignored the request, but the third time, the archangel poked his finger into Aubert's skull to get his point across. This time, Aubert complied, and had the relics of the archangel transferred from Mount Gargano in Italy to the Mont-Tombe, as Mont Saint-Michel was known then. The sanctuary was dedicated to Saint Michael in October 709."

"The angel poked a finger into Aubert's skull?" Naomi asked and scrunched up her face. "Yuck."

"According to legend." Caroline shrugged. "The relic of his skull, including the hole, is on display in the Saint-Gervais Basilica in Avranches."

While listening to Caroline's story, they had wandered back into the small village and met the rest of the group at La Mère Poulard. Once seated and looking at their menus, Harry complained, "Omelets? We're supposed to eat breakfast for dinner?"

"You can order something else, but omelets are what Annette Poulard served when she and her husband Victor opened this restaurant in 1888," Caroline explained. "They..."

"Oh, no, do I sense another love story? How many die this time?" Harry grumbled.

Julia put her menu down and said, "Please continue, Caroline." She sat next to Harry but avoided looking at him.

Others also encouraged Caroline and looked at her with interest.

"Okay, so.... In 1872, the well-known architect Édouard Corroyer was appointed to restore the Abbey of Mont Saint-Michel. Édouard frequently traveled from Paris to the Mont, bringing with him his wife, child, and their maid, Annette Boutiaut. Annette was an incredibly good cook, and Édouard was a gourmet. He liked to brag about her skills, and said she was able to cook everything he asked for.

"One day, when they arrived in the fog by a horse-drawn carriage, the island appeared dark and forbidding to Annette. The tide was rising fast, and she didn't know how to get out of the carriage without getting soaked. The son of a local baker, Victor Poulard, recognized her dilemma and carried her onto dry land, and soon, while Édouard worked on the old Abbey, Victor grew closer to Annette. He wasted no time, and the two were married in January 1873." Caroline paused to raise her glass and take a sip of her wine.

"Later in 1873, the young couple acquired their first hostel business on the island and began to offer meals. Meanwhile, after news spread about the abbey Édouard had restored, more visitors began to arrive at the Mont. For a long time, it had only been of interest to shrimp fishermen and convicts' families, but now scholars, archaeologists, and pilgrims came. Annette remembered her own arrival on the Mont, remembered being hungry and cold, and decided to add a lunch menu.

"But serving lunch guests caused a problem. She never knew how many people would arrive between tides, and planning ahead was difficult, if not impossible. Annette started to invent new, lighter recipes, avoiding heavy meals of red meat, using more local products from the bay, the land, and the sea between Normandy and Brittany. Her most famous meals were her light, fluffy omelets.

"A few years later, Victor and Annette sold their first establishment and bought another property here on the

Mont, closer to the gate. They opened an *auberge* in 1888, and later added three annexes where we are sitting right now.

"Annette didn't travel, and she rarely left the Mont, but she loved to listen to her guests' stories, and often asked them for a photograph or a drawing as a memento, a practice which has continued till today. You'll want to look at the pictures later," Caroline pointed at the walls. "Annette and Victor lived happily until Victor died in 1923 and Annette in 1931."

Andrew raised his glass and said, "To Annette and Victor!" and most of their group joined him by repeating the toast.

Before they left, Stella and Naomi checked out the photos on the walls.

"Wow, the question isn't who was here, but who *wasn't*?" Stella said.

Naomi put her hands to her heart and sucked in a breath. "Harrison Ford was here! Right where we're standing. I can't believe it." She put her face closer to his photo and took a selfie.

"You and your hero. I'm surprised you're not kneeling. But look over there! Pablo Picasso! And there's Theodore Roosevelt," Stella said in a similar awe-inspired voice. "Oh, and Ernest Hemingway."

"Who?" Naomi asked with a wide grin and linked arms with Stella.

Leaving the island, they listened to frogs and crickets serenading their potential mates, and in the approaching twilight, the marshes looked very mystical.

When Naomi noticed the long line of people waiting for the next shuttle bus, she said, "The evening is too beautiful to squeeze into a bus with tons of sweaty strangers and overtired babies. Let's walk back to the hotel, it only took us thirty minutes this afternoon."

"I'd like to come back in the fall or winter months. Can you imagine how it would look with dense fog covering the lower half of the island?"

"The only thing missing would be one of your ghost-tour guides swinging a lantern back and forth. Boo!"

"Ooh, spooky," Stella laughed, and they made up stories about ghosts hiding in the marsh grass on their way back to the hotel.

"We missed the press conference," Stella sat on their balcony and poured them both a glass of the wine the hotel gave them as a courtesy gift.

"Why are you so interested in the hostage situation? We don't have anything to do with it."

"I don't know, maybe because we're so close to it?"

"I bet the whole thing will be forgotten as soon as something else comes up," Naomi said. "Imagine the national scandal if a visitor leaves his sticky fingerprints in the Hall of Mirrors at Versailles."

"Could be. John seems to follow the reports, and I'm sure he'll tell us if there's a new development."

For a moment, they sat in silence. The pastureland, where only hours ago sheep had grazed, was covered by water again. The surreal light of a full moon created the illusion of countless tiny sparkles.

And in the distance, the island seemed illuminated by thousands of flickering candles, their warm yellow glow also reflecting in the dark water.

"Can you imagine anything more beautiful than this?" Stella sighed. "I liked the story of how Victor and Annette met and how he carried her onto dry land. And it had a happy ending, too, for a change."

"Yeah, it was lovely. Oh...speaking of happy endings. Look at our honeymooners going for a late-night stroll under the full moon. How cute."

"Aren't you even a little bit jealous of them?" Stella asked, watching Andrew and Sarah leave the hotel.

"No. Andrew said they had to deal with many roadblocks before they got where they are now," Naomi said and topped off their glasses. "I'd rather take the direct route, no detours, and no hoops to jump through."

"Wouldn't we all?" Stella muttered.

CHAPTER 21

Stella—July 2018

Stella wrapped a scrunchie around her hair then let the ponytail fall over her shoulder. On her way past a low table in the hotel's lobby, a headline on the front page of a newspaper caught her eye. "Naomi. There's Kai!"

"Where?" Naomi craned her neck at the large urn where she was helping herself to a cup of coffee.

"Here, in the paper. Ugh, it's all in French. What's Kai doing on the front page of *Le Monde*? Oh my God, he's at the same place we saw on TV yesterday. What happened?" Stella's voice rose.

"If you'd give me a minute, I'd be able to read it and tell you," Naomi held out a hand for the newspaper.

But Stella had just spotted John, Michael, Karen, and Jenna sitting in an alcove of the lobby, concentrating on something on TV, and pulled Naomi along to join them.

"Jeeesus, Stella, slow down." Naomi freed herself from Stella's iron grip. "Hi, guys, what's going on?"

"There's something about the catacombs. Looks like a repeat of last night, though," John said.

"Oh good, it's in English." Stella was relieved—until she recognized one of the two men standing in front of a dark green, almost black, shack-like building.

"This is Leo Wu, and I'm reporting from the catacombs of Paris, where an unknown man took three hostages two days ago. With me is Kai Olders." Leo looked up at Kai, who was a head taller than the reporter. "Kai, you came face-to-face with the captor and the hostages. Tell us what you saw."

"Oh, no!" Stella grabbed Naomi's arm again. "Did you hear him?"

"Stella, for cryin' out loud, I don't wanna spill coffee on my white shorts," Naomi hissed and set the coffee cup on the table next to her.

"Leo, let me clarify. I didn't come face-to-face with him. I only saw his back," Kai replied.

"We were told the tours have been suspended. What were you doing there? And isn't it illegal to be in the catacombs after hours?" Leo prodded.

"I guess it is, but I was also told it doesn't bother the police too much. And it's an open secret that there's lots of business going on after the tunnels are closed. So anyway, this one guy from our group knew about a cave that was set up with tables, chairs, air mattresses and blankets. There were also snacks, beer and bottled water. Three of us decided to stay and have some fun."

"Why did you want to sleep in an underground tunnel full of bones and skulls?"

"Such a chance doesn't come up too often. I guess it's the grown-up version of telling ghost stories at a sleepover," Kai grinned.

"When did you run into the kidnapper?"

"We were on our way out of the tunnels around nine in the morning when we heard voices. It was strange, because, as you said, the tunnels are closed. At first we ignored the voices. But then we heard a crash, and someone screamed."

"What kind of crash?"

"As if someone threw a coffee maker against the wall."

"A coffee maker?" Leo's eyes narrowed to slits.

"Listen, you asked what kind of crash. It sounded like someone dropped a small appliance, and glass shattered, okay?"

"And what about the person who screamed? When was it?"

"The scream came right after the crash. It was a woman's voice. The guys and I just looked at each other and decided to check out what was going on. Now...the tunnels can be low and narrow, and at times you must be on your hands and knees to get through. And it's like a labyrinth down there—one wrong turn, and you end up who knows where." Kai stopped talking and raked his fingers through his hair.

"After a few minutes, we came around a bend and the voices were much closer. I was in front. No idea how I got there because I'm not familiar with the tunnel system, but there I was, and my half-forgotten military training from almost twenty years ago kicked in. I got on my belly, slid to the corner to peek around, and saw a man holding a gun maybe ten to twelve meters away."

Leo asked, "How well could you see in those tunnels? Isn't it dark?"

"There are electric lights on the walls every few meters, and they're bright enough to see where you're going. Anyhow, this guy had his back to me and couldn't see me. He yelled at two women and gestured farther down the tunnel. They refused to go, and when he reached for one of them, she stumbled and fell backwards. The other woman rushed to her and shouted at the guy, but I didn't understand what she said. It was all in rapid French."

"Can you describe how the hostage-taker looked?"

"He looked bulky, like someone who works out a lot, and he was wearing dark blue cargo pants, a wind jacket, and something like combat boots. Similar to tactical gear. He also wore a safety helmet with a light."

"Where was the third hostage?"

Kai took a quick swig from a water bottle. "A man was sitting on the floor of the tunnel. His hands and feet were bound with duct tape and it looked as if there was blood trickling down the side of this face. I can only assume it was blood. It looked dark."

"What happened next? Why didn't you try to help the people? It sounds as if they could've used it," Leo said.

"Listen, Leo," Kai said, shoving his fingers through his hair again, making it stand up in a few spots. "True, there were three of us, but Bulky had a gun. And we might've been brave—or stupid—enough to stay overnight, but we hadn't signed up for a gunfight. Plus, we didn't know if he was alone or if there were more. We figured we'd be of more help if we alerted the authorities."

"How long were you there? How did you manage to leave without him noticing you?"

"We couldn't have been there more than a minute or two. You'd be surprised how much can happen in only a minute. I signaled the guys to retreat," Kai demonstrated his hand signal while he talked, "When we backed away from the scene, the man on the floor must've sensed us and gave us a slight sideways jerk of his head. As if he was telling us to get the hell out of there. And the woman who yelled at Bulky made enough noise to cover any sounds we might make. We left the tunnels as fast as possible and went straight to the police. You know the rest."

"And you didn't hear anything at all during the night or early in the morning?" Leo asked.

"Man, I don't know how much effort you put into the research of these tunnels, but there are hundreds of kilometers of tunnels, and hidden caves you can only access by crawling. The sewer pipes make noise, and the subway rattles above those tunnels. I can assure you, we took the fastest way out, and it still took us about forty-five minutes. Our nerves were kind of stretched thin by the time we saw daylight again."

"Were your friends able to contribute anything to help the police?" Leo asked.

"They were behind me and couldn't see anything, but they were able to confirm what we heard."

"Thank you, Kai," Leo looked into the camera again, straightened his tie, and finished, "reporting from Paris, this is Leo Wu."

"Oh, my God, how terrible," Jenna said. "I hope there's a way to provide those poor people with food and fresh water. They must be freaking out."

Stella had paled while watching the recorded interview. She shook her head and looked at Naomi, who had been silent through the interview.

"We should've tried to stop Kai," Stella said, wringing her hands.

"Nobody knew this was going to happen. And why should he have listened to us?" Naomi asked and reached for her coffee.

"Wait, you know this man?" John asked.

Naomi explained, "We stayed at the same hotel in Paris and had a drink together on Sunday afternoon. He told us he had a night tour of the catacombs planned."

Caroline joined them and said, "I watched the press conference last night, where a spokesperson from the organization in charge of maintaining the tunnels, the Inspection Générale des Carrières, verified the names of the two scientists, who entered the tunnels to take material samples and check the walls and ceilings for possible water damage which can impact the stability. They also confirmed their approval for a non-employee to accompany the women. His name and the purpose of his presence haven't been shared."

"Why would they keep it a secret?" Karen asked.

"It's possible the authorities haven't been able to reach his family yet," Caroline said. "I can't imagine they'd want his relatives to hear about it on the news first."

Suddenly, Stella and Naomi had a vague connection to the hostage situation. Granted, it was far-fetched, and they didn't even know Kai well, but three days ago they had laughed with him. She was also amazed at how calm he appeared on TV. She wouldn't have been able to say one coherent word, let alone rehash the whole story. And the reporter was a schmuck. Kai held his ground very well. Stella wished she could tell him so.

Caroline said, "Did you all have breakfast yet? We need to get going if we want to make it to the Loire Valley in time to visit a few of the *châteaux*."

All six of them shook their heads.

"Well, it's eight o'clock now. Let's get something to eat and meet at the bus in one hour. I'll let François know we won't leave at 8:30 as planned but at 9. Sounds good?"

"Sounds good," six voices answered, and everybody got up.

Thirty minutes later, on the way back to their room, Stella asked Naomi, "How are you doing it?"

"Doing what?"

"You just polished off a hearty breakfast with all the doings, while I had to force myself to nibble on a croissant and a yogurt."

"You know I never lose my appetite. Would it change anything if I don't eat?"

"I guess not," Stella admitted.

Before they reached their room, her phone rang. "It's Luca! What does he want?"

"Pick up and find out. Put him on speaker!"

Stella greeted her brother by saying, "Did Mom or Dad ask you to check on me? Making sure I'm staying out of trouble?"

"Damn, Stella, it's good to hear you," his strained voice came through the cell phone. "Is Naomi with you?"

"Yes, hi, Luca, I'm right here. You're on speaker."

"Good. Where are you right now?"

"Halfway down the hallway in our hotel," Naomi answered. "Care to know the color of the carpet, too?"

"Where in France are you?" Luca's voice was tense.

"Mont Saint-Michel, but we're heading out within the next half hour," Stella said. "We're off to the Loire Valley today. I'm so excited, and..."

"Girls, can you go somewhere where we can talk in private?" he interrupted.

"Almost at our room, hold on." Stella mouthed, *What the heck?* to Naomi. "What's so urgent? Are Mom and Dad okay?"

Before he could answer, her phone played another ringtone, followed by a text message.

> Please call me ASAP, D.

She almost dropped the phone.

"Are you kidding me?" Naomi looked over her shoulder. "What does *he* want now?"

"Stella, Naomi, what's going on?" Luca voice boomed. "Are you in your room?"

"Just walked in," Naomi said and closed the door with a firm push.

Stella said at the same time, "David wants me to call him."

"Since when are you in touch with David again?" Luca asked. "No, don't answer. It can wait. But back to why I'm calling. Did you know Revan is in Paris?"

"I didn't," Stella said. "I thought he was somewhere in India."

"What? Since when?" Naomi asked.

"He called to tell me something exciting had come up and he planned a stopover in Paris for a photo op."

"Oh, if it's only a photo op, it means he'll be home in a few days," Stella looked into the distance, where Mont Saint-Michel basked in the bright morning sunshine, bracing itself for another day with thousands of tourists congesting its ancient streets.

"Luca, what's going on? You're not just calling to tell us to meet with Rev for dinner, are you?" Naomi said in a tight voice.

"I'm not quite sure what's going on, but I wish it was as simple. His parents got a call from the Bureau of Consular Affairs. They were told he's being held captive in some underground mine together with two other people."

Naomi shrieked and grabbed Stella's arm. They looked at each other, not able to say a word.

"They announced the women's names on TV, but nobody mentioned the man's identity. Are you sure it's Revan?" Stella said, finding her voice again. "Wouldn't it be a huge coincidence if it was him?"

"There's no doubt it's him. His name hasn't been released because the American Embassy had to get involved first. The women's names could be made public because they're employees of the inspectorate, and French citizens. Rev is an American citizen and is there as a visitor."

"How are his parents holding up?" Naomi asked. She was as white as the wall.

"Alicia's freaking out, and Robert is trying to hold it together for her sake. I thought of taking the first flight to Paris today, but I wouldn't get there until tomorrow. And I don't know how much I'd be able to do. Instead, I drove to Philadelphia this morning to be with Rev's parents. They haven't even told Dinah yet. She's away at a summer camp this week, but they're bringing her home this evening."

"We're going back to Paris," Naomi said resolutely. "Right now."

"Yes, we have to be there," Stella agreed. "Like you said, Luca, there may not much we can do, but at least we'd know we're close enough to help him."

"I don't think it's necessary for you to cut your trip short. I just wanted you to know what's going on. Weren't you supposed to be back by tomorrow evening anyway? Hopefully, Rev and the women will be free by then."

"There's no way I'm strolling around fucking wannabe castles and watching lovey-dovey couples for the next day and a half, while knowing Rev is rotting in a stinking cave with some gun-toting lunatic. He could be dead for all we know. Kai said he was bleeding," Naomi said fiercely as she marched toward the door. "I'll go find Caroline and drop us out of this carriage ride through the French countryside."

"Kai who?" Luca asked.

"Someone we met in Paris. He's the guy who alerted the police. Look up the news footage," Naomi called out.

"You can bet I'll check it out," Luca said, "Okay, if you're serious about returning to Paris, I'm sure Alicia and Robert will appreciate it. Stella, call me when you get there. Do you need help arranging for a hotel?"

"No, I'll call the hotel where we already have reservations and see if they can accommodate us earlier," Naomi yelled from the door before stepping into the hallway. "Bye, Luca. Stella, meet me downstairs."

"Let me know if there's anything I can do from here," Luca said. "Keep in touch!"

"Will do—and give our best to Alicia and Robert," Stella said. "Love you!"

"Love you back! Be careful!" Luca said.

CHAPTER 22

S<small>TELLA</small>—J<small>ULY</small> 2018

Most members of the tour group were still in the restaurant when Naomi and Stella rushed in and repeated the phone conversation. Naomi finished by saying, "I'm sorry to do this, but we have to cut our trip short. We need to be in Paris as soon as possible."

"I think I'm speaking for all of us when I tell you we're sorry you're leaving us, but we understand. You need to do what your gut tells you."

"Thank you, Caroline. Thank you, everybody. Now, what's the fastest way for us to get there?" Naomi asked. "I guess I could look it up online, but I haven't had time yet."

"Let me check a few things. There are plenty of bus and train connections from here to Paris. It's a popular day-trip location." Caroline pulled out her tablet and started typing.

"We apologize for causing all this trouble and holding everybody up," Stella said. "You're on a schedule, so please don't let us keep you. Naomi and I can figure it out ourselves, or we'll ask the reception desk for help."

"Nonsense!" John said.

"Stop it!" Michael said.

"We don't want to hear about it," Andrew said.

"Okay, guys, thank you!" Stella was grateful for the support.

"Here's what will work best for you, I think." Caroline put her tablet on the table. "There is a high-speed train going between Rennes and Gare Montparnasse in Paris several times a day. It takes less than two and a half hours. Rennes is on our way to Angers, where we're visiting our first château. We'll drop you two off at the train station and continue on."

"Works for me," François said. "And I know where the train station is in Rennes. It's just a small detour. No problem!"

"I've only heard the last part, about Naomi and Stella taking a train to Paris, but I'm going with them," Julia said from the doorway. She stood there with her suitcase, her body rigid. Her purse was clutched under her arm as if it might try to escape.

"Thank you for the offer, Julia, but I don't think it's necessary," Naomi said.

"We'll be fine, but thanks," Stella added.

"Oh, I'm not worried about you," Julia said. "But I can't spend one more minute in the company of he who shall remain nameless." She looked over her shoulder at Harry, who sauntered toward the restaurant.

"Jules, what the hell's that supposed to mean?" He looked even more disheveled than he did on Monday morning, when they all met.

"Stop calling me Jules or JuJu. In fact, don't talk to me at all," she hissed.

"What's your problem?" he shrugged.

"Stop playing dumb. Do you really want me to say it again? Fine!" Julia pointed a finger at him. "When you tried to stop me from going into my room last night and groped me, you crossed a line. I don't want you anywhere near me. Not your hands, not your face, nothing. And I'm telling you one thing right now. Emily won't like it either when she hears about it."

"What's Em got to do with it?" He scratched his belly.

"Yup, just what I thought." But she wasn't done yet. "By the way, I doubt Emily asked you to go on this trip. I have a feeling you told her to stay at home because you *wanted* to go. Even though I don't know why. I hope you didn't think you could start something with me."

"Come on, don't be such a Miss Prim. I may've had one drink too many last night, but I was lonely and thought you'd enjoy some male company. If Em hears your little sob story, she'll prattle on about a divorce again."

"And I hope she'll go through with it this time. I can guarantee you I'm not going to try to talk her out of it. You're despicable," Julia spat. She stepped closer to Stella and Naomi and said much more calmly, "I'd like to get on the train with you, and maybe I can even be of help in Paris."

"What do you mean?" Stella asked.

"I have connections to the American Embassy. It can be difficult to get through to the right people. Especially given the delicacy of this matter."

"Why should they tell an accountant what's going on?" Harry asked while he heaped toast, scrambled eggs and a few sausages on his plate. With his fingers, he snagged a chunk of cantaloupe directly out of a bowl and popped it in his mouth.

Caroline signaled a waitress to take away the fruit bowl.

"I am not an accountant," Julia said through her teeth, emphasizing each word, "and you know it."

"Well, you do Emily's taxes." He bit into one of the sausages and looked around for support. His face fell. "What, do you all believe her over me?"

"I'll only say you're lucky none of us guys saw what Julia just described," Andrew slammed his hand on the table and pushed his chair back. Sarah put her hand on his arm.

"A few of us women might also have figured out ways to step in," Lynn said. She waved a travel-size can of hairspray in Harry's direction. "Works almost as well as pepper spray, which is what I carry at home, but I was afraid it would be confiscated at the airport."

Oh, my goodness, this would be funny if it weren't so serious, Stella thought. *Go, Lynn!*

"Look, Harry, I know you think you're God's greatest gift to women and expect us to worship at your feet. But...not happening," Julia looked at Caroline, then at the group. "I apologize for this scene. It's unacceptable for you to have to witness this exchange. I was confronted with Emily's change in travel plans when it was too late to drop out. I tried to make the best of it, but after last night I can't relax and enjoy the last two days. I'm going back to Paris. Again... sorry!"

"Don't you dare apologize to any of us, Julia," Steve said. "We're sad you're leaving. I wish we'd known about all this and been able to help keep the situation from escalating. But we understand your decision."

"Thanks, Steve," Julia said.

"What are your connections to the Embassy, Julia?" Naomi asked.

"Well, I'm a tax attorney and work for the Department of Treasury. I know people here in Paris, and will do whatever I can to get information about your friend. I don't know how much I can help, but at least I can try."

Naomi stood up to hug Julia. "Thank you so much!"

"I think it's settled, then," Caroline said. "Let's meet at the bus in fifteen minutes, and we're off to Rennes."

⌒⌒

Getting on the bus, Caroline told Harry, "I suggest you sit with me in the front."

"Oh, it's fine, I don't mind mingling."

"This is not a discussion, Harry. Sit here, please." Caroline pointed to the seat behind François.

Bless her! Stella was impressed with how Caroline put him in time-out like an unruly child.

When the bus pulled out onto the street, Stella looked at Mont Saint-Michel one more time, vowing to return.

Julia, who sat across the narrow aisle from Stella and Naomi, asked, "Where are you staying in Paris?"

"At a hotel in Montparnasse," Naomi said. "I'll call them as soon as we're on the train to ask if they have something for us. What are your plans?"

"I have reservations at a hotel in Versailles. But if you don't mind, would you ask your hotel if they have a room for me until Saturday? It would help make things easier if we're staying together."

"No problem. It's the least I can do!"

"But we don't want you to give up your plans to visit Versailles," Stella said. "You must've looked forward to it."

"Don't worry about it. I've been there before. This is more important." Julia opened an app on her phone and chuckled. "Let's get to work, girls. I'm the queen of to-do lists. Thank goodness for the Notes app."

Stella stared at the phone in her hand. "I have to call David. It's been over an hour since he texted me while we talked to Luca."

"Quite frankly, I don't care what he wants," Naomi said. "I'm worried about Revan right now. Period."

Then she looked out the window for a moment, and said, "Sorry, I'm acting like an ass and it's not fair to you. If you feel you need to call him back, do it." Naomi reached for her hand and squeezed it.

"I really do. He must have a good reason if he wants me to call him. What if something happened to him, too?"

She pulled up his contact and looked at the image she had assigned to it.

For more than a year she'd been wanting to call him, or write back to him, asking for an explanation. But she was hurting so much, she'd preferred to live in a cocoon and have no connection to anything related to David—not even his sister, who had tried to stay in touch.

Never in a million years did she imagine they'd meet again under such bizarre circumstances. Yet here they were...

She typed a message.

I got your message. Can I call you later?
Stella

Within seconds, her phone rang. She had no choice. She needed to pick up. Her hands shook when she touched the green button.

CHAPTER 23

DAVID—JULY 2018

D avid stood in front of the open window of his hotel room. He tuned out the noises on the streets below him and focused on the trees in the park. He didn't care about the climate-controlled air escaping into the summer heat. Since he left Stella the message to call him an hour ago, he debated how to tell her what he'd seen on the morning news.

David clutched his phone and waited for her to accept his call. It only rang a few times before she said, "David?"

Hearing her voice caused a sensation in him he could only describe as free-fall. Like a roller-coaster going over the highest point and barreling toward the bottom at the speed of light. The heart-in-your-throat, adrenaline-rushing-through-your-veins experience.

His mouth was dry.

"David?" she asked again. Her voice was quiet, and she sounded defeated. No, not defeated. Scared.

Two pigeons flew up and perched on the small ledge outside his window. Their cooing irritated him, and he shut the window.

"Hi, Stella...umm...where...what..." He leaned his forehead against the glass. *Focus, Danvers!*

"Stop it, David." Her voice sounded stronger, and he grinned. *There she is! Coming out of her shell.*

"Let me try again," he managed a strangled laugh. "I'm so glad to hear your voice. Where are you?"

"On my way to Rennes. Why? What's going on?"

"Have you been following the news?"

"A little...I assume you're talking about the hostage situation?"

"Yes. I don't know how to tell you... Revan is involved." He held his breath. "I didn't want to believe it, but they showed photos of him and the women."

"What, in the catacombs?"

"No. The women's pictures looked like their work IDs, and Revan's must've been from a media kit. I texted you as soon as I saw it. I didn't want you to hear it on the news."

"Luca called us at the same moment you texted. But we didn't know they announced Rev's identity." David heard Naomi's voice in the background. Stella made an affirmative sound to Naomi, then said to him, "Naomi and I are on our way back to Paris."

"Is there anything I can do to help?" he asked.

"To tell you the truth, I don't know yet what we'll do, or what we even can do. We haven't had time to digest any of this." He noticed how she emphasized the word *can*. "We should be in Paris in about three hours. One of the women in our group has connections to the American Embassy, and she's trying to help us get in touch with someone there, but who knows how much they'll tell us."

"Call me when you're at your hotel. I'm not going anywhere until I talk to you again," he said, then added, "Please, let me help you."

"Okay, I'll be in touch later."

"Promise me!" David said.

"Yes, I promise I'll be in touch this afternoon. I've got to go, David. The connection is breaking up."

"Until later, bye, Stella."

David tossed the phone on his bed. He had no clue what he could do, but he knew he'd do his best to support Stella and Naomi while they waited for news and Revan's rescue.

He needed to be ready and have his wits about him when they arrived, which wasn't for another few hours. He couldn't sit here, he had to move. Maybe he should go for a walk.

Without paying attention to where he was going, he let his feet take him away. When he reached a busy intersection, David wasn't surprised to find himself in front of the

Opera House. *Talk about coming full circle...* No, the circle would only be closed if he were here with Stella.

Instead of going inside, as he had for the past three days, he sat on the steps and looked down the straight avenue leading back to his hotel.

His conversation with Jerome two days ago came to mind. David apologized and told him the naked truth before they began the auditions. "As soon as we entered the box, I saw someone...very special to me in the auditorium."

"What is so special about her?"

"She's my Christine," David admitted, keeping it simple but to the point. "And I renounced her last year."

"Sounds like the stuff opera is made of. Were you able to talk to her?" Jerome asked.

"She was gone before I could get there," David said and—to his embarrassment—had to swallow back tears.

"Then you better make sure you catch her next time," was Jerome's advice before he handed him a sheet of music, "Now, let's hear you sing."

And while David sang "The Anthem" from *Chess*, his thoughts strayed to Stella. *Ask me why I love her...*

Somehow, he nailed his auditions. One day he'd be able to laugh about the list of songs Jerome chose for his impromptus. If David didn't know better, he'd suspect Aaron had a hand in the selection.

He strolled back to his hotel, but couldn't stand the thought of being cooped up in his room. Instead, he crossed the street and sat in the park again, his hand on his cell phone in case Stella called. The rumbling of heavy equipment at a nearby construction area, and people shouting out to each other, made it almost impossible to hear his phone, but he'd feel it vibrate.

He checked the time again. Only an hour had passed since he talked to her. In a few hours, he would get to see Stella again. Because he knew, after hearing her voice, it wouldn't be enough to simply talk to her on the phone.

He needed to see her in person.

And he wanted to hold her again.

Would she let him?

CHAPTER 24

Stella—July 2018

After hasty goodbyes to their group, Stella, Naomi, and Julia sat in the dining car of the luxurious modern train and perused the menu.

"This is impressive for a train restaurant," Naomi said. "In fact, the entire atmosphere is more country club than mass transportation. Buying the tickets and jumping on the next available train is no different than hopping on the subway in any American city. I have to mention it in the package I put together for European vacations. A lot of our customers will love this."

"Yes, traveling by train is very popular in Europe," Julia said. "I use them all the time when I'm here. And if you don't mind spending a few extra euros for first class, you get excellent service."

When a waitress stopped at their table, all three women ordered a *salade niçoise*. "And a bottle of Blanc de Noirs, please," Julia added.

"A black white wine?" Stella wondered.

"No, but close. It's a sparkling wine, like champagne, made from black-skinned grapes and goes nicely with the salad."

"Are you sure we should drink alcohol, considering what's waiting for us in Paris?" Stella asked. "We have to stay alert."

"Three women sharing one bottle of wine is no more than two glasses for each, and we'll have a hearty meal with it. All the protein in the salad and the carbs from the baguette will soak up the alcohol," Julia raised her water glass. "*Santé.*"

"I'll call the hotel now to see what I can arrange for rooms," Naomi said.

"And I'll text my contact at the Embassy," said Julia.

Stella asked, "What can I do?"

"Call your brother. See if we can get written permission from Revan's parents to talk to people at the Embassy. I know he's a grown man of legal age, but it can't hurt to have something to wave in front of the bureaucrats."

"Should they fax it directly to the Embassy?"

"No, have them email it to you and copy me. We don't want it to get lost in the shuffle at the offices. And we don't know who we'll end up talking to."

"Got it!" Stella said and texted Luca,

On the train now. Julia says it would be helpful to have a written consent from Rev's parents saying we can speak to an officer at the Embassy on their behalf. Email it to me and copy Julia. I'll send you her contact details.

Luca's reply came within seconds,

Of course, I should've thought of it myself. Will tell Robert ASAP. Alicia's on her way to pick up Dinah. They're holding up okay.

Thanks. I'll let you know when we're at the hotel. Naomi's on the phone to arrange rooms. Love you.

"Luca's on it," she said after closing the message window.

"What does he do for a living?" Julia asked.

"He's a news director for Bloomberg in their New York City office."

"Ah, good to know. Maybe we'll need to tap into his pool of media contacts."

"Ladies, we're all set at the hotel." Naomi put her phone down and took a swig of her freshly poured bubbly. "Yum! I needed some fortification." She took a photo of the bottle's label. "This one's going on my list of favorites."

"Did you get a room for Julia?" Stella asked.

"Yes and no. We'll have to share a room for one night."

"Fine with me, I'll sleep on the couch," Julia said.

"Not necessary," Naomi grinned. "For tonight, all they have available is a family room with three twin beds. We can discuss everything else when we get there."

"Great, thank you. My news is, we won't be able to speak with an officer in the American Citizen Services office today, but my friend in the IRS office said he can meet us after work. Alexander is trying to get an overview of what our options are, but he says there's likely not much they can do to help us since the hostage situation is still ongoing."

"I'd like to meet with him. Anything's better than twiddling our thumbs in the hotel room," Naomi said. "When and where?"

"He suggested we meet in front of the Embassy at five."

"Tell him we'll be there," Naomi said, then nodded to the approaching waitress. "Now let's eat. I see three salads coming our way..."

"Why don't you tell me a little bit about Revan? It might help if I have an idea of who he is," Julia asked.

Naomi looked at Stella. "How can we best describe Revan in a few words?"

"Oh, boy. He's one of those people you have to meet in person to get the full picture."

"What does he do for work?" Julia asked. "How old is he? Girlfriend, wife? Hobbies?"

"He is thirty-five, the best friend of Stella's brother, and his work is his hobby, or vice versa. Revan works as a documentary photographer, but he's also doing freelance photography. He goes to politically unstable countries and war zones with a news team, and then combines the assignment with a private side trip to some other hot spot. Heaven knows how he comes up with all his destinations."

"Sounds as if he's looking for adrenaline kicks?" Julia asked and picked up a chunk of tuna with her fork.

"You can say that again! And it's why he doesn't do relationships. He says it's not fair to a woman to live in constant worry over whether he's coming back alive or in a wooden box," Stella added with a side glance at Naomi.

"Even though there might be women who understand it's part of who he is." Naomi twisted her mouth and looked at her hands. "He's the best friend you can imagine, and he'd do anything for those he loves." She quickly wiped her eyes with the back of her hand and reached for her fork.

Stella gave Naomi's shoulder a gentle rub. Her friend could put on a tough show, but in one case she wore her heart on her sleeve. And everybody in their small group of friends knew it...all but one.

"I can't wait to meet him," Julia said with an encouraging smile for Naomi.

"Are you going to call your friend and tell her you cut the trip with Merveille Tours short?" Stella asked, trying to change the subject.

"Yeah, tonight, from the hotel. I don't think she'll be surprised to hear it. Harry had affairs for years, but he never tried anything with me or anybody else who's close to Emily. This was a new low, and it will be the last straw for her. She started divorce proceedings about two years ago, when their youngest kid finished high school, but Harry begged and whined and, for reasons that baffle me, she called it off."

"Maybe she still loves him," Naomi said, her voice steady and strong again.

"No, and I don't know if she ever was in love with him. They met when she was a senior in college, at a career fair where he was one of the recruiters for some large company. She got pregnant not much later, and believed marriage was the right thing to do."

"So, he's older than she is?"

"Yeah, quite a bit. Even back then I thought it was sleazy when he started something with her."

"What about their children?" Stella said. "How will they react if she files for divorce?"

"They've witnessed enough scenes over the years, and they aren't close to him. I was serious this morning when I told him I won't try to stop Emily. She's young enough to find someone who treats her with respect and shows her real love."

"Will he make it difficult for her?" Naomi wanted to know.

"With him you never know, but I don't think so. He owns a head-hunting business, even though he prefers to call it consulting, and it wouldn't be good for his reputation if this got out. In the past it was hard to prove anything, because the women he approached kept it quiet. But this time he made the mistake of putting his hands on me. And I don't shy away from the media," Julia speared an olive with her fork before putting it in her mouth and biting down slowly.

Their hotel was in a well-kept neighborhood, mainly residential, but with little stores and small restaurants scattered throughout. Stella found the combination charming.

After they finished checking in, she looked around the lobby. Mix-and-match chairs and sofas in vivid patterns invited guests to make themselves comfortable, and Andy Warhol-style artwork covered the walls.

She said, "Revan would love this hotel. At home, he prefers monochrome décor, but I know he loves bold accents."

"Let's hope we'll be sitting here with him soon," Naomi replied. "As soon as Julia's done at check-in, we'll decide what to do next."

"I have to write to Luca, and I also promised David to let him know when we're here."

"You know you broke your promise—no, our *deal*—not to mention his name on this trip. Ha! I'll get to pick your first date after we're back at home."

"Go ahead and scroll through your Rolodex of discarded dates. I can manage to get through an evening listening to baseball statistics or stock market trends." She yawned for good measure.

Naomi laughed, "No, I'll find someone more exciting for you. Scout's honor!"

"Are we back to Girl Scouts? You haven't been a Scout in how many decades? Anyway, they don't count anymore."

"Okay, I'm done," Julia announced, and waved her key card.

When they walked into their room, all three stopped and laughed. Three beds stood close to each other, headboards against the wall, with just enough space for nightstands between them.

"Somebody's been sleeping in my bed," Naomi whined and plopped on the middle bed.

"As long as nobody's been eating from my bowl of porridge, I'm fine," Stella said.

"Guess I'll take the broken chair," Julia laughed.

"Which bed do you want, Julia?" Stella said.

"I don't have a preference, go ahead and pick yours. All I need is a pillow and an outlet to charge my laptop and phone!"

"Then I'd like the one near the balcony."

Julia put her purse on her bed and shoved the suitcase next to it. "How 'bout we all get settled in, and in thirty minutes go look around the neighborhood. The Luxembourg Gardens aren't far from here. And the Montparnasse Cemetery is also close by. We could take a self-guided tour there before they close at sunset."

"Are you switching professions? Shall I call you Caroline?" Naomi rolled over on her stomach.

"Sure, go ahead, Goldilocks," Julia countered without missing a beat.

Stella went to the small breakfast table in the room's kitchenette and messaged Luca,

At our hotel now. It's lovely. Too sad our visit here's overshadowed by the mess. Julia's contact at the Embassy is meeting with us at 5 pm. I'll let you know later what her friend said. Talk soon. Stella.

Next she sent a note to David. Just thinking about him made her heart beat faster.

At our hotel. Naomi, Julia and I will go for a walk, then meet with a friend of hers at five at the US Embassy. I'll keep you posted. Stella.

Right away, she saw three small dots dancing at the bottom of the screen, then his reply came,

> Thanks for letting me know you're here. What can I do for you?

Nothing right now, thanks.

Half an hour later, Julia held up her phone and said, "We have three options for how to get to the Embassy. We can call a cab, which can take us there in about fifteen minutes, traffic permitting. Or we can take the metro, which takes about twenty-five minutes. And the third possibility is walking. It should take about forty minutes. We're meeting Alexander in a little over an hour. What do you want to do?"

"I'd say walk," Stella said. "Naomi and I haven't seen much on this side of the Seine yet."

"I agree," Naomi said and licked her lips. "And maybe we'll pass an ice cream shop."

"Well, then, girls, put on your walking shoes," Julia said. "The ice cream is on me."

They walked along the Luxembourg Gardens, crossed the Seine on Pont du Carrousel, and strolled through the Tuileries Garden toward the Place de la Concorde. Along the way, they stopped to take photos and admire the sights.

"I know where we are," Stella called. "We were here last Sunday. First on the bus, and then when we walked to the Arc de Triomphe. Look, Naomi, there's the obelisk."

"Hard to believe it's only been a few days. I'd like to see some of those buildings when they're illuminated at night."

"Me too. And depending on what we can do to help Rev, maybe we have time to go into the Louvre before we fly home?" Stella looked over her shoulder to the imposing museum at the other end of the park.

"I'd love to join you when you go," Julia said.

"Where one goes, we all go!" Naomi declared and raised her hand for a high five. "We're in this together now."

They dodged taxis and tour buses, crossed the Place de la Concorde, then sprinted through more cars, bicycles, and pedestrians until they reached a copse of tall chestnut trees.

"There's Alexander. Oh, great, he has someone from the Citizen Services office with him." Julia waved to two men standing in front of the black wrought-iron fence surrounding the Embassy of the United States of America.

Stella saw the man next to Julia's friend.

"No, he doesn't," she whispered.

CHAPTER 25

―――――⊶∘⧉⌒⧉∘⊶―――――

Stella—July 2018

"What's *he* doing here?" Naomi snapped and stopped walking.

"How would I know?" Stella replied. She rubbed her arms but couldn't get rid of the goose bumps.

"Did you ask him to come?" Naomi narrowed her eyes at Stella.

"No, I told him I'd keep him posted." She didn't care for Naomi's aggression.

"And you just happened to mention where we're meeting?"

"What's up with all the questions?" She tried to hold Naomi back when she started to march toward the two men.

"I don't know what's going on," Julia said. "Do you know the man with Alexander?"

"He's my ex-boyfriend. It's a long and somewhat bizarre story. I'll fill you in later," Stella answered.

She couldn't take her eyes off David. He was here, and she'd be face-to-face with him in a moment. She couldn't believe it.

"That's one way to describe it," Naomi said over her shoulder. "Shitshow would be more accurate."

"You don't need to tell me anything." Julia rubbed Stella's arm. "He looks familiar, though."

Naomi reached the men first. She nodded to Julia's friend and said a quick, "Hi." Then she put her fists on her hips and looked at David. "And what brought *you* here on this sunny afternoon?"

His eyes briefly met with Stella's before he looked at Naomi. "Naomi, before you say anything else, calm down."

"Calm down? You just happened to walk by this building and just happened to start a conversation with a random stranger, and it just happened at exactly five o'clock?" She accentuated each 'happened' with a jab of her finger against David's chest.

"First of all," he replied, "this is a free country, and I can walk wherever I want and talk to whomever I want whenever I want." He ticked off each of his rights on his fingers, then held up his hand to stop her from interrupting. "But the reason I'm here is because I want to help. And I can't if I'm hiding in my hotel room."

"Well, you've been doing it for a year. You should've managed a few more days, if you ask me," Naomi fumed, her index finger poised for another jab.

"Naomi, put your finger away before you chip a nail. You're acting childish, and people are looking," Stella reached the two brawlers and pulled Naomi away from David. "The last thing we need is for security to show up and take us away in handcuffs."

"Hi, David," she said, and attempted a smile.

How do you greet your ex-boyfriend after a year of silence? Is a hug appropriate?

He solved the problem when he leaned down and breathed a kiss on her cheek, sending a pleasant shiver through her. She longed to let muscle memory take over and move a little closer to him.

"Hi, Stella. I couldn't wait for your next text message, I had to see you're okay and decided to meet you here. When I arrived a few minutes ago, Alexander was already waiting, and I asked him if he was meeting you three ladies," David explained, without breaking eye contact. "I hope you don't mind."

She felt dizzy. How on earth was she supposed to react to him? The touch of a hand on her right elbow broke the spell.

"Stella? I want you to meet my friend Alexander," Julia introduced in a firm but warm voice.

"Nice to meet you, Stella." Alexander reached out and shook Stella's hand, forcing her to turn his way. She was afraid to let David out of her sight and scolded herself for being so silly.

Stella guessed Alexander to be around fifty. His salt-and-pepper hair was cut short, and his dark eyes didn't seem to miss a beat. He cut a striking figure in his well-cut business suit.

"As David said, he introduced himself, and we started talking about the latest development in the case," Alexander said.

"What...what latest development?" Naomi whispered. She looked from Alexander to David with wide eyes.

"You must be Naomi," Alexander said, holding out his hand. "Nice to meet you."

"Likewise," Naomi took his proffered hand, then asked, "So, what happened?"

"Well..." Alexander began, but David interrupted him. "Excuse me, can I make a suggestion?"

"Depends... I'm not sure I want to hear a word you have to say." Naomi was obviously not done with him.

Stella wanted to tell her to shut up, but David was faster.

"Naomi, stop it!" he said in a clipped voice, then looked at Julia and said cordially, "Sorry, we haven't met yet. I didn't mean to be rude."

"Pfft..." came from Naomi's direction.

He held out his hand to Julia and said, "David Danvers."

"Oh, wow," Julia looked from him to Stella and murmured, "That's why he looks familiar." She looked back to David, "I saw one of your shows in Denver a few years ago and loved it."

"I'm glad you enjoyed it."

"Great. The monthly fan club meeting has been opened. Now let's move on to the next item on the agenda," Naomi muttered.

"Really, Naomi, enough," David said as a muscle rippled in his jaw. "I know I'm on your shit list, but for now, let's be adults and find a way to get along. Whether you like it or not, I also consider Revan a friend of mine, and I want to help in any way I can."

"Well, I don't think even *you* can lure the kidnapper out of there by singing. But..." she held up a hand when Stella opened her mouth. "I agree it doesn't help Rev if I'm acting like a bitch. But be warned, buddy, I'm saving it for later."

Then she looked at Alexander, "Can you now please tell us what you've heard?"

"I suggest we go somewhere else. Since it's clear none of you checked the news in the past two hours, let's adjourn to a small, pleasant bistro where we can talk without being disturbed."

"Why not now?" Naomi challenged him.

"I meant to suggest the same thing before I was interrupted," David gave Naomi a pointed look.

"Alexander, I like your idea." Julia took his arm and they began a quiet conversation as they walked ahead.

Stella, Naomi, and David fell in step behind them, with Stella in the middle. Stella's heart pounded; she was hyperaware of David's presence next to her. She was tempted to touch him to assure herself he wasn't just a dream.

"Do you think there's a story between those two? They look chummy," Naomi asked her.

"Maybe. Let's try to worm it out of her later, when we're back in our room," she answered, grateful for the distraction.

They followed a labyrinth of residential streets, smiled at children kicking a ball or riding their bikes, leaving the hubbub around the tourist attractions behind them, when Naomi cleared her throat several times.

Stella stopped walking. She was running out of patience. Today wasn't the best day for Naomi to go on a vendetta.

"Is there something you want to say, Nam? Just spit it out."

David leaned around her and rested his hand on her hip in a familiar gesture she'd missed.

"David," Naomi croaked and cleared her throat once more. "I'm sorry I went off the way I did. It isn't fair, and I know you really want to help us."

"Don't worry, Naomi," David replied easily, giving Stella's hip the hint of a squeeze. Both knew how hard the admission must've been for Naomi. "I'm sure we can manage to be civil to each other. And if you want to yell at me after Revan is safe, you and I will go somewhere alone, and you can let me have it."

"Count on it! Because I have a *lot* more to say," Naomi promised. She stepped around Stella and stood in front of him.

Then she hugged him and said in a low voice, "Man, you messed up big time."

He said in a grave voice, "You're not telling me anything new, Naomi."

Julia and Alexander waited for them in front of the bistro, where guests sat outside under trees and colorful sun sails. The brutal heat was beginning to give way to a pleasant summer evening, and outdoor fans helped to circulate the air. Nevertheless, Alexander asked for a table inside, giving them some privacy.

None of them were very hungry, but they ordered a few appetizers to share and a carafe of their house wine.

"So, I think we've waited long enough. What did we miss?" Julia asked as soon as the waitress had left.

"Both women were released this afternoon," Alexander said.

"And Rev?" Naomi asked. She slid around on her chair and played with the napkin in front of her.

"He's still in there," David said. "One of the women developed a health problem."

"Were the women able to tell the police anything?" Stella asked.

"Nothing else has been released yet. I'm sure they'll have a statement for the press later," Alexander said. "There's a TV on the wall. Let's ask them to turn up the volume if something comes up."

"Alexander, how can the Embassy help?" Julia asked.

"I'm sad to say, but there's not much they can do," he looked at Stella and Naomi first, then at Julia. "Their hands are tied as long as Revan is being held hostage. The Embassy staff's job is mostly concerned with diplomatic matters, and right now the local authorities are in charge."

Naomi said through her teeth, "Looks to me as if the asshat who's keeping him is more in control than the cops. And speaking of police! What the hell are they doing? Are they just standing there doing nothing? Why haven't they gone in and flushed the guy out?"

"I've been doing some reading about the catacombs. The tunnel system is so vast, people have gone missing in there, and even sending search dogs doesn't guarantee they'll be found in time," Alexander said.

"I can't stand this." Naomi was close to tears. She smacked her hand on the table. "This waiting is driving me bonkers. I have to do something. I think I need to go to the entrance of the catacombs and see the place for myself."

"I can't imagine they'll let anybody near it," Stella said.

"Oh, I'm sure the entrance is guarded like the National Archives right now. But still..."

"Don't get in their way, and don't give up hope." Stella leaned over and gave her a hug. "Revan is tough. He's never been the victim of a crime, but he's been in some pretty scary situations and always keeps a cool head."

"I hope you're right. But what if something happens to him?" Naomi's voice shook, and Stella had no answer for her friend.

Shortly before seven o'clock, a reporter's familiar face showed up on the TV screen, and Alexander asked the owner to adjust the monitor and turn up the volume.

"This is Leo Wu, and with me is Commissaire Charles Rousseau of the Police Judicaire. We received word of a change in the hostage situation. What can you tell us?"

"Both female hostages, Dr. Marianne Caron and Dr. Claudine Bisset, were released today." Rousseau was a man in his sixties with close-cropped gray hair. He looked exhausted and not thrilled with being interviewed.

"Why did the kidnapper let the two women go?" Leo asked.

"Dr. Caron developed serious health concerns. According to the IGC, she had no preexisting conditions, or she wouldn't have had clearance to enter the caves. But either the prolonged exposure to the limestone or the combination of the humid climate and low temperatures caused her distress." Rousseau spoke English with a heavy accent.

"What's the issue with limestone?" Leo interrupted.

"The existence of limestone made those quarries the perfect place to deposit corpses in the eighteenth century, when the city's cemeteries were overflowing, because it masks the stench of disposing bodies. Limestone is an alkaline product and contact with skin can result in abrasions ranging from mild irritation to bad burns, and if the dust is inhaled or swallowed, it can cause severe respiratory problems."

"When did Dr. Caron start having trouble?"

"Yesterday. Dr. Bisset said the kidnapper at first believed Dr. Caron playacted when she developed breathing issues, but he realized today the situation was worse than he assumed and decided to let them go. He escorted the two women a short distance and then told them to keep walking without looking back."

"What about Mr. Forrester? Why didn't he leave with the women? What's his condition?"

"According to Dr. Bisset, Mr. Forrester appeared to be in good health when they left. He was kept bound on his wrists and ankles with duct tape most of the time. When the kidnapper left with the women, he chained Mr. Forrester to stone columns or pipes."

"What a scumbag!" Naomi cried out. "To leave him all by himself!"

Leo continued, "Were the women able to give more information about where they were held?"

"For Mr. Forrester's safety, I can't comment. I assure you we're doing everything we can." Rousseau attempted a smile but didn't quite manage one.

Or maybe it's just a twitch because he's annoyed by Leo's questions, Stella thought.

"A source told us the kidnapper sent a note with the women in which he wrote 'Don't try to find us. Remember 2008.' What does that mean?" Leo asked.

"No comment."

"Come on, give me something."

"I've told you what I'm at liberty to divulge at this point. We still have an active hostage situation and will not risk anything that might threaten the safety of Mr. Forrester." Rousseau looked around and nodded to someone out of the camera's view.

Naomi jumped up and walked around the table until she stood in front of the TV. "You were a little prick when you interviewed Kai, and you're still the same little prick. Get it, Leo? They only tell you what they wanna tell you."

She sat back down with a sigh, and Julia put her arm around her shoulders.

"Were the two women able to tell you how they survived without food or water for almost three days?" Leo didn't give up.

"Dr. Bisset confirmed they had access to bottled water and some food," Rousseau said.

"Where are the women now?"

"Both will be monitored overnight at a hospital."

"One more question, Commissaire Rousseau. How far would the police be in their investigation if Mr. Olders and his friends hadn't discovered this situation on Monday?" Leo challenged the policeman.

"No comment," Rousseau said with a bite in his voice and exchanged hand signals with someone.

"Thank you, Commissaire Rousseau." The reporter smiled into the camera, "This is Leo Wu, live from Paris, where the two female hostages were freed this afternoon."

"He's unbearable," Naomi said. She looked at Alexander, then David. "This morning, we watched a replay of his interview with Kai, and this Leo clown doesn't care one bit about what's really going on, it's all about him."

"With the women out, we might hear more about Revan soon," Stella said.

Naomi shook her head. "They'll go 'round and 'round about the two women. Which I understand, don't get me wrong. I'm glad they're out of there."

David asked, "Who's this Kai? You've mentioned him a few times."

"The man Leo referred to, Mr. Olders. He stayed at the same hotel as we did last weekend, and we had drinks together. This is all a weird coincidence," Stella explained.

"Now I understand Naomi's reactions earlier, when she got so mad during the interview," David said.

Naomi looked at Julia and Stella. "I think I'll take a taxi back to the hotel. It's been a long day, with a lot to digest. I need some time to think. What about you two?"

"I'd like to spend a little more time with Alexander and catch up, but I won't be too late. Why don't I see you at the hotel, maybe in two hours or so?" Julia said. "We'll stay here and take care of the bill."

"Okay, thanks. We'll square up later," Naomi said.

Stella had often glanced at David while they were at the bistro, and he in return watched her. But they didn't have a chance to talk.

David's hand inched toward hers but stopped halfway. "Give me an hour or two with you. I'll walk you back to your hotel."

A walk sounded good. It meant spending time together without being completely alone with him. "Okay," she agreed.

David stood and looked at everyone at the table. "Please, let me settle the bill on my way out. No arguments!"

Alexander nodded, "Thank you."

Stella met Naomi's eyes and said, "I'll meet you at the hotel, okay?"

Naomi looked from David to Stella and said, "Be careful!"

CHAPTER 26

Stella—July 2018

"Thank you for walking with me, Stella," David said after they left the bistro and strolled back through the same streets as earlier. "You have no idea what it means for me to see you in person."

Yeah, I think I do, she thought, but didn't say anything. She wasn't ready to bring up their personal issues.

They passed the American Embassy and continued in the direction of the Tuileries Garden.

"I've spent a lot of time in this park in the past few days." David said, and shoved his hands in the front pockets of his jeans.

"It's a beautiful park," Stella said. "And so many people are still out for a walk or letting their children run off some energy. I wouldn't want to live in a city the size of Paris, but if I had no choice, I'd like to be near a park. The way your apartment in Chicago is so close to Grant Park."

"I often think back to going there with you and sitting at Buckingham Fountain," David said. He ran a hand over his head. "Stella, listen, I don't know where to start, but there's so much I have to say to you."

Did he just say he thought about her? "We need to talk, there's no doubt, but not now. Not here."

She felt David's hand close to hers and pulled away, reaching for her purse strap, although it didn't need adjusting. What if she took his hand? Would it be like holding out the proverbial olive branch?

"How long are you staying in Paris?" she asked.

"I go back to London on Saturday."

"London, wow. Aren't you needed there now? No performances?"

"My understudies fill in for me. You know I rarely use them, but this is—you are—more important than the show."

"What production are you in?" she asked, his last words still ringing in her ears.

"You'll laugh—the *Phantom.*"

"Why should I laugh? The musical is still such a huge worldwide success after more than thirty years, it's amazing," Stella said. "What were you doing here in Paris?"

"I auditioned for *Don Giovanni*. When you saw me at the Opera House, Aaron and I had just been on a tour of the theater. Auditions were on Monday and Tuesday."

"Did you get the role?"

"Yes. I signed the papers yesterday to sing here in the spring," he said.

"How wonderful for you. Congratulations." Stella smiled and stopped walking. She was happy for him and his successes. "I remember you telling me once how it can be difficult for Americans to get contracts in Europe, and you've been here for eighteen months now. You made it!"

He winced. "Thank you..." She waited for him to say more, but he didn't.

"Are you looking forward to performing in Paris?" She asked while she followed him to a bench.

"Yes, I'm looking forward to it, but..."

Before she could stop herself, she blurted out, "David, are you happy?"

He sighed deeply and patted the bench next to him, inviting her to sit, which she did. "It's a question I've asked myself very often. One I don't have an answer for, to be honest."

Stella regretted asking him. She shouldn't care whether he was happy or not, and she didn't want to feel sorry for him.

"How are your parents doing? How's Sabrina?" She hoped it was safer territory to ask about his family.

"They're doing well, thank you for asking."

Stella folded her hands in her lap. Their conversation seemed so...stilted and superficial, and it pained her.

Is this what's left of us?

David leaned back and linked his hands behind his head, then sat up again and rested his forearms on his knees. "Dad's still with United, but says he wouldn't mind a golden handshake. Mom has cut down on her teaching at the High School for the Arts. She wants them to travel more while they're still healthy."

"Oh, my. Can you imagine your parents being around each other all the time?" Stella liked them both, but couldn't picture them in retirement.

"No. I see Dad signing up for adult history classes at some college in Chicago, and Mom accepting a volunteer job somewhere teaching little kids early dance steps. And Mom's also dropping hints about grandbabies, in general aimed at Sabrina. She's telling her not to wait till they're too old and weak to hold a baby."

Stella laughed, "Old and weak is not how I see them anytime soon. Does Sabrina have a serious boyfriend now?"

"From what I hear, she's still in her on again-off again relationship with Kyle. She threatened Mom and Dad that she wouldn't come home anymore if they don't stop the emotional blackmail. I have a feeling she's putting on a show, and would like a commitment from Kyle, but I'm staying out of it."

David turned to look at her. "What about your parents and Luca? What are they up to?"

"They're doing fine. Dad still teaches Math at UPenn, and Mom still works for Innovative Rehab. Luca doesn't have a lot of time to come home and visit, and Mom and Dad miss seeing him. I think they still hope he'll come back to Philadelphia and settle down."

She kept her eyes on the fountain while she talked, but could feel David watching her. She wanted to slide closer to him, but her head told her to stay where she was. When she looked at him, his eyes mirrored the same longing she felt.

"Oh, God, Stella," he said and reached out to brush the backs of his fingers over the side of her face. "I can't believe I'm sitting here with you." He pushed a strand of hair behind her ear. "What are you doing tomorrow?"

"I don't know yet. I assume Naomi will have a battle plan worked out by the time I get to the hotel. You know her. She needs action. Being passive and waiting for others to act is hard for her. Which reminds me, I should get back."

"What's the address? I'll pull up the directions," he asked. "Or would you like me to call a taxi?"

"I'd like to walk, and I have a basic idea where we need to go," she pointed toward the Louvre looming in the not-too-far distance. "This way, then take a right and across the Seine."

They walked side by side, both lost in thoughts, when David asked, "Can I see you tomorrow?"

"You must have other things to do," she glanced at him.

"Stella, the most important thing for me is to be there for you," he repeated his earlier statement.

"Thank you. How 'bout if I text you after breakfast? Naomi might complain, but I think, deep down, she's grateful for your support."

They had left the park and stood in front of the glass pyramid. "Julia and I talked about visiting the Louvre. I mean, we have tons of time, but it just feels wrong to go sightseeing while Revan is in danger."

Talking about Revan brought back the reality of why they were here. This wasn't some random picking-up-where-we-left-off, and it wasn't about her and David. She tried to blink away the tears puddling in her eyes, but a few managed to roll down her face.

He reached out and rubbed them away with his thumb, every nerve in her body responding to the feel of his skin on hers. She stepped a little closer and could smell his aftershave. He must have showered and shaved before meeting them, because she couldn't see the usual stubble on his chin.

David continued his gentle caresses of her face and said, "You need to distract yourselves. We can check the news online throughout the day. If there's any new development, we'll hear about it. Or Alexander can let us know."

Stella noticed how he said, *we'll* hear about it. Not, *you'll* hear about it. It was reassuring, yet there was no *we* anymore. Best to ignore his slip.

She stepped away from him, out of the reach of his touch. "I'll ask Julia if she can arrange it."

Crossing Pont Royal, they passed an accordionist sitting on a three-legged stool, playing a soulful melody. Stella stopped walking and looked up and down the river.

"Naomi and I went on a boat tour last Sunday and came by here. You know, I never thought I'd like Paris as much as I do."

David reached for her hand and laced his fingers through hers. He pulled her closer and sang a few lines, in perfect harmony with the musician. The old man smiled at them and nodded.

She wanted to scream, "What are you doing to me?" But she remained silent. She'd figure it out later.

And she'd never listen to "La Vie en Rose" again without remembering this moment.

David pulled change out of his pocket and dropped a few euros into the man's tin bowl. Still holding hands, they continued walking in silence until Stella pointed with her free hand and said, "There's our hotel. Thank you for walking me home—well, not home, but here."

"Stella, please call me first thing in the morning," he said in a pleading voice, then pulled her into his arms and brushed his lips to the top of her head.

She closed her eyes and didn't want to let go of him. The comfortable familiarity between them wasn't lost on her, and she wanted to bask in it for the short time they had.

Stella nodded, "Bye, David. See you tomorrow."

Without looking back, she walked into the lobby, and spotted Naomi sitting at the bar, deep in an animated conversation with—Kai.

What is he doing here? And didn't she say she was tired and needed time to think? Stella shook off her confusion and joined them.

"Well, this is a surprise. What brings you here, Kai?"

"Hi, Stella." Kai stood and hugged her.

"You won't believe it, but listen to this!" Naomi said in a cheerful voice. "On my way back to the hotel, I walked past the entrance to the catacombs..."

Stella interrupted her and laughed. "Nice try, but to get to the catacombs from the bistro, you had to walk past our hotel, and probably keep walking for another ten minutes. Mmm-hm...Don't give me that look. You did *not* just happen to walk by, you went there on purpose. You probably took a taxi from the bistro and got dropped off right there!"

"Yeah, well...anyhow," Naomi waved her hand, "it doesn't matter how I ended up there. But who do you think I ran into? Ta-da..." Naomi pointed to Kai. "The man who was face-to-face with the kidnapper!" Naomi copied Leo's voice.

Kai grinned at Stella and said, "Your friend is fierce when she wants something."

Stella rolled her eyes. "Tell me something new. But isn't the area packed with police and news crews? How did you find each other?"

"I went there because I had nothing better to do, when I heard a commotion and saw a tall woman arguing with one of the cops." Kai gave Naomi a stern look, then continued, "As soon as I recognized Naomi, I tried to pull her away before she was arrested. I don't know what she told the poor guy, but he looked like he was running out of patience."

"It doesn't matter, I was ready for step two," Naomi said.

"What's step two?" Kai asked.

"It involves a lot of crying," Stella explained.

Kai laughed and said, "Is there a step three?"

"Don't ask," Stella grinned. "So, what else is going on?"

"I just told Naomi about the interview with this Leo guy. Oh man, I didn't want to be there, but he kept pushing his microphone in my face."

"Oh, right! I guess you got more than you signed up for. Weren't you scared?"

Kai answered, "I can tell you it wasn't what we expected when we woke up Monday morning." He sighed, then smiled and said, "But enough of that. What would you like to drink? My treat."

"I'm going to make a quick trip to the room. But I'll have a glass of pinot noir when I return. Thanks, Kai." She turned to Naomi, "Is Julia back yet?"

"I haven't seen her come in. Maybe *catching up* with Alexander is taking a little longer?" Naomi winked, then said to Kai, "Okay, so you were saying about Leo..."

Stella wasn't interested in any Leo stories, and she needed a few moments to get her emotions sorted out. She already missed David and wondered where he was right now.

As she crossed the lobby, the music playing in the background couldn't have been more fitting. "Time to Say Goodbye." But she wasn't ready to think about goodbyes, not when they just had their hello.

A glass of blood-red wine was waiting for her when she returned and found Naomi and Kai sitting on the outdoor patio.

"Those tall orange flowers look exotic. Our backyard at home is also sheltered and gets plenty of sun in the afternoon. I think I'll try to recreate this setup. And I need to get one of those wrought-iron bistro sets with yellow or orange cushions."

"As long as you don't put candles everywhere, Revan won't mind," Naomi said.

Kai put down his beer. "Revan... Wait! The man in the catacombs is the same guy you told me about on Sunday! Who loves motorcycles?"

Naomi just nodded.

"Okay, it's all coming back to me now. Weren't you supposed to be on some tour?"

"We dropped out of the tour this morning and came back as soon as we heard," Stella said.

"But you also had plans to go to Normandy, didn't you?" Naomi asked Kai. "Why are you still here?"

"After my unexpected adventure, I decided to stay here for the week and see what's happening next. Just didn't feel like driving around anymore."

"Then you can keep us company while we're all waiting. There's not much else we can do," Naomi said, then jumped up and waved. "Julia, we're out here! Grab a drink at the bar and join us."

"Be right there!" Julia called back.

"Another friend?" Kai asked.

"Interesting story, but yes. We met Julia on the tour," Naomi said.

"Julia, this is Kai," Naomi said after Julia sat down.

"I saw you on TV. You're the one who..."

"...almost came face-to-face with the kidnapper," Kai laughed. "Yes. My two seconds of fame."

"Well...you did. Almost," Julia said.

Stella thought it was time to change the subject, and turned to Julia, "Alexander seems nice. *Very* nice. What's up with you two?"

Naomi put a hand over her mouth, trying to stifle a giggle. "Since when do you ask such personal questions?"

She gave Stella a piercing look, then a knowing smile slid over her face. "I know! You just don't want to talk about David!"

Stella studied the wine in her glass long and hard, took a sip, then focused on Julia and prompted her, "We're all ears..."

"Wait, who's David?" Kai asked.

"Stella's ex-boyfriend," Naomi explained, then added, "he's in disgrace."

She eyed Stella. "And since you, my friend, promised Julia earlier to fill her in about David, you might as well tell both Julia and Kai. I have a feeling we'll be seeing more of the Troubadour over the next two days, so everybody might as well know what he did."

Stella didn't think Kai needed to know her personal business, and she would've preferred to tell Julia on her own terms, but too late now. If Naomi thought she could rush her, well...

She took a few deep breaths, pursed her lips, tilted her head to the side and, putting her chin on the knuckles of her right hand, said in her best Storytime voice, "Once upon a time, there was a young woman who fell head-over-heels in love with..."

"You can fast-forward a tad, thank you," Naomi said.

"We dated for two years, but he was away more than with me..." Stella said.

Naomi explained to Kai, "Famous opera singer, Broadway star, on tour nine months out of the year or something like it."

"Do you want to tell my story?" Stella asked, then returned her attention to Kai and Julia. "Anyhow, we were fine, but then out of the blue he broke up with me last year. We hadn't been in touch since then, until we ran into each other last weekend. The End."

"Okay, but why is he in disgrace?" Kai wanted to know and looked at all three women.

Julia gasped.

Stella's shoulders slumped and she said, "Hmph."

"Tsk, tsk, tsk...only a man would ask." Even Naomi shook her head.

"Sorry, a dumb question, I guess. New topic. What do you think of this heat wave crippling Europe right now?" Kai leaned back in his chair and stretched out his long legs.

"Ah, the weather! Always saves an iffy situation," Stella laughed.

"It wasn't too bad near the beaches," Naomi said. "And we cooled down with lots of ice cream."

"I hear the city of Paris allows people to use the water basins to stay cool. A few days ago, there was a photograph in the local papers of hundreds of people standing in the basins at the Trocadéro Gardens," Kai said before he yawned. "Ladies, I think it's time for me to head back to my hotel. What's your plan for tomorrow?"

"I'd like to go to the police and find out what they can tell us. But after my experience today, I don't think we'll get far," Naomi said.

"My suggestion is to wait until morning before making any decisions," Julia said. "Maybe there'll be news by then, and if not, we can't do anything but wait. We definitely can't force our way behind the police lines at the catacombs," she looked at Naomi, "and play *Rambo*."

"Well, I thought more *Charlie's Angels*. Can't you see us? Styled hair, designer dresses, hidden shoulder holsters?" Naomi pretended to pull a gun, then stopped. "How do you know I went there earlier?"

Julia tapped the side of her nose, "Call it a hunch."

Kai snorted, "I hope you're not traveling with weapons."

Naomi wiggled both eyebrows, "A woman is born with weapons."

Kai choked on his last mouthful of beer, and Julia said, "Okay, I have to go and check on a few emails. Bye, Kai. Girls, I'll see you upstairs."

"Yes, ma'am," Stella and Naomi giggled.

"Kai, how 'bout we'll be in touch in the morning? I told David the same thing." Stella shot Naomi a loaded look and pressed her lips together. She didn't want to hear her opinion.

"Naomi has my phone number. Text me in the morning, but I'm warning you. I never reply before nine o'clock. I like to go jogging before I talk to anyone." He got up and reached for his motorcycle helmet sitting next to the chair.

"See you tomorrow, Kai. Thank you for helping us," Stella said.

"I haven't done anything."

"Oh, yes, you have. Who knows where we'd be without you and your buddies," Naomi said, and gave him a quick hug.

CHAPTER 27

"Stella, Naomi, wake up!" Julia called from the small kitchen table without taking her eyes off her laptop.

"Why are you yelling?" Naomi asked. "What time is it?"

"I'm not yelling. I'm making sure you hear me. Alexander texted to let me know there's a press conference at eight. It's quarter past seven now."

Naomi jumped out of bed and hurried to the bathroom. "I'll leave the door ajar so I can hear what you're saying, but no peeking."

"Where did you get the coffee? Did you go to the breakfast room?" Stella asked as she crawled out of her bed. She stuck her nose in the air and follow the smell of java.

Julia pointed behind her. "There's a pod machine over there. We never looked in the cabinets yesterday, but it's equipped with mugs, utensils, even plates and glasses."

Stella called, "Naomi, hurry up in there."

"And where did you get the pastries?" Naomi came out of the bathroom and went straight to the kitchenette, where she eyed the assortment of brioches, madeleines, turnovers, and croissants in a bowl next to the coffee machine and rubbed her hands together. "Ooh..."

"Those are from the bakery down the street. I was up an hour ago. Since all European cities have bakeries around every corner, I didn't have to go far. Help yourselves. I also bought milk for the coffee and some orange juice."

"I like this setup," Naomi said. "I think the three of us should stay in this room instead of paying for separate rooms."

"Works for me," Julia said.

"Yes, let's stay in this room. We'll let the hotel know when we go out later," Stella said as she came out of the bathroom. She narrowed her eyes at Naomi. "What are you wearing?"

"A T-shirt," Naomi reached for something at the bottom of the bowl.

"Isn't that one of Revan's shirts?"

"It might be," Naomi shrugged and pulled at the fabric reaching her thighs.

"You're poking the dragon, and you know it."

"I don't think he's missed it," Naomi replied with a wide grin.

"I don't know what the story behind the T-shirt is, but that's a nice Harley on it." Julia said before sipping some coffee, then taking a bite of her chocolate croissant.

"Let's just say Revan loves two things. His camera and his Harley. And nobody's allowed to touch them," Stella explained with a side look at Naomi, who shrugged.

"I see... So, do you want to hear about the press conference?"

"Yes!" Stella and Naomi answered together.

"Okay, sit down." Julia pointed to the other chairs at the table. "It's on French television, and I don't know if they'll have a translator there. I assume there'll also be individual interviews afterward, so we should try and catch one of those."

"I've been wondering why they do press conferences... and why isn't there more on social media?" Stella asked.

"The authorities seem to keep a lid on it, and the newspapers can only print whatever statements they release. As for social media, there might be something, but we're better off not reading unfounded stories," Julia said.

Five minutes before eight, Stella, Naomi and Julia lined up on the sofa in front of the wall-mounted TV, their eyes glued to the screen showing one woman and three men seated behind a rectangular table. The camera moved from face to face and lingered a little longer on the woman. She tried to smile, but her tired eyes betrayed her exhaustion.

A forest of microphones and recording equipment on tripods was set up in front of the four people.

Stella couldn't understand one word of what was being said by a still-invisible moderator. "Too bad there aren't any subtitles. Maybe we can at least learn their names. We've seen the cop before," Stella said.

"I could try and translate, but if they talk very fast, it'll get hectic," Naomi said. "I have a feeling the reporters can't wait to fire off their questions as soon as they get the green light."

"Don't worry, we'll catch a summary later," Julia said. "Oh, they're starting with the introductions."

First was the already-familiar policeman. His name plate said, "Charles Rousseau, Commissaire."

Next came a man who was introduced as Louis Pelletier, Inspecteur Générale, Police Judicaire.

The woman's name plate read, "Dr. Claudine Bisset, Inspection Générale des Carrières (IGC)."

Last was Manuel Savoy from the French Ministry of the Interior.

After introductions, Louis Pelletier spoke for a while. "My head is spinning just trying to follow any of what he's saying. I'll have to wait until they give interviews later," Stella said.

Naomi muted the TV but didn't turn it off, and they watched while the cameras volleyed back and forth between the reporters and the four people being quizzed.

"Julia, is there enough food so we can have breakfast in the room?" Stella asked.

"Sure, there's plenty. So, let's go through our plan for today."

"Without knowing what the latest development is, we can't plan anything," Naomi said.

"I agree," Stella said, then smirked. "And while we wait, Julia, you can tell us about you and Alexander. We never got to it yesterday."

"There's not much to say. We've known each other for a long time." Julia leaned back in her chair, cradling her coffee mug. "He and my husband were very good friends."

A husband? She never mentioned being married. But then we've only known her for three days.

She watched while Julia twisted a delicate ring on her left hand. She hadn't paid attention to Julia's jewelry before, but now she saw a small, square diamond with baguette-cut emeralds on each side.

"They met in the Special Forces. Alexander made it home from the battle of Mogadishu in 1993, Matthew didn't." Julia swallowed a few times.

"I'm so sorry. Now I feel terrible for prodding you." Stella reached for her hand.

"You couldn't know, and it's been almost twenty-five years. I can talk about it without falling apart. Alexander was a tremendous help getting me through all of it, and we stayed close. It was hard for him, too. He had to watch helplessly when Matt's helicopter was shot down and left the military as soon as he was eligible."

A bashful smile crossed her face, "And who knows...? Maybe I do like him a little more than just as a friend."

"Does he return your feelings?" Stella asked.

"Yes, he's made it clear for many years that he's only waiting for me to give him the right signals," Julia blushed. "We shared one kiss a long time ago, but I was afraid to lose him, too, if the friends-turned-lovers thing didn't work out. But do *not* repeat what I just told you."

She set her cup on the table. "On the other hand, maybe it's time for me to practice what I preach. If I tell Emily to be open for new love, then I guess I should be as well. Like her, I'm only in my late forties."

Stella asked, "In all those years, have you never thought about marrying again? Or children? You must've been young when it happened."

"I was twenty-three when Matt died, and I put all my energy into work afterward. There were a few casual relationships, but never anything serious enough to consider marriage again. And there have always been those underlying feelings for Alexander, which I've tried to ignore."

She sighed. "I can tell you, it's a bittersweet deal. By the time you make it to the top of the ladder as a woman, you've missed your chance at having a family, children."

"Would Alexander consider moving back to the States? How long has he been in France?" Naomi asked. She licked chocolate off her fingers and with her other hand reached for another pastry.

"Five years, but he was at the Embassy in Germany before then for a number of years. He wants to be back stateside next year. Like many of us, he's dealing with aging parents. But to be honest, I wouldn't mind living here with him for a year or two. I've established a rewarding career, but would give it up in a heartbeat to be with the man I love."

She sighed and finished her coffee. "But enough of me. Look, there's Leo again."

And there he was, standing in front of the entrance to the catacombs, this time with Dr. Bisset.

Naomi sucked in a deep breath and said. "I hope this is the last time we have to see him. Now he's making the poor woman stand there for his interview!? Where she emerged from just yesterday!"

"She works for the IGC and has to go down again at some point," Stella said. "I know I wouldn't. What a creepy place."

"Good morning, this is Leo Wu live from Paris. I'm here with Dr. Bisset, who escaped the tunnels of death yesterday afternoon." Leo flashed his white teeth at Dr. Bisset, who adjusted her sunglasses and gave him a forced smile.

"Good morning, Mr. Wu. I wouldn't call it the tunnels of death, but I don't have the time or energy for semantics." Dr. Bisset spoke in a calm voice with only a light accent.

"*Slap!* There ya go, Leo!" Naomi cheered.

"Dr. Bisset, can you describe in your own words what happened last Monday morning?"

"First of all, I would like to say I spoke with Dr. Caron this morning. She is doing well and will be released from the hospital soon." She gave Leo a pointed look, as if trying to tell him this should have been his first question.

"*Slap two*, Leo!" Naomi sang out. "Three and you're out."

"Her respiratory distress was caused by the prolonged exposure to the humid conditions in the tunnels. And the oxygen levels in the tunnels always fluctuate. It is possible we were in an area with low levels, which worsened her condition."

"I'm happy to hear it," Leo said. "Now, please tell us more about your actual encounter with the kidnapper, whose identity is still being kept secret. Did he share his name with you?"

"No, we didn't exchange personal information. Dr. Caron, Mr. Forrester, and I had been in the tunnels for about an hour and had just reached the area where cataphiles discovered a new cave last week."

"What was Mr. Forrester's reason for being there with you? He's not employed by the IGC," Leo interrupted.

"If he doesn't stop interrupting her, we'll never find out," Naomi complained.

"Mr. Forrester was invited by the IGC to take photographs of the area. He is a highly accomplished professional who has a worldwide reputation for taking amazing and accurate images in challenging conditions. We have worked together on several occasions.

"As I started to say, we began to set up our equipment. The cave is not yet accessible, and can only be seen through a narrow crack in the wall. All of a sudden, we were approached by a man wearing a police uniform and demanding to know our business in the tunnels."

"A police officer?" Leo's eyes widened and his thin eyebrows almost reached his receding hairline.

"Fuck, Leo, keep your trap shut," Naomi grumbled. She glanced at Julia and said, "Sorry."

Stella reached for her hand and gave it a squeeze, while Julia said, "Nothing I haven't said myself a time or two."

"We showed him our IDs, but also asked what he was doing there, since the tunnels are closed. Police units often use the mines for rescue trainings and drills for their canine units and SWAT teams, but none had been approved by us at that time. He got angry when we questioned him, and we reminded him we were the authority in the mines, not the police.

"Mr. Forrester was setting up his camera equipment and told him to let us work. He even said we weren't interested in his business and pointed to the man's duffel bag. This comment upset the man. When he reached inside his jacket, Mr. Forrester's radar went off and he swung his camera at the man."

"Mr. Forrester attacked him first?" Leo gasped.

"No, you moron, he offered him a lollipop and waited to be shot," Naomi fumed. "Why can't they put someone a little brighter than this idiot in front of the camera?"

She jumped up and glared out the window. "I can't watch this any longer. And to imagine Rev is still with the creep."

"Yes, it's scary, but we have to believe in him. I'm sure he's working on a plan for his escape," Stella said.

Julia paced between the sofa and kitchenette. "If it's true and the guy's a cop, then it could explain why they haven't shared his identity. I assume the authorities are trying to figure out if he's working solo or if there's a whole slew of criminal activities going on under their noses."

"What a mess! And we can't do anything but wait," Stella said.

"You both promised friends or family members to keep them informed," Julia reminded Stella and Naomi. "Why don't you assure them you're well and share what we just learned? I'll write to Alexander, but I'm sure he watched this interview, too." She typed a short text.

"And then?" Stella asked.

"Then we get out of the hotel and do what tourists do. Explore the city, keep ourselves distracted. Sitting here stewing about it doesn't help anyone. Ask David and Kai to meet us for lunch. We're a ragtag bunch of friends here, and we'll get through this together."

Julia looked at her phone, "Alexander says he watched the coverage."

Stella sat on her bed and wrote her message to David,

Hey, did you see the interview? We're still in shock. To stay busy, we want to do some sightseeing. Want to join us?

Stella's heart gave a little jump when she saw three dancing dots on her message screen. He'd been waiting to hear from her!

You don't need to ask me twice. The Montparnasse Tower is close to your hotel. Have you been there?

"David suggests going to the Montparnasse Tower. Is it something you'd be interested in seeing?" Stella asked Naomi and Julia.

"Sure," Julia said and looked at Naomi.

"Works for me," Naomi started typing on her phone. "I'll text Kai, just because we told him we'd stay in touch."

"What time should we meet?" Stella asked. "Is ten good? It gives us enough time to get ready."

Naomi and Julia both nodded, then went back to their phones.

Stella typed,

Sounds good. Meet there at ten?

> Yes. I'll be there.

Then came another message,

> I can't wait to see you again.

Stella didn't reply. She couldn't wait, either. And she wondered if maybe it should bother her.

Seeing him yesterday and talking to him had felt so... normal. Almost as if the past year hadn't happened—or had been nothing but a strange dream.

But it was real—twelve long months of silence. It couldn't just be swept under the next rug and ignored.

Stella knew what Naomi's advice would be. "Be sure you know what you're doing. And do it for the right reasons."

She didn't know when she and David would have a chance to talk in private, but before she flew home on Saturday, she'd get answers to the questions which had haunted her for so long.

CHAPTER 28

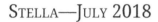

Stella—July 2018

David was already waiting for them in front of the tall, black glass and steel construction. He sat on a low wall in front of the building, looking up and down the street. Stella fought the urge to run to him.

"Have you been here long?" she called out as she climbed the wide stone steps from street level.

His face lit up at the sound of her voice and he stood. "No, only a few minutes. I wasn't sure how busy it was at this time of the day and wanted to find a spot where I could see you. You still snuck up on me."

He hugged Naomi and Julia and pecked their cheeks, then pulled Stella close and leaned down to kiss her. She turned her head just enough for the kiss to miss her lips.

"How are you today? You look beautiful," David tucked a strand of hair behind her ear. She wore it in a ponytail, the way she knew he liked it, but some of it had come loose and blew across her face. And she also might've picked the emerald-green dress because she knew he liked the color on her.

So what? Nothing wrong with wanting to look nice for the man you love...used to love...still love... Ugh!

"I'm fine. At least I was able to get some sleep last night. I think I was exhausted from all the walking," Stella smiled. "And you?"

"I didn't sleep much, but now I'm good," he said for only her to hear before he looked at Naomi and Julia. "Are we waiting for anybody else?"

"No, you've got the three of us all to yourself," Naomi said. "Kai has other plans."

"Alexander hopes to meet us after work," Julia added.

"Let's go up," Stella said. "Apparently, the tower isn't well liked by Parisians because it's such an eyesore, but the views are supposed to be phenomenal."

"Did you read about it after David suggested meeting us here?" Naomi nudged her shoulder.

"Maybe a little," she admitted.

After buying their tickets, they rode one of the twenty-five elevators to the 56th floor, where they took the stairs to the observation deck on the 59th floor.

"I have no words," Julia said in an awed voice. "The view is stunning."

"Yeah, I don't care how ugly the tower is from the outside, I'm glad someone built it. It's hard to believe how far you can see," Naomi said.

"Excuse me, would you mind taking a photo of us?" a young woman asked David.

After taking a few pictures, she offered, "Would you guys like a group picture?"

David looked at Stella, Naomi, and Julia. "You okay with that?"

"Of course," Julia said, and moved closer to David.

"Go ahead," Naomi sighed.

Stella hesitated before she said, "Sure." She didn't have to keep the photo.

After opening the camera app on his phone, David gave it to the young woman, then pulled Stella to his side. Her body molded to his as it had done so many other times.

Stella felt a pinch on her thigh and saw Naomi's hand when she looked down.

"Why did you do that? It hurt!"

"Making sure you're not daydreaming." Naomi side-eyed her.

"Geez, we're taking *one* group picture," Stella hissed. "We don't have to keep it. Maybe Julia will enjoy having it."

When David got his phone back, he typed something, then said to Stella, "I've forwarded it to you."

"Thanks, I'll send it to Naomi and Julia later. It'll be a nice memory of our time together."

David made a popping sound with his lips and looked at her with his dark eyes. *So he hadn't been able to break his habit of making that sound when he had something on his mind but wasn't sure how to say it.*

Julia and Naomi had wandered off by themselves, and she and David began walking around the roof terrace.

She pointed to the Sacré-Coeur Basilica in the distance. "We stayed at a hotel in Montmartre last weekend and walked up the hill to the church. It's majestic, and I felt so small, but I also felt like she—the basilica—protected me. Sounds silly, I know."

"Not at all," he said and kept his eyes on her.

"Have you seen it?"

"No, but if we have time, maybe you can show it to me?"

"Maybe…" A few days ago she had wished she could see it with him, but now she was afraid it would be too much.

David reached for her hands. "Let me take you out to dinner tonight," he pleaded.

"I don't know. What's the point of this, anyway?" She pulled her hands back and leaned against the railing with her back to the city.

"We'll figure it out together." His voice was tense with emotion. She felt his breath on her face as he pulled her close and she inhaled the familiar scent of him; bergamot and cedar—and a hint of lavender. La Nuit, the aftershave she gave him for their first Christmas.

"Are you still putting small sachets of dried lavender in with your clothes?"

"Yes. Busted," he said and cleared his throat.

Stella looked up at him. She was wrapped in his arms and he didn't seem able to let go of her any more than it was possible for her to step away from him. She noticed it yesterday, too, when he reached for her hand. It felt so right—and was also so...wrong.

"Stella, we need to talk, and..."

Be strong! You want answers. Get them.

She stepped out of his embrace and turned away. "You have no idea how messed up I am. Yes, of course we need to talk. Because I need closure. Otherwise, I'll never be able to move on."

Stella heard the quick intake of breath behind her. She propped her elbow on the railing, resting her chin on her knuckles and sucking in her lower lip.

Without looking at him, she said, "Where do you want to meet? I don't think a restaurant is a good idea. It's too public. You know it's only a matter of time before someone recognizes you."

"The restaurant at my hotel is fantastic, and they have smaller rooms for business meetings. It may not be the same atmosphere as the main restaurant, but we'd have privacy."

"Yes, it's fine. I don't need atmosphere," she said and thought, *The more sterile, the better.*

"Can I make a reservation for seven?" He sounded hesitant, and she wanted to assure him everything would be fine. But it wouldn't be, so she kept quiet.

"Sure. Now, let's find the others."

When they left the Montparnasse Tower a while later, Naomi said, "Kai just texted me about a park with open-air concerts and shows. He asked if we wanna go there with him tonight around 7:30."

"I'm meeting Alexander at 5 pm. You're all welcome to join us, and we can have dinner together," Julia said.

Stella looked at David first, then said, "We thought we'd sit down and talk tonight over dinner."

"If you two have dates, then I'll hang out with Kai for a few hours."

"Sounds like a great idea," Stella agreed. "But we'll get together at our hotel later for some girl time. Deal?"

"Deal!" agreed Julia and Naomi.

David asked, "What do you want to do next? We still have the whole afternoon."

"Has anyone checked the news on their phones since this morning?" Naomi asked.

"Alexander will let me know as soon as he hears anything," Julia said, then took out her phone. "Nothing."

"Is anybody hungry? What about lunch?" Stella asked.

"I should go back to the hotel," Julia said, and looked apologetic. "I know we said we'd do everything together, but Emily asked if we can FaceTime. She's contacted her lawyer and has a few questions for me. I didn't expect her to move this fast, but I want to support her."

"I'd like to go shopping," Naomi announced. "I spotted another Galeries Lafayette store over there," she pointed to her left, "and then I'll hang out at the hotel until I meet Kai." She didn't look at Stella.

"As long as you don't try to sneak into the catacombs..."

Naomi mumbled something, but didn't clarify when Stella gave her a questioning look.

"How are you getting to the park? Do you know where it is?" Stella asked.

"I'll look it up and take the metro."

"I have an idea," David said.

"Uh-oh," Naomi quipped.

"Stella and I are meeting at seven. Let me arrange for a taxi to pick you up at quarter of seven," he said, "It can drop Stella off first, then bring you to the park to meet your friend."

Naomi nodded and said, "Good thinking, Danvers. You've earned yourself a check in the plus column."

David shook his head with a grin, then asked Stella, "Wanna go to the Eiffel Tower? You said you'd like to go to the top, and afterward I can either walk you back to your hotel or we'll find something else to visit."

"Can we grab a sandwich somewhere on the way? I'm really hungry again."

David laughed, "What happened to the old Stella?"

"She changed..." Stella said quietly.

CHAPTER 29

DAVID—JULY 2018

David sat in one of the oversized chairs in his hotel's lobby. It was classy, with a touch of modern, decorated in shades of beige and white, with the inevitable black item of furniture as an accent. Huge flower arrangements and potted plants were scattered throughout the wide space, which now basked in the fading sunlight of the early evening beaming through the domed glass ceiling.

His attention didn't sway from the entrance doors, except for the occasional time check on his phone. It was 7:05.

Where is she? She's always on time. His palms were sweaty—and sitting still was almost impossible. What if she changed her mind?

After spending today with Stella, being around her and watching her take in as many details of Paris as possible, he was happier and more content than he'd been in a long time. *You know exactly since when...*

But did she feel the same? Did she only let him hold her hand and kiss her cheek to placate him? He didn't get that impression this afternoon. First, they visited the Eiffel Tower, and then went to the Centre Pompidou. David recalled her reaction when she saw the Stravinsky Fountain in front of the contemporary museum, how she stopped walking and gasped.

The memory of her eyes widening and the slow smile spreading across her face filled him with longing.

They spent a long time at the fountain. She wanted to know what it represented, and he summarized a quick google search result, "There are sixteen sculptures, and each is inspired by one of Igor Stravinsky's compositions. The black metal sculptures were made by Jean Tinguely, and the abstract, colorful ones by his wife, Niki de Saint Phalle."

"I love how all the pieces are spraying water while they twist in different directions."

He thought of the fountain as a complicated, animated 3D puzzle. Every piece of art in the water basin seemed to dance to their individual rhythms, but if one stopped moving, the whole effect would be destroyed.

He knew he needed to fix what he destroyed last year. And he knew it wasn't going to be easy. Saying sorry wasn't going to cut it. Tracy Chapman nailed it in her song, "Baby Can I Hold You." He just hoped he'd somehow find the right words.

In his mind, he formulated dozens of apologies, but he knew none were good enough.

Would he be able to share his biggest fear with her, something he'd never told anyone else?

Or would he lose her before he had a chance to win her back?

And—*where is she*??

A waiter crossed the lobby and asked him, "May I bring you anything to drink, monsieur?"

If he ordered a whiskey and a glass of Stella's favorite wine, would she think he presumed to know what she wanted? The Stella he used to know wouldn't. But he wasn't sure how the new Stella would react. What was it she mumbled earlier about the old Stella? "She changed..."

Time changed people.

Disappointment changed people.

He remembered when Stella almost guiltily ordered a glass of champagne with lunch at the charming *patisserie* on their way to the Eiffel Tower, and how much she enjoyed it.

"A bottle of *Dom Pérignon*, please."

"How many glasses?" the waiter asked.

"Two. Thank you." He didn't drink on a regular basis, but he allowed himself an occasional glass of whiskey or wine with dinner on days when he wasn't performing.

David jumped out of his chair when Stella walked into the lobby, and for a moment time stood still. Her black sleeveless dress hugged every perfect curve of her beautiful body. He wanted to memorize every detail. His eyes soaked her in, down to the dark pink nail polish on her toes.

Hell, Danvers, don't go all soft and mushy over nail polish. But it was *her* nail polish, and on *her* toes, and its effect on him was the opposite of soft and mushy. Very opposite, and very inappropriate timing.

She waved when she saw him and hurried toward him. He met her halfway. "Stella, you look amazing."

"Thank you." The corners of her mouth curled up and he wanted to kiss her.

A pearl pendant hung from a delicate gold chain, resting below her collarbone. David remembered reading about an ancient belief about pearls being created from angels' tears. He hated the idea of Stella crying, but after his dipshit move last year, she must have enough pearls for a triple strand necklace.

He cleared his throat and put his mouth close to her ear, "I love your nail polish and have to ask, um...what's the color called?"

Her boisterous, buoyant laughter had people in the lobby turning to see the source, but so what? Hearing the carefree sound was worth it.

She beckoned for him to come closer again. "Shower with Flowers. Do you like it?"

"You have no idea," he admitted before sending a mental message to his treacherous body part to behave.

He kissed her cheek, "Thank you for coming."

The waiter approached them with the champagne and two long-stemmed crystal flutes. "Where would you like me to serve, monsieur?"

David looked at Stella, "I remember what you had at lunch today, and ordered a bottle. I hope you don't mind. We can get something else if you prefer."

"No, it's very nice. Thank you."

"Shall we go to the courtyard?"

"Yes, please."

"The courtyard it is," he informed the waiter, who nodded, turned, and led them outside, where they were seated behind a cast-iron trellis covered with pink climbing roses, giving them a bit of privacy.

"What is it with Paris and courtyards?" she asked while the waiter opened the bottle and filled their glasses. "I'm planning to get a bistro set and bright throw pillows, maybe plant a large pot with colorful flowers."

"I'm sure it'll look pretty. You could also get a small backyard fountain," he pointed to the statue of a curvaceous woman sitting in the middle of a small basin, feeding a fat fish.

"What a great idea! But maybe not a naked woman," Stella said.

A waitress brought a platter with an assortment of cheeses, crackers, some fruit, and olives and said, "With compliments of the house, Monsieur Danvers."

"Is there anything else I can bring?" asked their waiter.

David thanked them both and handed one glass to Stella before holding up his own. "What do you want to drink to?"

"To Paris."

Both took a few sips of the refreshing beverage, then she reached for the cheese knife the same moment he did. Touching a live wire couldn't have caused a stronger reaction than the skin-to-skin contact of their hands.

He pushed the platter closer to her and reached for the olives. "We never got to talk about your trip this afternoon, or what brought you to France in the first place."

"It was the weirdest coincidence. Last week, Naomi asked me if I wanted to join her on this trip because her mom couldn't go. I already had this week off and wanted to visit Luca for a few days."

She held out both hands with her palms up. "Hmm... New York or France? The decision wasn't too hard. Naomi and I left Philly on Friday, spent Saturday afternoon and Sunday sightseeing, and our tour started on Monday."

"What was the group like?"

"There were fourteen people, plus the driver and our tour guide. Most members of the group were nice, except for one guy, but let's not talk about him."

She took another sip of champagne. "Mmm, this is really good!" She smacked her lips.

David thought it was incredibly sexy, and his body signaled its agreement. *Not again...* At this rate, it promised to be an extremely uncomfortable evening.

"But listen to this... Naomi didn't tell me the details. Only on the bus did I find out it's a tour to romantic places in France. I asked her if we were on *Candid Camera*, since she knows I've been feeling down because it's the anniversary of...well..."

She chewed on her lower lip and looked at her feet, and he hesitated, knowing she was trying to find the right words.

"Because it's been a year since I sent the letter?" David finished the sentence for her, feeling like dirt.

She nodded. "I had finished my annual reading of *The Phantom*, and..." He watched helplessly as she swallowed a few times and tears threatened to spill out of her sad eyes. If someone had dumped a pot of hot oil over him it couldn't have hurt more than hearing—and seeing—Stella's heartbreak.

After what he did to her, she still read it.

He reached out to touch her hand, but she held it up and said, "Let me finish this, and then we have to talk about something a little more uplifting... Anyway, I put the book and your letter in one of my storage bins and planned to have a ceremonial send-off fire later, but I could never burn any of it."

253

David couldn't stop what happened next.

In one fluid move, he turned his body toward hers, took her face in his hands and followed the wet trail of her tears with feathery kisses, until he reached her lips and slowly put his mouth on hers.

It was a soft, gentle kiss, meant to say, *I'm sorry.*

He pulled back a scant inch and looked into her eyes. He saw confusion and pain.

His next kiss was harder and searching, begging her, *Forgive me.*

When he stopped this time, he guided her head to his chest and wrapped his arms around her, kissing the top of her hair, letting his lips linger there. He hoped she'd understand his silent, *Let me hold you, baby.* He wanted to sit like this forever.

Carefree laughter at another table broke the mood.

He used his thumb to wipe away a last tear and couldn't resist again tucking a lose strand of hair behind her ear. When she leaned into his hand, his heart was beating so fast, he could feel it in his throat.

Did this small gesture mean there was hope?

She leaned away from him, "I hope I didn't cause a scene."

He again reached for one of her hands, needing to maintain their fragile connection. "You didn't. You have no reason to apologize for anything, my angel." His old pet name slipped out before he realized it.

She cleared her throat and said, "Okay, so...do you want to hear more about the trip?"

"You bet." He still couldn't bring himself to let go of her hand.

She told him about the places they visited, about the meals they enjoyed, and even related Caroline's romantic stories, the happy and sad ones. He listened, laughed, and asked questions, and wished he could've been there with Stella.

"Did you have a favorite place?" he asked when she was finished.

She rested her chin in the palm of her hand and thought about it, then reached for her champagne glass. Before her lips touched the rim of the glass, she looked up and said, "Mont Saint-Michel."

"Any special reason?"

"To me, it's the perfect combination of magic, history, passion, and strength," she mused. "And so beautiful, it takes your breath away."

As are you, my angel!

"You would've liked it there. I have tons of photos on my phone, but it would take forever to look through them now. Maybe I'll put a slideshow together when I'm back at home and send it to you."

"I can't wait to see it." He hoped to find a way to watch it together with her, not away from her.

One step at a time, Danvers...

Their waiter topped off their glasses, and told them their table was ready at their convenience.

"I think we'll finish the champagne first," David gave Stella a questioning look and when she nodded, he said, "Give us a few more minutes, please."

"I have a table reserved in a side room as we discussed, but we can also go to my suite and order room service. The manager assured me the menu is the same."

"Do you have a preference where we eat?"

He rubbed the back of his neck with one hand. "I think we're both more comfortable if we can speak freely, and without wait staff interruptions."

"You're right. In case there's more crying like I just did. Ugh... Can you see the headlines in tomorrow's papers? *Weeping Woman Wrecks David Danvers' Dinner.*" Stella snickered. "Yes, let's eat in your room."

He didn't care about his reputation or being recognized right now. But he needed to protect Stella from gossip and scrutiny.

After David informed the waiter about their new plans, she asked him to tell her about his performances in Hungary and England, about living in Budapest and London.

Giving her a summary of his past year, he realized the experiences sounded unbelievably similar—big stage, big city—and the only difference was the language in each country. But such was his professional life.

There was nothing to tell her about his personal life.

CHAPTER 30

---❖◦◗◯◖◦❖---

STELLA—JULY 2018

David held the door to his suite open and Stella walked into a room warm with orange evening sunlight. Through the large floor-to-ceiling windows, she saw part of the Louvre and the Tuileries Garden. Like the public areas of the hotel, the spacious corner room was decorated in shades of beige with black accents.

A round table with a white marble top stood in front of the corner windows, with two comfortable-looking chairs inviting guests to sit and relax. *A perfect spot for reading—or just enjoying the views.*

To the side, the door to the bedroom stood ajar and she saw part of a king-sized bed. She was relieved to see the sitting and sleeping areas were separated. Otherwise, the next few hours could be very awkward.

She dropped her purse on the sofa. "Do you mind if I take off my shoes?"

"Not at all, please make yourself comfortable. The powder room is there," he pointed at a door to his right, "in case you need it."

"How convenient to have a separate guest bath. Yes, I would like to wash my hands, but maybe I shouldn't look too closely into the mirror. I must look a mess," she sighed.

"Not at all, but if you want, I'll go in and cover it with a towel," he offered with a wink.

"I'm trying to be a big girl, but thanks for the noble offer!"

One look into the mirror confirmed her suspicions. Red-rimmed eyes and blotchy cheeks frowned back at her. And—invisible but imprinted on her skin—a burning sensation where David's lips touched not long ago. Her fingers went to the spot and lingered for a moment.

"What can I get you to drink?" David asked when she came out of the bathroom. "I can order some wine if you'd like."

"Just water for now, if you have some."

He took two bottles out of the minibar refrigerator. "Your choices are Perrier sparkling water, or Evian spring water."

"Sparkling, please. I like Perrier. Thanks." She sat down on one side of the sofa.

"Would you like to have a look at the menu first? I'm in no rush, but I don't know how hungry you are."

"The appetizers were filling, so I'm not too hungry. It was a nice gesture to bring them with the champagne. But let's check the menu and then decide whether we want to wait or order now." She reached for the menus on the table and gave one to him.

"Sure, why not?" he agreed.

"Oh no! Ugh, big mistake..." Stella put the menu down. "Did you just hear me say I'm not hungry? Well, I'm really not, but this all looks so *good*. Do you know what you want?"

"Yes, I do," he said and looked at her.

"What is it?"

He mumbled, "It's not on the menu."

"I'm sure they'll make it for you."

"They can't."

"David, I don't need to remind you, but this is a five-star hotel."

"Believe me," he said quietly.

She shrugged and let it go. "Why don't we go ahead and order before it gets too late? It might take a while to prepare the meals."

"Hold on, let me get a notepad." He went to the small writing desk in a corner of the spacious room, and she couldn't help thinking how good he looked in his black dress pants and dark gray shirt, with the sleeves rolled up to his elbows. He wore a burgundy tie earlier but must've taken it off along with his shoes while she was in the bathroom. She liked this casual look on him...always had. He walked with the confidence of someone used to being in front of thousands of people every day, but without being cocky about it. He was the image of masculine grace, but sleek and powerful. She could sit here all day and night and watch him.

Liar! You wanna do way more than look at him.

When he kissed her in the courtyard, it took all her willpower not to crawl into his lap and kiss him back the way her body and heart urged her to. The memory alone sent a tingling sensation to her core.

"Stella? What can I order for you?" David's voice interrupted her daydreaming. "No, wait, let me guess..."

"Go ahead," she said, entering into their old game of guessing what the other ordered. And later they'd share their meals. Or used to...

"You're going with the Viennese veal cutlet and a side salad, but will substitute French fries for the pasta." David looked confident to have gotten it right.

"And you're having the fillet of cod with herbed potatoes and olives. Correct?"

"Yup," he grinned. "What about dessert? Want to keep playing the guessing game?"

"Sure! You'll order, hmm," she tapped her bottom lip, "the selection of sorbets with the Madeleine cake."

"And you the crème brûlée," he said.

"I thought so at first. But the waffles Grand-Mère with chocolate sauce and apple compote also sound good." She sucked in her lower lip, rolled her eyes, and put an index finger under her chin. "Oh, I simply cannot decide!"

He laughed and said, "There's an easy solution, then. We'll order dinner first and wait for dessert until later. And if you still can't pick one, we'll get all three."

"Deal." She held up her hand for a high five.

He high-fived back, but locked their fingers before she could pull away. Then he kissed the back of her hand and released it.

"Would you like some wine with dinner?"

"Yes, please." Her skin prickled where his lips had touched.

While David was on the phone, she gazed out the windows. How would this evening end? She hoped they could remain friends after they cleared the air.

When he joined her at the window he said, "I ordered a bottle of Shiraz. I know you prefer reds over whites, and it'll go well with both the veal and the fish. But I can change it."

"It's fine." She turned, and said with a smirk, "I just re-membered something; I broke my promise to Naomi. She'll milk it so much, I'm almost afraid to see how she makes me pay."

"What did you promise her?" he asked.

"On Monday, I promised I wouldn't mention your name for the rest of the trip." She looked up at him. Judging by the sparkle in his eyes, he didn't seem hurt by her comment, only curious.

"Why is it important to her?"

"Because she wants me to move on. Last year she said she'd grant me a three-month bereavement period—her words, not mine, and don't look at me like that. You know Naomi—and after my time was up, she started telling me I can't continue to live in the past."

"You said she'll make you pay. What was your deal?" The curiosity in his expression was replaced by something else, but she couldn't put her finger on it.

"Well, we agreed if I break our deal, she gets to set me up on a blind date with a guy of her choosing."

His eyes widened and he propped his fists on his hips. "Come again?"

"She'll set me up on a blind date," she repeated, and almost laughed. His reaction was hilarious.

"You can't go out with a stranger. Especially not with one of her shady ex-boyfriends." David went to the table and picked up his phone. Then he put it down again. And started pacing between the table and the windows.

"Excuse me? First, I'm free to go on a date if I want to. Second, she'll send me on a dinner date, not into an arranged marriage. And third, nobody says I have to go on a second date with whoever it is."

"Right, because there won't be a first date to begin with." He pierced her with a look.

"Huh?" She went to get her water glass and said over her shoulder, "Shouldn't that be my decision?"

He was quiet, but she could feel his eyes on her. Then he asked in a voice so low she almost didn't hear him, "Did you go on any dates in the past year?"

"Well... I sort of went out twice," Stella said, and could feel her face getting warmer. She imagined Naomi telling her, "You don't have to explain anything to him, let's not forget *he* dumped *you.*"

"I wouldn't call them dates. Both times, Naomi had a date, and her date had a friend or a cousin visiting from out of town, and the friend or cousin needed someone to keep him company...blah-blah-blah... you get the picture."

"So, you were the designated babysitter?" He stood right in front of her now. The earlier curiosity in his eyes had been replaced with fire.

"That's actually a very good description," she grinned and touched her forehead. "But you know, then I got those sudden headaches and had to go home..."

She hadn't thought it was possible, but she swore something was boiling in his eyes. He ran a hand over his head and down the side of his neck.

Before she realized what happened, she was in his arms and he kissed her. Unlike his earlier kisses, this one was hard, demanding, and the message was clear.

It told her, *You're mine.*

For a moment, she got lost in his kiss, but then broke the connection and pushed away. What did he think he was doing? After everything he put her through...

"Listen," she needed to take the upper hand here and get them back on neutral ground. Kissing didn't give her the answers she was seeking.

"I'm sorry, Stella, and I apologize."

"Don't apologize for the kiss," she whispered.

"I didn't mean the kiss, baby. I'd never insult you by apologizing for wanting to kiss you. I apologize for what I did to you last year." He sat down on a chair.

She sat on the other chair, facing him. Was this it? The moment she'd been waiting for?

"I don't want your apology. I don't *need* your apology," she leaned back in her chair. "But I need to understand what happened. Was I not enough for you?"

He stared at her and reached for her hands, but she pulled them back and clasped them in her lap.

"Oh, my God, no! It was all me," his voice dropped to a whisper. "I... I panicked."

"Why?"

He jumped to his feet and paced between the door and the windows, the longest distance in the room. He rubbed the back of his head and neck again and stared at the carpet.

Like a caged animal. A few steps in one direction, a few back...

"Did you feel imprisoned? Did I take away your freedom?" Stella stared at him. Had *she* sabotaged their relationship without knowing it?

"No! You didn't do anything wrong. Nothing." He stopped in front of a window and looked outside.

His voice was almost impossible to hear when he said, "I was afraid one day soon you'd realize I was not enough for you. It happened to me once, and I couldn't bear to go through it again. Especially not with you."

Her head snapped up. "What are you saying?"

He turned around. His dark, soulful eyes were glittering with unshed tears. He walked to the sofa, sat down, and rubbed his hands over his thighs.

She wanted to comfort him but stayed where she was. Whatever was going on here, he needed to be the one to work his way through it and then explain.

"Adrienne and I met in 2009. We were the leads in a theater production in Chicago. It wasn't quite as big as Broadway, but got lots of attention, and we had a good run. We started to spend time together offstage, and one thing led to another until we had somehow transitioned from hanging out to dating."

Stella imagined hundreds of scenarios in her many sleepless nights, but not once had it occurred to her that she'd hear him refer to another woman. She knew he'd been in a few relationships, but he had always said they were casual. She was torn between getting up and leaving and staying to hear what else he had to say. Why had he never told her about this?

"I went on my first touring show in the fall of 2010, Adrienne to a stage production in New York. You know how difficult it can be to get together in person, and it's never for more than a few days, a week at the most." He looked at her and winced. "In the spring of 2011, I heard the first rumors about her being seen in compromising situations with the lead of her new show. When I asked her, she waved it off as gossip. But I kept hearing more stories, all very similar to the first one."

He sipped some water, then took a deep breath. "Each time, she tried to explain it as friends-meeting-for-dinner or so-and-so-is-going-through-a-rough-time. I wanted to believe her, but then she started to accuse me of never being there for her. She told me she needed the physical side of a relationship as much as the intellectual side. I felt guilty, but I didn't know how to change the situation. Did she expect me to drop everything so she could have more attention and her daily fix in the bedroom? When I learned from a friend of mine that she blamed me for forcing her into having affairs, I couldn't take it anymore. I flew to New York and broke off with her."

He regrouped before he continued, "We had agreed to keep our relationship out of the spotlight, but later I learned she had no qualms about throwing my name around to get her special privileges, like admittance to clubs and dinner parties."

David looked at Stella and said, "I realized too late how good she was at blaming everyone but herself. She threw at me that I should've asked her to travel with me, should've gotten her roles in my shows, knowing perfectly well that I couldn't do it. But later I wondered if there was some truth in what she said, even though I'd done the best I could."

"Did you love her?" She wasn't sure what she wanted to hear, but she had to know how important this woman had been to him.

"I had strong feelings for her, or I wouldn't have been in the relationship, but I wasn't in love."

He got up and crouched in front of her, reaching for her hands and rubbing them between his.

"*You* are everything I've ever wanted, from the moment I saw you in the park, with your nose buried in your oversized purse. Those six weeks in Philly were some of the happiest of my life. In the two years we dated, I could hardly wait to see you again, to spend time with you. And having your support when I went to Hamburg meant so much to me.

"But when I accepted the job in Budapest, I honestly didn't know how much longer I'd stay in Europe. All of a sudden, I began to see couples and young families every-where, and I thought of you, thousands of miles away.

"You never gave me one single reason to think you were unhappy. But I began to worry. How would you be able to build a family with me, if I was always somewhere else? And it wouldn't have been fair to ask you to travel with me, knowing how much you love Philadelphia and how important your friends are to you.

"I began to ask myself what I had to offer you. I loved you so much, and I was afraid I couldn't give you everything you deserved. Afraid you'd grow tired of waiting for me. I was scared I wasn't enough for you, and I'd lose you."

"Are you crazy? I loved you with all my heart." Stella couldn't hold back her tears.

He reached for her hands. "For one stupid moment I thought if I let you go, it wouldn't hurt as much because I was the one to cut the strings."

"What about *my* pain?" she whispered and pulled her hands free and rubbed her forehead.

"We had agreed to talk about our future after your stint in Germany. But then you just dropped me like a rotten egg. And not even in person. You wrote a shitty letter!" Her voice rose at the last five words.

She remembered how she found his letter in her pile of mail. How darkness engulfed her after she read it. How she reached for the phone to call him, not caring about the six-hour time difference or whether he was asleep or not. And how she froze just before she hit the call button. A freeze which lasted for an entire year.

"I've regretted writing the damn letter since the day I dropped it in the mailbox. But sadly, once a word is said, it can't be taken back." He shook his head, his eyes full of regret, and she could see the pain in them.

But her own pain was also fresh and bitter.

He reached for her hands again, and she didn't pull away.

"I've written many more letters to you since the first one. But I was too ashamed to send any of them, or to call you. I sacrificed you to my own cowardice, and I know it's unforgivable. When I saw you at the Opera House last Sunday, I thought fate was playing tricks on me. I mean, what were the chances running into you here, of all places? But I knew I couldn't give up until I saw you again and we talked in person. Aren't hope and love the last to die?"

David dropped his chin onto his chest. "I've allowed my insecurities to control me, and knowing I've let you down hurts more than it would have if you'd broken up with me."

"Why didn't you tell me?" she couldn't believe it. They never had secrets—or so she believed.

Words he said to her three years ago came back and realization hit her.

Gently, she lifted his face and looked deep into his eyes as she said, "You *did* try to tell me, David, didn't you? Before you left Philly, you asked me to let you know if I ever felt neglected."

He nodded. "I should've told you the reason, too. I know I have no right to ask you for anything, and I can't take back the letter, but I hope you'll give me another chance and let me make it up to you. You're everything to me."

Stella slid out of her chair and knelt on the carpet with him.

"I've never stopped loving you, David. You're all I ever wanted, and I didn't mind waiting for you to come back to America." She kissed his tears away as he had kissed hers earlier. "Maybe I would've gone to get you if you stayed away much longer. But you never gave me the chance to find out."

"Do you believe in second chances?" he asked.

"I believe in love, and I believe in destiny," she said. "And I've always believed in us. Which is why I was so stunned and didn't know how to reply to your letter."

He pulled her close and hugged her. "I know we belong together. Please, can we put this behind us?"

"You should've trusted me, David, should've told me about your fears. Then it never would've gotten to this point. A kiss and a hug won't be enough to get us through this. But I want you..."

His mouth was on hers before she could finish the sentence. He crushed her to his chest, never breaking the kiss. She put her arms around his neck and pressed her body against his. He was her lifeline, and she couldn't let go.

He stood up with her in his arms, and she could feel how much he wanted her. "Baby, let me show you..."

Sleeping with David probably broke every rule in every self-help book available. But she had longed to be in his arms for what had seemed to be forever, and she was willing to throw caution to the wind.

He walked them toward the bedroom, but when he pushed the door open, she broke the kiss, pressed her face against his shoulder and panted, "Stop."

"Baby, I swear I didn't plan this. I mean, yes, I want to make love to you, but if you think it's too soon, we'll wait." He set her down on the bed.

"No, I want this as much as you do." She looked at him and bit her lower lip. "But I can't."

"What am I missing?" he asked as he sat next to her sliding his fingers up and down her arm until she shivered. It was such a simple gesture, but incredibly erotic, and she had missed it so much.

"The timing's not good." She looked away, almost bashful.

"Are you afraid dinner will get cold?"

She giggled and shook her head. "No, but... Aunt Flo is traveling with me."

"You don't..." She saw the moment he understood. He grinned from ear to ear when he said, "Oh, I promise I'll find other ways to satisfy you without going the whole way."

She kissed him. "I know you would. But maybe it's better to take things a little slow for now. Let's not rush into anything."

"Slow it is. For now." He looked at her swollen lips and leaned closer. "I like it slooowww."

"You're terrible." She gave his shoulder a little push, which was a big mistake. She needed more physical contact and wrapped her arms around his neck again and pulled him down.

A loud knock on the door startled them, followed by a muffled voice. "Room service."

"And I thought that only happens in movies." She sat up, grinning and trying to straighten her hair.

Laughing, David got up, pulled his shirt out to cover the front of his pants and went to answer the door.

Stella took a moment to collect her thoughts. *Could being with David again really be this easy?*

CHAPTER 31

DAVID—JULY 2018

The waiter wheeled in a small table with a white table-cloth and set with their covered meals, water, wine bottles, and an array of glasses. David signed the bill and tipped the waiter.

Having Stella in his arms again, knowing she still loved him, was more than he had dared to hope. He couldn't believe she was willing to grant him a second chance, and he'd be the biggest idiot in history if he blew this.

When she emerged from the bathroom, her lips were still red, but she'd fixed her ponytail and washed her face. He hated knowing he made her cry.

"Ready to eat, my angel?" With a punctilious, formal bow, and a wink, he pulled out a chair for her. The heavy cloak he'd worn for a year had been lifted off his shoulders, and he felt so much freer, lighter, happier.

"Look at this setup." She took it all in with a big smile. "Fine china, silver domes covering the food, wine already poured. And—aww, how sweet, a single yellow rose."

She brought the rose close to her nose, then held it out to him. "Here, smell it. It's a lovely fragrance, not too heavy."

He sat down opposite her and said, "It's beautiful, but nothing compared to you."

He watched her closely for a reaction, but she only smiled.

"The food smells delicious, too," Stella said. "And I have to say I'm glad we decided not to eat in the restaurant."

"Me, too, believe me," he agreed. He touched his glass to hers and said, "To new memories."

When they uncovered their plates, she chuckled. "You've got mine! Some things never change."

He cut off a small piece of the cutlet with his fork. The breaded crust was crunchy, and the cutlet cooked to perfection. He held the fork in front of her mouth. Simply watching her eat this tiny piece of meat aroused him all over again.

She fed him a piece of the fish. "Open," she said, and he was pretty sure she was squirming in her chair, too, when his lips closed around her fork. This could turn out to be an interesting meal.

After they swapped their plates, she said, "Okay, let's talk about the elephant in the room."

"That's what you want to call him now?"

"No! Well, maybe," she chuckled again before she turned more serious. "If we're going to rebuild our relationship, we need to be able to see each other more often. But fact is, you're living in London, and then you're going to Paris, and I'm in Philadelphia."

David nodded and put his silverware down. He reached for one of her hands, needed to touch her to reassure himself she was really sitting here with him.

"My contract in London runs till October. And I don't have to be in Paris till mid-January. I also have a few other contractual obligations I can't ignore. But you're more important than anything else, Stella. I don't have a master plan I can pull out of my hat right now, but I promise I will find a way to make this work."

He took a bite of his herbed potatoes. "Mmm, we have to buy Herbes de Provence. Try it." He fed it to her.

"I think I have most of the herbs in my backyard. I'll have to look up the best way to dry and store them." She licked her lips, and he couldn't stop looking at her.

Danvers, you are one lucky man. Don't screw this up again.

"About my contracts, et cetera... I had planned to go to Chicago in November and put my apartment on the market since I'm never there anymore. But why don't I come to Philadelphia first for a few weeks, then go to Chicago for

Thanksgiving, and spend Christmas and New Year's with you?"

"I think it's a wonderful idea. The coming to Philadelphia part, I mean. What you do with your Chicago apartment is your decision, because it's your home. I wouldn't dream of telling you what to do with it."

"Oh, no. No more unilateral decisions. At least not on my side," he said. "I'm going to include you in each and every decision from now on."

"You said you're finished in London in October. When, exactly?"

"End of October. Good thing I haven't bought my ticket yet, because I'm flying to Philadelphia first to spend time with my leading lady," he winked at her.

"Great! I'll make sure the kitchen is stocked with your new favorite herbs," she said, then hesitated before asking, "How long are you going to be in Paris? Another four or five months?"

"We're performing from the middle of February to the end of March."

"And afterward?" David could hear her hesitation, and a chill slid down his back.

"I have no plans yet. But I think it's time to leave Europe and go back home."

Damn right, Danvers. Keep your butt stateside, closer to your girlfriend.

"Can you see yourself going on a Broadway tour again?"

"I don't think so. Something more permanent would be nice. I'll get Aaron on it as soon as I'm back in London."

He didn't want to think about London, because it meant he had to say goodbye to Stella. But one way or another, parting was inevitable. At least they knew it was only temporary.

She set her silverware on her empty plate and wiped her mouth with a napkin. "I'm full. There's no room for dessert right now. Good thing we didn't order it right away."

"I agree. Do you want to go for a walk?"

"Sure, why not? Walk off some of the calories," she laughed. "And then I should think about going back."

"Let's walk first, then come back here for a few more minutes, maybe a cup of coffee, before I call a taxi for you," he suggested.

"Okay. I'll leave my purse here then. Now, where are my sandals?" her eyes roamed the room.

She used his arm to steady herself when she slipped her sandals on. "Thank you for a delicious dinner."

With one arm, he pulled her close and kissed her. "Thank you for agreeing to have dinner with me. And for listening."

Holding hands, they walked the short distance to the Louvre pyramid. He heard her sigh.

"What's on your mind, love?" He couldn't refrain from calling her all the pet names he'd stored up.

"Whenever I saw couples being happy and in love, I envied them their closeness. Now we're one of them.

Today was wonderful, David. And it's been a relief to think of something other than the hostage situation, especially since I know if something happened, Julia or Naomi would've texted me."

He heard the fear in her voice and wanted to comfort her. "I agree with you, but don't forget, Revan is tough."

"I know, but still..." she said, and his heart jumped when she snuggled closer.

Twilight had turned to night, and stars glittered in the dark sky. David pointed up. "There's Polaris. I can't tell you how many times I looked at it and wished I was with you."

He touched her charm bracelet. "When I saw you're still wearing this, I began to hope it wasn't too late for us."

Instead of answering, she rose on tiptoe and kissed him. "I never took it off."

They took their time strolling back to his hotel. Before they entered the lobby, Stella saw the lined-up taxis and said, "I'll grab one of those after I get my purse from your room."

"I'm coming with you. I don't like the idea of you being alone with a stranger who might not speak English," he said.

"You don't have to, but I won't say no," she smiled.

In his room, she picked up her purse and the rose. "The first flowers you gave me were yellow roses, do you remember?"

"I do. The florist around the corner from you recommended it as the color for friendship, but also for joy and caring." He didn't take his eyes off her as she traced the petals with a fingertip.

"And today? Did you ask for this color?"

"Yes. Because it also conveys gladness and affection, as well as good luck, welcome back, and remember me." He kissed her. "Aren't you impressed with my knowledge of the language of flowers?"

Her carefree laughter was music to his ears.

"I am. And thank you. Umm... What are you doing tomorrow?"

"Seeing you, I hope. Do you have anything planned?"

"Julia and I keep talking about visiting the Louvre. Would you be interested in meeting us there?"

"Do I really need to answer?" He tightened his arms around her.

The kiss started out slow and patient, but soon he couldn't keep himself from deepening it, and their tongues met. Her hand came around and cupped his neck. He took the rose out of her hand and placed it on a table.

"It doesn't have thorns, but I'd rather not be distracted when you're in my arms," he whispered.

She dropped her purse on a chair and stretched to reach both hands behind his head, pulling him down to kiss his eyes.

"When I saw the anger and the fire in your eyes earlier, I knew you were serious about regretting what you did. Don't even think about pulling something like that ever again."

"I promise you, baby. I'm not about to make the same mistake twice," he said, and kissed her again.

Coming up for air, he said, "We didn't have dessert yet. Would you like to have something before you have to go?"

"I can't eat anything, but maybe..." Stella started to unbutton his shirt and followed each button with a kiss on his bare chest.

His body responded in a flash, and he knew she was aware of every hard inch of him. He stopped her teasing fingers with one hand.

"Stay the night. Please. I'll take you back to your hotel as early as you want in the morning," he begged as he skimmed a hand up and down her back, pulling her closer.

"I didn't bring a change of clothes or a toothbrush," she said.

"I always travel with a whole set of new toothbrushes. And the hotel has courtesy kits. Do you need anything else, any umm...woman stuff?"

"No, I have enough 'woman stuff.' Why can't men use the proper terms? Repeat after me. *Tam*-pon," she said and wiggled her eyebrows. "But I didn't bring anything to sleep in."

"You can wear one of my T-shirts, although...you might not need it."

"Do you want to sit on the sofa and look at the moon?" Stella asked. She pressed her body against his, from hip to chest.

"No," he growled. "I want you in my bed. In my arms. I'll be happy to just lie there and hold you."

"Okay, then. I'll text Julia to let her know I'll be back very, very late."

"Why Julia and not your BFF?"

"To avoid too many questions. It would take away time I'd much rather spend with you!"

"Then, by all means, please text Julia." Laughing, he walked into the bedroom. "Let me get you a toothbrush and a fresh T-shirt."

"Done!" Stella announced a moment later as she put her phone away, then took out her cosmetics pouch and followed him into his bedroom before she disappeared into the bathroom.

When she emerged, she looked so damn sexy in his shirt he wanted to take her right there, and the flash of dark purple underwear he glimpsed when she climbed into bed next to him was almost the last straw.

Yeah, this would be a rather uncomfortable night. But it was worth it.

Stella snickered as she snuggled into the crook of his arm. "Wait until Naomi finds out one of her new panties made it on the catwalk today."

David almost choked on his saliva. "You're wearing Naomi's panties?" He lifted the hem of the T-shirt. "Why?"

"Because she made a big deal about buying them last weekend and said maybe they'd see some action. She doesn't know I stole this pair. I wanted to feel sexy when we had our big talk."

"I can assure you, you're sexy as hell. And not because of the lingerie, though it's a pretty bow on a gorgeous package. But a gentleman knows when to shut up and appreciate what's so beautifully presented."

Her hands trailed up and down his chest and abs, where she made little circles with her fingertips.

"Baby, you better tell your hands to behave or my boy can't sleep." He had a hard time talking. Or breathing. And concentrating well enough to do breathing exercises was impossible right now.

"Okay, then I'll sleep now. Goodnight, love." She tapped a fingertip on his erection, then kissed him on his mouth and snuggled her face against his chest.

He couldn't get comfortable after Stella settled by his side. He stroked her arm and held her tight. If they only had this one night together, and the day tomorrow, he wasn't going to waste precious time by sleeping. And he had to find a way to see her again before November.

When her breathing was slow and steady, he kissed her hair and said sotto voce, "I love you, Stella. Till the day I die."

A while later, he got out of bed and walked into the large walk-in shower in his en suite bathroom.

He couldn't see Stella open her eyes when he turned on the water.

He didn't see her hug his pillow, inhaling his scent, and he didn't see her wipe away a tear when she whispered, "I'll always love you, too."

CHAPTER 32

STELLA—JULY 2018

Fingers danced over her skin—gentle, caressing, teasing.

Stella moaned.

Phantom fingertips barely touched the side of her breast and found their way to her hip. They continued down the side of her leg. And up again. They slid under her T-shirt and circled her breast, cupping it, and playing with her nipple.

She needed more. This was too much. And it was cruel. Those hands hadn't touched her so intimately in so long.

The fingertips went down again, stopping just above her knees, moving to the inside of her thighs. Only one fingertip branded her, taking its time going upward. The fingers reached the edge of her panties, traced them, until they slid under the silky material.

Please, yes. Just once.

She didn't often have erotic dreams, and this one was more than she could take. Seeking release, she reached down.

She touched the back of a hand. *His* hand. Their fingers interlaced over her throbbing spot. With just the right amount of pressure, he circled it and pressed down. She arched into his hand, shaking with the force of her climax, and cried out the only name that mattered to her.

Still trembling with the aftershock, Stella opened her eyes.

In her dream, David held her while she slept, undisturbed by nightmares. But it wasn't a dream. She *had* slept in David's arms all night, and he just made her come with a single touch.

He kissed her shoulder, then rolled her on her back and covered her mouth with his. His kiss was demanding, challenging, owning. He removed her T-shirt.

"Let me see you, my angel. Come again for me." He never stopped the teasing of her sensitive spot and took her over the top again when he pulled a nipple into his mouth and suckled like a baby.

"You're not a dream." She reached for his face and stroked her fingers over his stubble before cupping his cheek.

"I can assure you I'm very real. But I don't mind proving it to you again." He smiled while his fingers embarked on another journey over her body.

She didn't know what to say, but she knew what she wanted to do. She let her hand trail over his chest and abs and heard him hiss when she reached the waistband of his boxer shorts.

"Baby, don't. Today is about you," he whispered in a husky voice and stopped her hand.

"No way. You give, you get." She took him in her hand. His erection pulsed while she stroked him. Her hair fell over her shoulders as she placed kiss after kiss over his belly and further down, following the straight line of coarser hair.

"You know I'm hot for you, and I'm not sure I can hold back," he panted.

"I know, love." She kissed every hard inch of him, teasing his swollen head with the pad of her thumb, until he groaned and pulled her up. He kissed her hard and her hand found its way back to his erection. She stroked and squeezed until he let out a guttural sound and erupted, ravishing her mouth until the spasms pulsating against her palm eased.

"Oh, my God, baby, what are you doing to me?" He reached for the tissue box on the nightstand and cleaned himself.

"Are you complaining?" she asked and gave him her best innocent expression.

"What a silly question." He kissed the tip of her nose. "And it sure beats the cold showers."

"How many did you take last night?" she asked while she played with the spattering of hair on his chest.

He only shrugged. "Are you ready for a nice, warm shower? I'll wash yours if you wash mine."

"David, you say the sweetest things," she snickered. "And then I need coffee!"

His deep laugh warmed her through and through, and the kiss he followed up with expressed more than a thousand words.

"I could get used to room service." She sat in bed, again wearing David's T-shirt, and reached for a croissant. She had already devoured chunks of a fresh baguette with butter and jam and was on her second cup of coffee.

"I'll keep it in mind." He stretched out on the bed next to her and took a brioche out of the breadbasket.

Stella pulled in her bottom lip and focused on the beam of sunlight coming through an open section of the floor-length curtains. She didn't have the courage to look at him when she asked the one question bugging her. "David, was there anybody else when we were apart?"

He put his half-eaten brioche back on his plate and held her face in his hands.

"No. I swear to you, I didn't even look at another woman. You're the only one for me."

"But you must've been lonely or had, umm...desires." She chewed her bottom lip. Yes, she wanted to believe him, but the nagging little voice wouldn't shut up.

"I was very lonely, and I had plenty of desires, but I was longing for you. You came to me in my dreams, your face was the one I saw in my sleep."

"You could've reached out to me. You know where I live."

"That's near the top of my long list of should-haves, my love."

An hour later, they got out of the taxi and stood in front of Stella's hotel.

"I'm a little bit nervous about going up to the room," she said. She touched the yellow rose to her nose and let its scent soothe her. She wished she could take it home and dry it.

"You have no reason to feel uncomfortable, baby." He opened the door for her to enter the lobby.

"He's one hundred percent right, Stella," Julia said from behind them.

"Where've you been so early?" Stella asked.

Julia held up a bag. "Bakery! Hi, David. How are you on this beautiful morning?" She winked at him.

"Good morning, Julia. I'm fantastic, and you?" he replied while he squeezed Stella's hand.

"Very well, thank you."

Stella squared her shoulders. "I better go up and face the inquisition."

"Don't let Naomi make you feel bad," Julia said. "I know she's your closest friend, and she wants the best for you, but she also needs to let you live your life the way you want to."

"I have everything I want." Stella looked at David.

"And if you need some leverage, she didn't return to the hotel until almost two in the morning."

"Huh? How very interesting. She must've had a fun time with Kai."

David squeezed her hand again. "I'll grab a cup of tea and wait for you here. And please, take your time. We're in no rush to go anywhere—as long as we're together."

"Julia, we're going to the Louvre. Wanna come?" Stella asked.

"Sure, I'd love to. Would you mind if Alexander joins us? He took today off to spend some time together before I fly home tomorrow. He wants to talk," she made air quotes.

"Oh boy, there's lots of talking going on among all of us," Stella said. Then she said to David. "I don't think I'll need long upstairs. Give me maybe half an hour?"

"I'm not going anywhere, love! Look for me right through those glass doors."

"A-*hah*, there she is."

Stella dropped her purse on her bed and went to the kitchenette to fill a glass with water. She put the rose in it and set it on her nightstand. "Good morning to you, too. Isn't it a gorgeous day?"

"You must've forgiven Prince Charming since you spent the night with him. I assume he had a convincing explanation," Naomi prodded.

"Well, yes, sort of, I guess."

"What kind of answer is *that*?"

"The only one I can give you right now."

"Why did you text Julia, not me?" Naomi looked sideways at Julia, who sat at the small table in the kitchen area. "No offense, Julia."

"None taken." Julia smiled at something on her cell phone.

"I knew you were with Kai and I wanted to let you enjoy your time. But you're right, I should've texted you both."

"Imagine my surprise when I came back to the hotel and your bed was empty. I was worried."

"Be fair, Naomi. I put a note on your pillow saying Stella was staying with David," Julia intervened.

"True, true," Naomi admitted. "So, how was dinner?"

"Dinner was great. We shared a bottle of champagne in the courtyard, and then we had dinner in David's suite, so we could talk without interruption."

"So, did you just pick up where you left off a year ago?" Naomi snapped her fingers.

"Nam, I really don't want to rehash everything right now. I haven't had time to think about it, either, so there's a lot I still need to process," she said. "How was your evening?"

"The park was fun. There were concerts, and they had food stands, and later Kai took me for a ride around Paris on his motorcycle."

"I'm glad you had a good time. And I think you should add the info about the park to the travel packages. Sounds like something the typical tourist wouldn't hear about. Now I'll change into something more casual. David's waiting downstairs. Why don't you both have breakfast with us?"

"He didn't feed you this morning?" Naomi grumbled. "Too busy tasting the other fruits?"

"Don't be crass. And yes, we had breakfast, but it was two hours ago, and we can call the breakfast here brunch or something. Maybe they'll serve champagne with it."

"Oh, man, it must've been quite the night. Bubbly in the morning!" Naomi rolled her eyes. "You're in an awfully good mood."

"Then be happy for me, since you seem to have gotten up on the wrong side of the bed," Stella said and pulled the dress over her head.

"What are you wearing?" Naomi narrowed her eyes and pointed a finger at her.

"What?" Stella looked at her dress in her hand. "You were with me when I bought this dress."

"Under it!" Naomi clarified and her eyes widened. "I... nooo, you wouldn't..."

"There is a slight possibility I might have grabbed one of your panties instead of mine yesterday," she drawled, then raced toward the bathroom and slammed the door, giggling.

Naomi's laughter followed her. "Yeah, fat chance...your thieving little fingers just happened to find their way into my suitcase? Aren't you glad we wear the same size, missy? And who was it who made fun at me when I went lingerie shopping? Huh?"

"Well, thanks to you, I didn't have to go in my white cotton bikinis, so you're right. I think I'll keep this pair, so let me know how much I owe you." She cracked open the bathroom door, blew an air kiss to her BFF, and closed it again.

Stella kissed David smack on his mouth when she joined him in the courtyard.

"The others will be down soon, and I promised them we'd have champagne. What do you think? Too much?"

He kissed her back and smiled, "Your wish is my command. Let me order it right away."

"Really, Troubadour, which bottle did you escape from?" Naomi crossed the courtyard. "I hope you got some sleep last night. Missy here isn't telling me much."

"Then what makes you think I'd tell you more?" He stood up, kissed Naomi's cheek, and held her chair for her.

"Very gallant. Thank you. I can see why she's is under your spell again."

"Naomi, you're such a sweet little lady. In fact, I really missed you, too. And what did you just call me?"

"Oh...Troubadour?! Kind of fits, don't you think?"

"You could've called me much worse, so I'll take it," he laughed.

"Believe me, I did—on more than one occasion," Naomi grinned. "Call you something worse, I mean."

"I don't doubt it."

"So, are we going to see more of you again?" Naomi challenged him.

"You sure will."

He signaled the waiter when Julia came running out into the courtyard.

"We've gotta go. Your friend is out of the catacombs, and he's at the hospital right now. Come quickly. Alexander is meeting us there. I told the front desk to call a taxi for us."

CHAPTER 33

Stella—July 2018

"Is there another route you can take?" Naomi tapped the taxi driver on his shoulder. "We've been sitting here for an eternity!"

"Traffic is bad," came the short answer in heavily accented English before he pointed to a sign above his visor. 'Do not talk to driver when vehicle is moving.'

"We aren't moving," she scooted out a bit from where she was squeezed between Stella and Julia on the back seat.

The driver let the car crawl forward a few feet.

"Would you like me to drive?" Naomi's chin almost touched the driver's seat.

"You want to get out?" he retorted and turned on the radio. French rap music blasted through the taxi.

Stella pulled Naomi back and said, "What did you expect? We're in the middle of morning rush hour traffic. A few minutes won't make a difference."

"Revan's all by himself, so he might think otherwise," Naomi hissed and tilted her head in the driver's direction. "Should I ask him in French? Maybe he doesn't like Americans. Our taxi driver last weekend was so *much* friendlier."

The driver muttered something and turned up the volume on the radio—this time to near earsplitting levels.

Julia reached for Naomi's hand and held it. "Revan's safe now. And we won't go away until they let you and Stella see him for a few minutes."

After an agonizing twenty minutes, the driver pulled into the drop-off area in front of the hospital's main entrance. Naomi glared at him through his rearview mirror and yelled over the music, "Are you sure this is the entrance we need? Shouldn't we go to the Emergency Department?"

"You asked for Pitié-Salpêtrière University Hospital. This is University Hospital. Twenty-five euros."

David handed cash to the driver with a short, "Keep the change."

"You just let this guy rip you off," Naomi fumed. She slammed the door shut and threw her hands in the air. "It was less than five miles. He shouldn't have charged more than fifteen."

"I know. There's a reason why I gave him exactly twenty-five and told him to keep the change."

"And it's still too much tip for the pigheaded ass, but thank you."

Alexander was waiting for them just inside the sliding glass doors. He shook hands with David and pecked Stella and Naomi's cheeks. Stella tried to hide a grin when she saw him kiss Julia a little longer than necessary and Julia blushed.

Naomi rolled her eyes and scrunched up her face. "Ahem...sorry to interrupt. But what exactly is our plan? Do you think the information desk will point us right to Revan?"

"I don't think so. And he might be under police protection, too," Alexander said.

He was wearing a pair of dark jeans and a light gray polo shirt, and Stella couldn't help but think he still had the posture and no-nonsense look of a former Special Ops soldier. And, to her great relief, he automatically took charge.

"First we need to find out which department has Revan. My guess is the Emergency Department, but he could also be in Intensive Care. We don't know what his health condition is."

Naomi tried to stifle a gasp.

"I suggest we don't approach the desk as a group. I should go with either Stella or Naomi—someone who has a personal connection to him, even though we won't give them details unless we have no other choice."

Naomi pleaded, "Stella, let me go, okay?"

She nodded. "You two go find out where he is, and the rest of us can wait here. I'll text Luca to let him know what's going on. At least the little bit we know so far."

David put his arm around her shoulders and led her and Julia to a table where they had a full view of the entrance area.

As they walked away, Alexander said, "Let me do the talking, Naomi. Just stand there and look desperate."

Stella watched while Alexander spoke to the youngest of three nurses at the help desk, who shook her head after typing something on her computer. He reached into his pocket, flashed an ID card, and swiftly put it away again.

"What's going on over there?" she whispered to David. Then she saw Naomi switch a ring from her right hand to her left before she pulled a tissue out of a dispenser on the desk and dabbed at her eyes.

"What's she doing?" Stella whispered to Julia.

Julia said, "I don't care, as long as it gets you girls through the first door."

Stella could hardly sit still when she saw Alexander accept something from the desk nurse and reach for Naomi's elbow to guide her back.

"How'd it go?" she asked.

"The nurse didn't want to give me any information, and only reluctantly after I told her I'm working at the

US Embassy. Revan's in the Emergency Department," he said. "We got three visitors' passes. Stella, why don't you come with us? Julia and David, I'm afraid you'll have to wait here."

"No problem. I'll check the news to see if there are any statements from the police," David said. He kissed Stella and hugged Naomi. "Go get him."

Stella, Naomi, and Alexander followed the signs directing them deep into the belly of the hospital. Soon, Stella had lost all sense of orientation. The arrows and signs led them down one hallway, around a corner, then up one flight of stairs, down another long hallway. All looking alike, the only difference being the colors of the doors. The whole place reeked of disinfectants and carbolic acid, combined with the human smells of fear and worry.

"They'll discharge Revan by the time we get to him. The taxi driver should've brought us here in the first place," Naomi grumbled and pointed to another sign directing them through this torturous route to the Emergency Department.

While they used a glass skywalk to reach the adjoining building, Stella saw several ambulances lined up in front of it. "We're getting closer."

Alexander reiterated, "We'll try to play the same card as before. Naomi pretends to be Revan's fiancée. I had to come up with something closer than friend."

Stella nodded, "I saw you switch the ring your grandma gave you for graduation. Lucky for us, it has a diamond in it."

"A ring from a toy capsule would've done as well," Naomi said and rubbed her hands up and down her arms. "Okay! Here we are! What if they don't let us see him?"

"Stay calm. We're almost there," Alexander encouraged her.

"Who am I, in case they ask?" Stella asked.

"You're who you are. The sister of Revan's best friend. We need to stay as close to the truth as possible. You're supporting your friend, his distraught fiancée, at this difficult time." Alexander winked at them.

Oozing self-confidence, he approached the nurse's desk. "Good morning, do you speak English?"

"Yes. How can I help you?" the woman answered. Her name tag identified her as Corinne. She looked seasoned enough to have been guarding the entrance to the Emergency Department for at least half a century, probably always with a grim determination to only allow a handful of people past her station.

When Stella looked down the long, wide corridor, she saw individual spaces divided by plastic walls and curtains for some privacy. They reminded her of oversized changing rooms, but instead of monotone background music there was a symphony of low voices and the constant beeping of the medical equipment keeping the staff abreast of patients' health changes.

One police officer, clad in a dark blue uniform and bulletproof vest, stood in front of a section not far from the nurses' desk. The off-white floor-length curtain for the partitioned area was closed, but swishing, as if someone was brushing against it from the inside.

"We're here to see Revan Forrester," Alexander told her.

"I am afraid that's not possible," Corinne replied without consulting her computer.

"We have visitors' passes." Alexander stood straighter and pointed to the temporary pass attached to his polo shirt.

"Those only allow you to walk through the hospital's hallways until you reach me," Corinne explained with a bored expression.

"I apologize, umm... Corinne. We should've introduced ourselves. My name is Alexander Whittaker, and I work for the American Embassy. These are Naomi Winters, Mr. Forrester's fiancée, and her friend, Stella Harrison." In one smooth move, he flashed his ID again.

"Sorry, but I can't help you," Corinne said. She hadn't even glanced at his card.

"I assume you didn't hear me say this is Mr. Forrester's fiancée. She is desperate to see him." Alexander put his arm around Naomi's shoulder while she pulled out her tissue again and held it in her left hand. In the cold fluorescent light, the diamond sparkled like a decked-out Christmas tree in a store window on Fifth Avenue in December.

"I heard you. Mr. Forrester has no approved visitors and I told you more than I should," Corinne remained firm.

She nodded at someone who approached them, "*Comment ça va?*"

It was another police officer, carrying three Styrofoam cups of coffee. "*Ça va bien, merci.*" He placed one cup on Corinne's desk.

Stella wondered if he was going to Revan. Before she could ask him, Naomi started sobbing and broke out in a loud wail. "I flew *all the way* from Philadelphia to Paris to be with my fiancé and you're telling me I can't see him? After everything he went through! He could've died! How am I going to explain to our babies at home that their daddy is all alone?"

She threw herself at Stella with real tears running down her face. Stella didn't know what reaction Naomi expected, so made do with rubbing her back and murmuring, "There, there..."

The police officer in front of the curtain looked over at them and gave a hand signal to the coffee cop. At the same time, the curtain parted and a nurse walked out carrying an empty tray.

Coffee cop turned around and said in English, "You are Mr. Forrester's fiancée? Come with me."

Naomi's tears dried up with astonishing speed. She blew her nose and said with a smile, "Oh, thank you! Thank you so much, Commissaire...?" She pulled on Stella's arm.

"Capitaine Pascal Clouseau. Your friends have to wait here, we only allow one visitor."

"Please, let her come with me. What if Revan doesn't recognize me after his ordeal? Oh, what did that monster do to him in those tunnels...tunnels of death?" Naomi started sobbing again and clung to Stella's arm. "Tell me, is he terribly disfigured? Is he in pain? Oh no, is he *dying*?"

Clouseau looked at his colleague and received a nod from him. "Okay, your friend can come."

"Our babies will be so happy to know I was able to see their daddy." Naomi beamed at him and wiped her nose.

"How old are the babies?" The cop asked.

"Oh, Harley and Porsche will turn one next month. Those two are keeping me on my toes, just like their daddy. Never a dull moment at our house," Naomi said and reached inside her purse. "Would you like to see their photo?"

At the same time, the other police officer pulled the curtain aside. "Mr. Forrester, you have visitors."

Stella and Naomi stepped inside.

Revan was propped up in a large hospital bed, covered up to his chest by a warming blanket. An IV was inserted in the back of one hand, with a blood pressure sleeve wrapped around his upper arm, a pulse oximeter taped to a forefinger, while a nasal cannula supplied oxygen. Behind his bed, an impressive assortment of beeping and blinking monitors made the small space look like a command center.

The grin on Revan's face went from ear to ear.

"Nugget, I thought I heard the angels sing when your charming voice traveled through the sterile air. Come and kiss your astonished fiancé hello."

Naomi went over to him and kissed his cheek. "You need a good shave." She wiped away a few fresh tears. "What did you get yourself into this time, Shutterbug?"

"That's how you greet a man who came back from the underworld? And what did I say about calling me that name?"

He flashed a lopsided smile and pulled her close with his free hand. "I think I deserve a real kiss." He crushed his mouth to hers.

Stella chuckled when Naomi had to put both hands to the sides of Revan's head to keep herself from falling on him.

Then his eyes roamed over Naomi's chest. "Nugget, you're a sight for sore eyes! Just what the doctor ordered."

Naomi reached for the front of her tank top and pulled it up an inch, but exposed her well-toned abs in the process. She mumbled, "Can't breathe without an oxygen tube, but is already misbehaving. *Someone* must be feeling better."

Revan didn't stop smiling—or looking.

"Don't hog the man. Others are happy to see him, too." Stella squeezed past Naomi and leaned forward to kiss his cheeks. "Hi, Revan. I'd like to say you look good, but you've looked better."

Revan laughed, "Cinderella, I'm tempted to believe it when you say it."

He focused on Naomi again and waved her closer. "So, we have twin babies? Show me their picture. I can't remember how they look."

Naomi retrieved a photo from her wallet. She leaned closer and whispered, "Aren't they adorable?"

Revan looked from the photo to her cleavage, "Mmm-hm..."

She held the photo next to his face and said, "And don't they look just like their daddy? I saw them at the dog shelter last month and am trying to convince my parents to adopt them. Look at their little pink tongues." Naomi copied the puppies' expressions and jumped out of Revan's reach.

"Wait till I'm out of this bed and home again. I think you and I have a few things to discuss." Revan smirked. "And listen, Nugget, don't you know lying to authorities is a crime?"

"Well, then don't tell them. When will you be released?"

"They said I'm in decent shape, but a little dehydrated. And my body temperature was too low. No surprise. I wasn't exactly on a sunny beach. They'll let me know in a few hours," he said and glanced toward the curtains. "The bigger question is, what are you two doing here in Paris? I mean, I'm glad to see your lovely faces. You are much nicer to look at than the company I kept recently."

Before they could answer his question, coffee cop stuck his head inside the cubicle and said, "Your time is up, I'm afraid."

Stella asked Revan, "How can we get in touch with you? Do you have your cell phone?"

"No, Macho-Man took it, and it's somewhere in the catacombs. My camera equipment, too. He better not touch it."

"We'll get you a new phone and come back later," Stella promised. "Anything else you need? Change of clothes? Toiletries?"

"I hope to be in a nicer room when you return. I'd love to see some trees for a change," he laughed. "A cheap cell phone would be great, but nothing else, thanks. I'll pay you back later. Someone from the police department went to my hotel room and brought my clothes. You can't imagine how abjectly grateful I was for fresh underwear."

He wiggled his eyebrows and grinned at Naomi, "I got a sponge bath after I arrived here. And let me add it's not something I need to experience again. Not as romantic as it sounds when they assign you a male nurse."

Naomi gave him an angelic smile and said, "I wouldn't have wanted anything different for my ailing fiancé. See you later," she blew him a kiss. "Make sure you tell your bodyguards out there to add our names to your visitors' list."

Stella and Naomi turned to leave, and Revan said, "Oh, wait. Can you let my parents know everything's fine? I'll call them as soon as I'm out of here."

"I texted Luca and told him you're in the hospital. He's been with your parents since Monday. But I'll let him know we talked," Stella said. "See you later."

"Thank you, girls." Revan reached for the yellow beverage on the table next to his bed and sniffed. "Lukewarm Gatorade, great. Let's see if they can at least round up some ice cubes." He pressed the nurse's button.

On the way out, Naomi stopped at Corinne's desk again and asked in a sweet voice, "Corinne, excuse me. What do we need to do to come back later with a few items for my fiancé?"

The nurse pinched her lips together and replied, "He should be transferred to a room in another department by then. The help desk in the front lobby can tell you when you return."

"Thank you," Stella said and pulled Naomi away.

"Where did you get those acting skills?" Stella asked.

"Did you forget we joined the stupid drama club in tenth grade? It was finally good for something," Naomi laughed.

"What if the cop wanted to see the photo?" Stella giggled.

"Then I would've been so surprised to discover it was gone and would've blamed the babies' granny."

"Well, congratulations. It was one of the best performances I've ever witnessed. And Revan seemed very happy to see you." Stella winked at Naomi.

"As he should be," Naomi sniffed.

307

⌒⌒

"What kind of phone should we buy for him?" Stella asked after they updated David, Julia, and Alexander.

Alexander said, "He needs something to get him through the next few days. Buy a refurbished phone and a prepaid SIM card, and he's all set. I assume he'll buy a new one when he's in the States again if he doesn't get his own phone back. It's what I'd do."

"I agree, I'd do the same," David added. "Do you know where we can find an electronics store?"

"No, but I'm sure there are plenty around. Here's the next question. What are you guys going to do until you come back?"

Stella said, "I feel bad going sightseeing when he's in the hospital, but there's not much else we can do. And it doesn't help Revan if we just sit here. At least we know he's safe and well taken care of. The way he's hooked up to the IV and other monitors, it might be a while until they move him to another room.

"Why don't we go to the Louvre as we planned earlier, have lunch, organize a new phone for him somewhere along the way, and then come back?"

"There are several nice cafés inside the Louvre. At one, visitors sit in a gallery surrounded by marble columns and paintings," Alexander suggested.

Julia said, "Sounds lovely. We can all go there together, and afterward Alexander and I will spend a few hours by ourselves. Maybe we can all meet somewhere later for our last dinner in Paris?"

"I'd love it," Naomi said. "Sounds like a good plan. Maybe Rev can join us, too, if they release him today."

"I'd like to meet him, if it's not too much for him," Alexander said.

"Knowing him, he won't sit in a hotel room. And I'm sure he'll be more than ready for something besides hospital food," Naomi said, and Stella agreed.

"Have you heard from Kai? I thought you wanted to text him," Stella said.

"I texted him before we left the hotel, and he wrote back saying he was leaving Paris today," Naomi said, and shrugged. "I don't know why he didn't tell me last night, though."

CHAPTER 34

Stella—July 2018

"The painting is much smaller than I expected. I thought it'd be more like the size of a movie poster," Naomi said. She pushed a lonely olive through the balsamic vinaigrette on her plate.

"But doesn't her smile fill the whole room?" Julia gushed. "No wonder it's one of the most visited pieces of art on Earth."

"Once you get close enough to see it," Naomi laughed.

Stella finished her caprese panini and took a sip of water. "I can't believe this week is coming to an end. So much has happened, it feels like we've spent a whole month in France."

"I'm sure you could've done with a little less excitement," Julia said.

Stella looked at David and nodded. "True, but there were also some unexpected but very wonderful moments."

"What are you two going to do now?" Julia asked, and looked from Stella to David. "Even though I've only known you a few days, it's obvious how much you care for each other."

David played with his water glass. "We haven't had time to come up with a plan. But I won't let anything come between us again." He leaned over and kissed Stella. "I promise!"

"I know," she said. "Maybe I'll come to London for Labor Day. If I leave on Friday and stay the week through Saturday, I'll only need four vacation days. It would break up the time till you come home in November. What do you think?"

"Baby, if you really need an answer, here it is..." he took her face in his hands and lowered his mouth over hers.

Finger-snapping right next to their faces interrupted the kiss. Naomi snapped once more for effect, then announced in a schoolmarmish voice, "You are in a public place, kids."

She glanced over to Julia and said, "A little support here, please?"

But when she caught Julia and Alexander sharing a quick kiss, too, she jumped up and said, "Time to freshen up. Unbelievable..."

Stella laughed and called after Naomi, "Wait, I'll come with you."

"Hmph…" was the only reply.

"I love you, too, Nam," Stella said, and followed her friend.

"I don't see the young nurse from this morning," Naomi said when they walked into the hospital again. "Let's see how many hoops we have to jump through this time." She asked one of the nurses in French, "Excuse me, we're here to visit Mr. Forrester. Can you tell us where we can find him?"

The nurse typed in Revan's name and asked, "May I have your names?"

"Naomi Winters and Stella Harrison."

"Thank you." After consulting her computer again, the nurse said, "Both your names are on the approved list. Mr. Forrester was moved to a general room an hour ago." She wrote the station and room number on a piece of paper, printed out their visitor passes and gave them to Naomi. Then she pointed to her right and said, "The elevators are this way."

"Thank you."

"Why didn't you give her David's name? We don't have a visitors' pass for him," Stella asked when they were out of the nurse's earshot.

"Because Revan doesn't know David is with us and couldn't put his name on the list of visitors." Naomi winked at David. "You just have to sneak in with us."

"How? He's not very invisible." Stella reached for his hand.

"Well, David has to trot out his own acting skills if we're being asked. Mine are exhausted," Naomi said. "And the nurse didn't even ask. She saw him standing with us."

"How big is this place? I wonder if people ever get lost in here," Naomi complained when they reached Revan's floor fifteen long minutes later.

"It's part of Sorbonne University, and one of the largest hospitals in Europe. I think that explains it," David said.

"Good! No cops anywhere, which makes it easier," Stella said when she looked up and down the long hallway. "At least we don't have to invent some crazy story about what relationship David and Revan have and why he wants to visit him."

"We could've recycled the fiancé story again," he said and stroked her hand with his thumb.

"You would pretend to be Revan's fiancé?" Naomi commented drily. "How sweet."

He laughed and knocked on the door to Revan's room, then opened it without waiting for a reply, letting Stella and Naomi walk in before he entered.

"Look who's here again," Revan greeted them with a broad smile. Dressed in jeans and a T-shirt, he was sitting on his bed flipping through the pages of a car magazine.

Then he zeroed in on David and said, "Man, what are *you* doing here?" He pointed his chin in Stella and Naomi's direction. "And you're in one piece? Amazing."

David shook Revan's hand and said, "Long story…good to see you!" He handed him a small shopping bag. "We hope this will help you for now. We've already added our contact information."

Naomi flipped her thumb in David's direction. "He's still on probation." She approached Revan's bed and gave him a small envelope, "Here, Shutterbug. I got this for you at the store where we bought your phone. In case you have another memory lapse."

Stella pulled a bag of gummi bears out of her purse. "I hope the hospital allows you food from outside. Or do they watch everything you eat and drink?"

"They don't care anymore. Haven't you noticed the absence of all the monitors? And no cops anywhere?" Revan said. "Soon I'll be a free man again."

Stella looked around and saw a regular hospital room, not a technology-enhanced mini-lab like the Emergency Department.

"What's new? How are you feeling?" Naomi asked.

"The doctors are happy with my lab results and everything else. I'm just waiting for my discharge instructions and then I'm good to go. I can't wait to get out and take a shower without any assistance," he looked at Naomi and grinned. "On second thought, what if I feel a little wobbly and need a helping hand?"

"I'm sure your hotel has a little stool you can borrow to sit on in the shower. But why don't you tell us what possessed you to go down into those mines?"

"I was supposed to take photos. Four days later, I saw the sunlight again." He winked, "And you, of course, Nugget. The highlight of my day so far."

"Nice try, Rev. We want the minute-by-minute scoop, not the edited version for your mother," Naomi sat down in one of the chairs. She slipped her feet out of her sandals and put them on Rev's bed. "Okay, I'm comfortable now. Start at the beginning. Best start with how you know the women who dragged you with them."

"Seriously? You want me to go back to Adam and Eve?"

The door opened and two women in white coats entered the room. The younger one said, "Mr. Forrester, I'm Dr. Petit. I want to go over the discharge instructions with you, and Suzette has made a copy for you of your lab work and test results. In a few minutes, you are free to leave."

"No shots or medicine?" Revan asked and accepted the envelope from the nurse.

"No, but we want you to follow up with your own physician as soon as you get home. Because you've been under strenuous conditions for the past days, we recommend you are not alone for the next twenty-four hours. Dizziness, nausea, or general weakness can still occur. Do you have someone who can assist you?"

"My fiancée is here and just said she won't even let me take a shower by myself. She's afraid I can't stand up long enough." Revan grinned and patted the bed. "Nugget, come sit with me. Don't be shy."

"Nothing will stand up in the shower if I'm there," Naomi muttered.

Thirty minutes later they walked together through the glass doors into the bright afternoon sunshine.

"Man, this feels really good." Revan took a deep breath. He closed his eyes and turned his face up to the sun.

"You can let go of my hand now," Naomi said. "The charade is over."

"We can't risk it. I might get dizzy. You heard the good doctor," he replied.

"You heard me, too. Let go of my hand."

"Okay, okay," he dropped her hand and put his arm around her shoulders.

"You're intolerable. Why do I even talk to you?"

"You're like a moth to my flame," he said and kissed her on the head.

"Moth to your flame? Did you hit your head a few too many times in those tunnels?" She patted his head.

Stella followed their exchange intently. Under different circumstances, Naomi would revel in being held by Revan, but at this moment, it was looking like she couldn't take much more. The stress of the past few days was ebbing, and now they needed to take time to work through everything they experienced.

Together, they walked to the nearest taxi stand and told the driver their destination.

"I can't believe your hotel is so close to ours," Stella said when they arrived.

"Isn't life just full of surprises," Revan said. "Why don't we all go to my room for a minute, but then I need some time alone. Don't get me wrong, I'm grateful to see you all, but give me an hour or two. And I guess my parents would appreciate a phone call, too."

Once in his room, they didn't bother sitting down.

"Do you need to be at the press conference at six?" David asked. Revan had mentioned one during their taxi ride.

"No, they invited me, but I have nothing to say. Let the big shots smile into the cameras and pretend they know what they're talking about. I want a big steak and something decent to drink."

"Here's a suggestion." David looked from Stella to Naomi and then back at Revan. "Why don't we all meet in three hours at the restaurant downstairs. I'll make a reservation on our way out. We can catch up on a few things, and celebrate having you back, man." He slapped Revan on his back.

Stella asked, "Can we invite Julia and Alexander to dinner, too?"

Revan said, "I don't know who they are, but it's fine with me. Okay, in three hours. Downstairs."

Turning to leave, Naomi stopped and asked, "Wait Rev, the doctor said you shouldn't be alone. Do you want one of us to stay here?"

"Nugget, what a kind offer. But no thanks. I love you like a sister, but I prefer to shower without being watched."

"I was going to volunteer the Troubadour." She smiled widely at David, but he only laughed at her idea.

Revan said, "I'm fine, and if I don't feel great, I'll call for help. See you all later."

"Like a sister! That man is insufferable. I don't know why I try to be nice and offer my help," Naomi fumed while she and Stella walked to their hotel. "Why do I worry so much about him?"

"Oh, Nam, cut him some slack for now. But maybe it's time for you to let him know what he really means to you. He's known both of us for most of our lives, and it's possible he just needs a little push to see what's right in front of his eyes."

"He needs a push, all right. But you heard him! He'll never see me as more than a sister," Naomi said and rolled her shoulders. "Ugh, I'll show him."

After a moment, Naomi said, "And what are you going to do about David?"

"What do you mean? You heard us earlier. I'm going to London in September, and he's coming back to the States in November."

"I heard it loud and clear. But aren't you worried you'll end up where you were last year?"

Stella thought about Naomi's question. Would they eventually end up back on the same slippery slope where they crashed before?

CHAPTER 35

STELLA—JULY 2018

As soon as they entered the restaurant at six o'clock, Stella spotted David and Revan at a table in a small alcove. Palm trees swayed outside the windows, and as she had admired in so many other restaurants, several bistro sets and yard furniture were spread throughout the outdoor area.

Stella went to David, who got to his feet and opened his arms. "I missed you."

"No more than I missed you, love."

Naomi said, "Rev, I want you to meet Julia. And Alexander, her..."

"Her boyfriend," Alexander shook Revan's hand and laughed. "You've caused quite the ruckus, and I'm glad to finally meet you in person."

"I don't mind a little adventure here or there, but usually I go in better prepared," Revan said. He pulled out a chair for Naomi, "Sit with me, Nugget."

Naomi ran a hand over the side of his face and chin, "Look at you, you shaved. And without needing a tourniquet. Wow."

Revan snagged her hand and held it. Then he said, "Listen, guys, I know you want to hear about the past few days, and I don't mind giving you a brief summary, but can we leave the topic alone then? I'd really like to talk about something else tonight." He looked from Stella to Naomi. "Starting with what you two lovely ladies are doing in France. You still haven't told me."

"Okay, Shutterbug, start talking!" Naomi said and pretended set a stopwatch. "You've got five minutes. Ready, set..."

"What will it take to get you to stop calling me that name," Revan grumbled.

"Clock's ticking, Shutt..." Naomi started, but a quick kiss silenced her. Julia and Alexander snickered, Stella and David laughed.

"Stop kissing me. Talk about an annoying habit." Naomi wiped her mouth with a napkin, then said, "Maybe I'll call you Caveman instead. Kind of fits."

322

Revan looked at everyone else with a lopsided grin and winked at Naomi. "I can see this will take time. No problem."

He beckoned a waitress over, they ordered beverages and appetizers, and asked to be given a little time before ordering their entrées.

Just after the waitress left, a couple approached their table. "Sorry to interrupt, but we didn't want to walk by without saying hi."

"Andrew! Sarah! What are you doing here?" Stella called out.

"This restaurant was recommended to us. How are you all doing? We heard the news about your friend. Have you seen him?" Andrew asked.

Stella pointed to Revan and said, "He's sitting right there! Revan, these are Sarah and Andrew. We met them and Julia on our tour."

Revan asked, "Why don't you join us? Then you guys can catch up. Pull up the table over there."

"Are you sure we're not interrupting?" Sarah said. "Hi, Julia! How are you?"

"Doing great, thanks," Julia said with a smile. She reached for Alexander's hand. "This is Alexander."

"Her boyfriend," he explained proudly. When Julia nudged him, he said, "What? I've waited over twenty years to be able to say it."

"I know, sorry." Julia kissed him.

When Sarah saw David, she said, "You look a little bit familiar..."

"David Danvers. It's nice to meet you." He stood and shook Sarah's hand.

"Oh no, that's impossible. Andrew, say something!" Sarah gushed and elbowed Andrew.

"Hi, David. You must be tired of this fan reaction." Andrew held out his hand.

David shook it and said, "Yeah, it happens occasionally. But it's part of the deal."

With introductions out of the way, Andrew and Sarah sat down, and once the drinks and appetizers arrived, Revan said, "You joined us just in time to hear the abbreviated version of 'Revan in the Underworld.'"

He drank some water, then continued, "You already know I was invited to take photos in the catacombs..."

"Rev, did we tell you we met the man who saw you Monday morning?" Naomi interrupted.

"Interesting coincidence. You'll have to tell me more about him later. Well, I'm sure you all heard how we ran into Macho-Man. We spent the first two days being shuffled around a bit. Our lovely *host* quickly became erratic, and I told Claudine and Marianne that I'd watch him for habits and routines. I wanted to get a reading of the guy. It was clear he didn't feel threatened by the women, but he didn't like me being there.

"When Marianne started to get sick, the asshole didn't believe her. My first goal then became to get them out of there. I figured I wouldn't have an actual fighting chance until it was just me and Macho-Man."

"Were you and the women able to communicate with each other?" Andrew asked.

"Not a lot. We never knew if he could hear us." Revan reached for his wine and took a healthy sip.

"You must've been frantically praying for the SWAT team to show up," Alexander said.

"Yeah, I wondered why nobody came, especially after he let the women go. But I assumed there must be a good reason, so I didn't worry too much. I'm not saying I enjoyed the situation, but I knew I needed to wait for my turn."

He helped himself to some crostini topped with brie and strawberries and took a bite. "Much better than eating stale energy bars for three days," he declared and rested his forearms on the table.

"Macho-Man... I never learned his name...was really starting to lose it after the women left. I snoozed whenever he left me alone, but he looked as if he was about to keel over himself. Now, I'm not saying I was in top shape. I hadn't slept soundly either, and the lack of nutritious food was beginning to take a toll. But I was his responsibility, not the other way around, which makes a big difference."

Naomi was silent while she stared at Revan, and pale as a ghost.

He leaned back in his chair again. "I knew I had only one chance to get out. If I blew it, he'd probably shoot me and leave me for the sewer rats."

"Oh no, Revan, how awful," Stella said.

"The moment I waited for came this morning, when he untied me for a bathroom break. Well, bucket break would be more appropriate. We both heard someone running, and it distracted him. I slammed my elbow in the side of his neck, which knocked the air out of him. Then I took off. I didn't care where I went as long as it was away from him. And eventually I ran into members of the SWAT team and their search dogs."

He winked at Naomi. "Seeing those cops in full gear was a sight almost as stunning as you this morning, Nugget."

Naomi had tears in her eyes and twisted a napkin between her fingers. Her mouth trembled.

"And you still don't know what his business was down there or who he was?" Stella asked.

"We watched the press conference earlier and can fill in a some of the blanks," Sarah said. "His name is Claude Voltaire, and he's a forty-six-year-old officer in the anti-drug squad. He stole over sixty pounds of confiscated crack cocaine from the safe at police headquarters at the end of his night shift on Sunday, and the police tracked him down after he didn't show up for work on Tuesday. And the note he sent with the two women had his fingerprints on it."

"So why didn't they send in a special unit earlier if they knew who he was?" Naomi asked.

Andrew said, "They weren't sure if Voltaire was working alone or if he was part of a ring of crooked cops. If he was part of a group, and his name was published, the others would have known they'd been discovered. The police department has had a series of scandals involving drug thefts by insiders over the past few years.

"In 2008, there was a standoff between crooked cops and a SWAT team in an old warehouse here in Paris, and everyone died when one of the bad ones pulled out a hand grenade and blew them all up."

Sarah added, "Voltaire has worked for the police force in Paris his whole life. He either remembered the case or maybe he'd been somehow involved in it. But the authorities couldn't risk a similar stunt in those tunnels. The catacombs are under one of the busiest arrondissements of Paris, so an explosion could've caused a massive collapse of part of the city."

Revan nodded several times during Sarah and Andrew's summary, but didn't ask questions.

"Did they say why they finally went in today?" Stella asked.

"Yes. The sound of running Revan described was two teenagers who had managed to sneak into the catacombs through one of the hidden entrances. The police were obviously monitoring all known entrances, but some are still unknown to most. The kids saw blankets lying in one of the caves Voltaire must have used and the bucket he used for his personal business. They reported what they found. Now the cops were able to narrow down the location of

Voltaire and Revan and decided to go in. And met Revan on his way out," Andrew explained.

Alexander nodded, "Paris has a huge problem with the consumption and trafficking of crack cocaine."

"Who knows how long Voltaire had this little side business going? Did they catch him, by the way?" Stella asked.

"Yes, they did. As soon as two cops took Revan out, the rest and the dogs went after Voltaire. When they found him, he was responsive, but didn't put up a fight," Sarah said.

"And he did have a hand grenade in his duffel bag," Andrew finished.

"I wonder if he used drugs himself. Could explain some of his strange behavior," Revan said. "Well, I had a feeling the guy was more muscle than brain. Imagine, literally his own shit gave him away."

He straightened and rubbed his hands together. "Now, let's order dinner. I'm hungry, and I really want to hear your story, girls."

CHAPTER 36

DAVID—JULY 2018

"Now you know how we all met," Stella finished her recap of events. While everyone was eating, she and Naomi took turns telling Revan about their first days in Paris and the tour, and Julia and Sarah added a few of their own anecdotes.

"And how I got you back, baby," David whispered in Stella's ear while he rested his arm on the back of her chair.

"Well, Cinderella, I have to admit, your story is as entertaining as mine," Revan laughed and wiped his eyes with a napkin. "I would've loved to be a fly on the wall and watch you and Nugget on your turtledove trip. How many boxes of tissues did you go through?"

"Don't you worry your little man brain about us. We had a wonderful time until you got yourself into a mess, Shutterbug," Naomi replied and patted his cheek.

"I'm nosy now, but what's up with the nicknames you have for each other?" Julia asked.

"Revan loves to assign nicknames," Stella said. "Years ago, Naomi found a small gold nugget in Alaska. She was so proud of it, she showed it to everyone she met. Not just once, but all the time, and Rev began to call her Nugget. At some point she had a goldsmith put a hole in it so she could wear it as a pendant," she looked at Naomi. "I don't think I've seen you without it for even one day."

"Nope, not one day without my little nugget," Naomi said and held it up. "I even wear it to bed."

"Thanks for the visual, Nugget," Revan said drily. "Now my little man brain has something to keep it occupied for a while."

"When she was a kid, Stella dressed up as Cinderella for Halloween several years in a row. It didn't take long for Revan to pick it up," Naomi explained.

"And Naomi thinks it's funny to call me Shutterbug because of...well, take a wild guess," Revan said. "Man, it makes me angry just thinking about my nice camera. I can't believe I trashed it. I hope the other one's still in one piece."

David looked at Andrew, who sat across from him, and said, "You mentioned earlier you're a doctor. What field are you in?"

"I'm a laryngologist and work with the Center for Music and Medicine at Johns Hopkins Hospital. The Center offers music-related treatment to patients with Parkinson's disease or dementia. If you're ever in Baltimore, I'd love to give you a tour of the Center, if you're interested."

"I definitely am. I'll call you and we'll set something up. And I bet Stella would love to visit and reconnect with Sarah as well. Maybe we can make it a long weekend," David winked at Stella.

Andrew handed him his business card after he wrote something on the back. "I included my private cell phone number. Call me anytime."

"Thanks. I don't have any business cards with me, but I'll add your contact in my phone later and send you a message."

After dinner, when Stella and Naomi said goodbye to Andrew and Sarah, David pulled Revan aside. "I'd like to go for a last walk with Stella, just an hour around the block. I know it's a lot to ask of you, since you must be dead on your feet, but would you mind walking Naomi back to the hotel? I don't want to impose on Julia and Alexander, they seem to need a little more time, too."

"Don't worry about it. It'll feel good to move, and hopefully I'll fall into bed and sleep through the night. So you're gonna to be around again?" Revan asked.

"Yeah, and I know how incredibly lucky I am to have Stella back in my life." He shoulder-slapped Revan, "Thanks for walking with Naomi."

"I've got it, man. Don't give it another thought," Revan answered. "Nugget, come go for an evening stroll with me."

"Why?" Naomi asked.

"Because our lovebirds need a few minutes alone to say goodbye. Which leaves you and me to keep each other company."

"Since you put it so nicely, how can I possibly say no to such chivalry." Naomi gave David a hug and whispered in his ear, "I haven't forgotten about our little talk. Next time in Philly, buddy."

He smirked and kissed her cheeks. "You tell me when and where. See you soon."

As he watched them leave the restaurant, he heard her say, "The Troubadour's still in hot water with me. I don't forgive as easily as Stella."

And David was very aware of it. If only he knew for sure Stella had completely forgiven him. He'd do everything in his power to prove she was his priority.

"Do you want to go to the Montparnasse Tower again?" he asked her when they started walking.

"Sure! I haven't seen Paris at night from above yet." She entwined her fingers with his.

For a few minutes they didn't talk. He didn't know what to say. He wanted to hold Stella in his arms, wanted to make love to her, wanted to *show* her what he felt instead of just saying it.

"Oh, good! There aren't any lines," Her voice interrupted his thoughts. He hadn't even realized they'd reached the Montparnasse Tower and were standing in the foyer until she spoke up.

"Let's buy the tickets." She pulled him to the ticket station.

On the elevator, she wrapped her arms around him and asked, "What have you been thinking about? You've been quiet all the way over here."

"Honestly? I've been thinking about what to say without making mindless small talk," he admitted. "There's so much I want to say, but we're running out of time. I'll miss you so much, baby."

"I'll miss you, too. But it'll be Labor Day weekend in no time." Her voice was soft, and he saw how she was trying to hold it together.

Stepping out on the observation deck, she said, "Now I can understand why Paris is called the City of Light. Not just all the streetlights, but the Eiffel Tower and other landmarks appear even more majestic with this light show."

She stood in front of him, firmly snuggled into his arms. He kissed the top of her head and let his lips linger there. He needed to inhale her scent, to store it until he held her again.

She sighed. "Paris brought us together again."

"I'm scared to say goodbye to you today, Stella. What if you change your mind and decide you can't trust me anymore?"

He turned her around so she looked at him. She took his face in her hands and caressed it. "As long as we both want to make it work, we're good."

"I love you, baby. Never forget it."

"I know, and I love you. More than words can say."

When they kissed, his entire being began to sing, intensifying until his soundless love song reached an epic crescendo. He poured all his feelings into the kiss, and hoped she understood his silent message.

Later, when they stood in front of her hotel, he said, "Let me know what flights you want to book for September, and I'll arrange the tickets for you."

"Thanks, but no thanks. Because we're still figuring out what went wrong and how to avoid making the same mistake in the future, it's important for me to buy the tickets, to know—and remind myself and you—it's my decision to come see you." She shimmied closer to him. "But I would accept if you were to invite me to stay at your hotel."

"I was hoping you'd stay with me, baby. I'm in a nice studio apartment in the theater district."

"Maybe we'll have time to watch a play in one of the other theaters? Of course I'll come to your performances, but it would be fun to sit together with you in an auditorium, too."

"We can do whatever you want. I'll send you my schedule, then you can do some planning."

He kissed her, full of longing. "Text me when you land in Philadelphia. I'll track your flight, but I want to hear from you directly. Please, baby."

"I will. I can't wait to see you in a few weeks," Stella said. "I'd better go in now. This isn't getting any easier. I love you."

"I love you, too, baby. Goodnight," he kissed her one last time, then watched her walk away.

Letting her go was the hardest thing he'd ever done.

CHAPTER 37

STELLA—JULY/AUGUST 2018

Stella stopped typing and looked out the window. In the far distance, she spotted a handful of other airplanes on the horizon, and over thirty thousand feet below them, freight ships were making their way from one continent to the other. Somewhere out there, under the same blue sky, David was now on his way to London.

Back when they first dated, she used to look up at the sky, and if the clouds were moving toward wherever he was at the time, she'd send imaginary thoughts and wishes his way. It was childish, but it helped her get through the days and weeks without him.

Or maybe she was just a hopeless romantic. Stella shrugged and got back to work.

It was hard to believe how different this flight was from last weekend, when she and Naomi were flying in the opposite direction. Only a few days ago she was looking forward to seeing Paris and escaping her pain, at least for a little while.

Now she'd found her happiness again, yet she had to leave half of her heart in Europe. But it wasn't in pieces anymore. It was one half of a whole now, and she knew the other half was longing for her as much as she was longing for him.

"What're you doing? You've been hacking away on your tablet for an hour, if not longer," Naomi asked and pointed to the dessert Stella had saved from her meal. "And you barely ate anything."

"David said I can make plans for when I'm in London. Theaters are usually closed one day per week, and sometimes his understudy takes over when there's only an afternoon performance, which gives us two full days to visit someplace outside of London."

"Look up Oxford and Stonehenge. They are a nice day trip, and can easily be reached by train. Bath and Wells are also pretty. Where are you staying?"

"With David. He has a studio apartment in the theater district."

"I know I've asked you this before, but do you think all will go well this time?" Naomi asked. "I don't want you to be hurt again."

Stella sighed. "I know. I really believe we can make it work. The irony is, none of what happened last year would've been necessary if only David had talked to me, and I need to follow up on his fear of being let down."

"What you told me about that Adrienne hussy sounds terrible. Makes you wonder why they hooked up in the first place."

"He said they slowly slid from a friendship into a re-lationship. Who knows? People connect for the strangest reasons. When he and I started to date, he told me he hasn't been in a serious relationship for a while. It was too difficult with him traveling so much. But I didn't ask more questions, assuming it was in the past and had nothing to do with us. Now I wish I had. Hey, I should google her. Find out more about the woman who messed him up."

"Let's do it now. We'll start with Facebook," Naomi said. "Thank goodness for inflight Wi-Fi. What's her last name?"

"Adrienne... let me think, hmm... Canasta."

"Hah! Here she is. Wow, she's nothing like you. The only thing you have in common is brown hair." Naomi held up her iPhone for both to see.

"David says we're not at all alike." Stella nodded.

Naomi narrowed her eyes. "And those girls of hers are fake, too. Man, what did he see in her?"

"I don't know. Does it say where she works now? I don't want her anywhere near David."

"What do you mean, you don't want her anywhere near David? If she's still performing, they might end up together on some stage. But if he's not strong enough to resist her, he's not worth your time." Naomi continued to flip through photos of Adrienne.

Stella waved a hand toward the phone. "Forget about her. He was devastated by her betrayal and wants nothing to do with her. She's history! But I thought about something else."

Naomi sighed. "Could it have anything to do with him?"

Stella ignored the comment. "I think we should invite Luca, Jo, and Rev for dinner. We could cook something French, serve French wine, and show them our photos. I took tons."

"I took plenty, too. But instead of cooking, can we just make a niçoise salad? Maybe with some baguettes and cheese to go with it? I don't feel like standing in the kitchen all evening when the guys are having a good time outside. We should try to get the sparkling wine Julia ordered on the train to make it authentic."

"Okay, we'll pick a weekend as soon as we're home. I assume Luca will still be in Philly when we get there, and I'll ask him. I'm sure he wants to see Rev in person, too. You can let Jo know. I haven't hung out with her in a while and can't wait to hear what's new."

"Yes, and I can't wait to grill her about Luca..." Naomi said with a gleam in her eyes.

"Let it go and leave them alone. You should think about what you want to do about *your* crush," Stella grinned.

"Nothing. You heard him!" Naomi made a face while she pulled a travel magazine out of the seat pocket in front of her and grumbled, "Sister!"

Two weeks later Naomi walked into Stella's kitchen and dropped an envelope on the counter. "Here's the printout of your e-tickets. I don't know why you don't download them on your phone like everybody else. It's so much easier, and you can't lose them."

"Because I like looking at them and holding them in my hand when I get to the airport," Stella said. "Did you bring marinated olives and baguettes? Wait, no need to answer. I can smell the bread."

"Here!" Naomi held up a bag and whispered, "And they had madeleines, so I bought some of those, too. Of course, I'll tell the guys I made them. Slaved in the kitchen all afternoon, dipping them in the chocolate, one at a time."

"Nugget, I can't see you spending more time in the kitchen than is absolutely necessary." Revan reached over her shoulder for the box with the madeleines.

"Take your sticky fingers out of there. Those are for later," she slapped his hands away. "But I meant to tell you something, Shutterbug. Remember the boxer puppies? My parents adopted them, and they came home last weekend."

Revan glared at Naomi and said, "Why am I not surprised? Do you always get what you want?"

341

"No, of course not. There was this one time...well, anyhow. The puppies are too stinking cute. You should swing by and meet them."

"I'll visit them after I get back from my next trip. Time to hit the road again. What are their names?" He leaned against the counter and crossed his arms in front of his chest.

"Scarlett and Dixon."

"I have a suspicion who's responsible for naming the poor puppy Scarlett," Rev looked straight at Naomi, "but where does Dixon come from?"

"Dad's been reading a book about some war recently. Maybe there was a General Dixon?" Naomi suggested, shrugging.

He shook his head and pressed his lips together. "Oh, Nugget, you're beyond words." He reached out and tousled Naomi's hair.

"I know. I told him he should name the dog Rhett, but he insisted on Dixon." Naomi looked sideways at Revan. "What's so funny?"

"Nothing, really. I hope you don't make Scarlett wear a bonnet when you take her for walks in the park. And please don't put her in one of those god-awful pet strollers. I'm sure she has four healthy legs and will want to run."

Naomi gave him a little shove and said, "I can't decide whether you're arrogant or ignorant, Revan Forrester. Why was I worried sick about you in Paris?"

Chuckling, he walked to one of his bookshelves and pulled out a *National Geographic History* magazine. "Here, take this home and read it. It has a great article about the Mason-Dixon line, with photos provided by yours truly."

"I'll put it on my nightstand, thanks." She took it without looking at it and set it aside.

"You'll have to open it to read it, Nugget." He grinned and walked to the bar. "Drinks, anybody? I'm not waiting for Jo and Luca to get here. By the way, do you know why he had to pick her up at the train station? She knows where we live!"

"It's what a gentleman does, but I wouldn't expect you to know that. I'll have a glass of red wine if you don't mind. You'll find me in the backyard," Naomi countered and went outside. "Nice backyard fountain, Stella. It looks beautiful with the new bistro set. Very French..."

"How're things at home, Rev?" Luca asked. "Your parents must be thrilled to know you'll be around for a few weeks."

"Mom's getting a little too clingy and calls every other day. It was great to come home after I had all my business finished with the police in Paris. But you know me, I need to be out there. I'm flying to Haiti tomorrow." Revan leaned back in one of the outdoor chaises. "Stella, I have to admit I wasn't so sure about your fountain idea, but it's not bad."

"Thank you. I've been sitting out here every minute I can. Listening to the water splash is so relaxing, and I love to watch the birds playing in it."

"And so romantic..." Naomi's voice trailed off and she batted her eyelashes. "Only David is missing."

"Yes, you're right. And stop being so snarky. Luca, can you set everything up so we can look at the photos on the big screen?" Stella asked.

"Sure. I assume you downloaded everything to your laptop?" He got up and walked inside. "Password the same as usual?"

"Yes."

Jo promptly followed him. "I'll grab another glass of wine. Anybody want something?"

Naomi poked Stella and said, "Did you see? She's going wherever he is. Something's going on..."

Rev looked around and said in a stage whisper, "I think so too. It's obvious. She's thirsty."

"Do you know anything? Aren't you Luca's best friend? Go ask him what's going on and how they spend their time in New York." Naomi snapped.

"Are you kidding me? I don't care if they sneak around together."

"Drop it, guys. There's no sneaking around. Jo and I go out for drinks every now and then. It's what friends do," Luca said from the French doors. "Everything's set up, Stella."

"I can't believe people are actually booking trips like yours. Nugget, are you really going to sell such sentimental hogwash to your customers?" Revan asked when they got settled on the chairs and sofa in front of the TV.

"You bet I am. I already have a few customers who are interested in it. It was a wonderful tour and very romantic. But one needs to have at least one romantic bone in their body to admire the beauty of what we've seen. You don't seem to have one, though, so the tour would be wasted on you."

"No need to worry, Nugget. Many women have told me how much they appreciate my romantic bone," Rev grinned.

"Ugh, just what I wanted to know..."

Stella laughed and said, "You asked for it."

For the next hour, they took turns sharing memories of their trip, often stopping the slideshow to relive a moment.

Stella gasped when a photo of her and David on the observation deck of the Montparnasse Tower filled the screen.

"When did you take this, Nam?" Seeing him in the photo made her heart miss a beat. She wished David could be with them right now.

"When you two were immersed in one of your many little *talks*. Looked more like flirting to me, though."

Stella's phone rang with a familiar ringtone and she jumped up to answer it. "David wants to FaceTime. Is it okay with you guys?"

"Sure, put him on," Luca said.

"Hi, baby, how are you?" Stella greeted David. "We're looking at the trip photos. Wanna say hi to the gang? Wait, I'll flip the camera setting."

"Bring 'em on, love," he smiled. "Hi, guys, how's it going? Luca, Jo, good to see you."

"Doing well. I hear you're out of the doghouse, but I'm warning you, all eyes are on you," Luca laughed. "Big brother and all…"

"I wouldn't expect anything different," David said. "I know I'll have to earn my way back into everybody's good graces. I really look forward to seeing you all in November."

"We'll make sure to get together. Let me know if you also swing by New York. We'll go out for a beer or two."

"Would love to; sounds good."

Stella switched the phone's screen back and stepped outside, holding her hand under the splashing water. "How was your day?"

"Good. The usual stuff. Did the new fountain finally get installed? I hear water in the background," he asked.

"Yes, I thought I mentioned it when it was delivered. And I got my tickets today. I'll arrive in London at ten in the morning on Saturday, September first."

"Perfect, I'll pick you up at the airport. I have a performance in the evening, but we have all day until around 5. Wanna come to the show?"

"No, not on the first night. I'll be too tired. But I'd like to go on Sunday."

"Sure." He lowered his voice, "I miss you."

"I miss you, too" Stella said quietly.

"I love you. We'll talk tomorrow. Okay, baby?"

"Okay. Goodnight."

Stella joined the others, but her mind was far away while they continued their slideshow. The amicable way David was being welcomed back into their group, how Luca playfully told him he'd be watching him, was calming her underlying jitters. He fit right in three years ago, when he came for the first dinner, and he'd fit right in again.

"Whoa, hold it there for a second." Revan sat up straight and stared at the screen. "Who's that?"

"Me, Shutterbug," Naomi said. "Do you need glasses?"

"I'm talking about the guy feeling you up."

"What? Are you stupid? Nobody's feeling me up."

"What's his hand doing under your shirt, then?" Rev got up and pointed to the spot in question.

"Who cares?" she shrugged it off.

"When did you have time to meet someone in Paris?" Rev stood close to Naomi and glowered at her. "So, who is Mr. Tentacle?"

"He's the guy who saw you in the tunnels, right after you let Creepy Cop truss you up."

"And what's your connection again? I don't think you ever told me."

"Oh, Rev, it's a long story and for another day. I do happen to meet people without your pre-approval." Naomi patted his cheek and walked away.

Stella followed her and pulled her aside, "What's up?"

"I don't know. This shit with Rev is getting to me more than it used to. I'm sorry, but I think I'll be heading home."

"I'm sorry. We can tell Rev to mind his own business."

"No, it's fine. I'll call you tomorrow."

They hugged and Naomi called out, "Bye, all. I'm going home. Puppy duty—I promised Mom and Dad I'll do the evening poop tour around the block."

"Hey, Nugget, don't talk to strangers," Rev called after her.

"Yeah, yeah. I'm a big girl."

CHAPTER 38

STELLA—SEPTEMBER 2018

Stella shoved her hands into the pockets of her jacket. They were still sweaty and trembling.

Before landing at Heathrow Airport, the Airbus A-330 had been forced to fly countless loops through heavy rain gusts, shaking the airplane as if it weighed nothing. *Is this storm an omen for what's to come? What if this week in London is a mistake?*

"Next!" yelled the middle-aged immigration officer.

"What's the reason for your visit?" he asked when Stella handed over her passport.

"Vacation," she replied. Why do their questions always make one nervous? They had no reason to deny her entry. But she'd be glad when she had her luggage and walked out into the arrivals area. With a little luck, straight into David's arms.

She couldn't wait to see him. No way was it a mistake to be here. And she'd never been to London, so that was an added perk. Plus she'd already collected a folder full of ideas for sightseeing and day trips.

The officer slammed an immigration stamp into her passport and handed it back to her. "Enjoy your stay," he said before he barked, "Next!"

At the baggage carousel, she watched dozens of suitcases go by. Most of them were black or gray, dented and scratched, wearing battle scars from being tossed around the depths of cargo areas around the world. Whole families congregated smack in front of the conveyer belt, fathers telling their children not to touch, but doing nothing to keep their offspring out of the way.

An older woman with a cane stood not far from Stella, and she wondered how on earth such a fragile lady would manage to pull her luggage off. If it arrived with hers, she'd get it for her.

She spotted her suitcase and fought her way closer to the luggage belt. A small amount of tension left her. It was a relief to know her luggage made it and wasn't on its way to another foreign destination.

Just as she reached for her light gray suitcase, easy to recognize thanks to the burgundy luggage strap, an elbow rammed into her side and almost shoved her into the older woman. A burly man reached around her and pulled his two oversized sports bags off the belt with one hand. *Show-off...* She caught a whiff of something unpleasant. Stella didn't like to smell cigarette smoke in general, but this was an extra nasty-smelling brand.

"Hey, watch it. I'm trying to get my suitcase, too," she said.

"Don't worry, it'll come around again," he said and sauntered away.

Was there an equivalent to road rage when flying? Some people acted like assholes once they saw the finish line—or in this case, the Exit sign behind the customs area. No patience or manners left at all.

Stella watched her suitcase moving farther away—*practice what you preach, be patient*—when she noticed the elderly lady shifting her cane from one hand to the other and reaching for a brown suitcase.

"Let me get it for you," she picked it up and placed it next to the woman. "Do you have more luggage? Do you need help getting through customs?"

"Only this, thank you, dear. I can roll it, and my son is waiting for me on the other side of the doors."

After Stella's own suitcase emerged from its unnecessary extra trip, she made her way toward the bright green *Nothing to Declare* sign.

She felt giddy. The last few weeks had gone by fast, but not fast enough. Only a few more minutes and she'd see David again.

"What do you mean, open my bags? I have nothing to declare," an angry voice shouted. She looked around to see the bully had been tagged for a bag check. She knew it wasn't nice, but she didn't feel sorry for him at all, especially when he seemed to take the same attitude with the female customs officer as he had with her.

"Come with you? I don't think so. I have a train to catch," he bellowed, as Stella saw two border force officers approaching him with their dogs.

She kept moving. Too bad she'd have to miss the end of the little drama.

The doors in front of Stella slid aside and she stepped out into a sea of expectant faces. And was swept up by strong arms.

"There you are! Oh, baby, I missed you."

"David," she laughed. "Let me at least put down my suitcase."

"Drop it. I'm not letting go of you," he replied and kissed her with an urgency that made her tingle all over. "Let's get out of here. And you're lucky—the rain just stopped, and the sun came out. Heaven smiles when angels travel..."

He set her down and reached for her suitcase but kept a tight hold on her hand. She didn't want to let go, either.

During the taxi ride, she stayed snuggled under David's arm with her head resting against his shoulder. She listened to him pointing out a few sights, but for the most part she was content simply knowing they had a whole week together.

His rented apartment was modern and comfortable, and she could understand why he preferred it to a hotel room. It had a homey feeling. After he finished showing her around, he offered to make coffee or tea. Stella longed for a cup of *real* coffee, not the junk served on airplanes.

"Who's doing the cleaning and laundry?" she asked as she got comfortable in one of the wide chairs in the living room, eyeing the low glass-top coffee table in front of them.

"Housekeeping comes in once a week, which is enough. Washers and dryers are in the basement, and I drop off my dress shirts at the cleaners. For cooking, I keep the basic staples, but most of the time I pick up takeout," he said from the open kitchen, where she could see him taking cups out of the cabinet.

"Do you sometimes sit on your little balcony?" She had spotted it outside the French doors as soon as they walked in, attracted to the bright sunshine streaming into the room.

"No, it's too narrow for sitting. Did you know they're called Juliet balconies?" David walked in with a tray laden with coffee mugs, sugar, milk, and scones.

"What an interesting shade of orange...or is it salmon?" She touched the short rose in a slim vase on the tray.

"I'll let you figure out the correct color name," he said with a wink.

There were more roses of the same shade on the mantel over the fireplace and on the small dining table, and she'd even seen a vase in the bedroom when she put her luggage away. She'd definitely google the meaning of the color later.

"I can't wait to start exploring London. You have to be my tour guide this time," Stella said.

"Let's have coffee, and then off we go. But don't expect too much from me. I haven't seen much myself."

They spent the rest of the afternoon walking around Piccadilly Circus, St. James Park, and Buckingham Palace, all within walking distance of David's apartment, and enjoyed an early dinner at a neighborhood pub before he left for the theater.

She promised to stay awake until he came home, but when her head dropped for the third time after a relaxing bath and over thirty hours on her feet, she gave in and crawled into the large bed.

"Goodnight, my love." David's arm came around her. His familiar scent comforted her, and she snuggled closer.

"What time is it?" her voice was heavy with sleep. "I tried to stay awake, but I couldn't..."

"Almost midnight. I got home a few minutes ago." His nose touched her neck. "Mm, lavender."

"I used one of the little bath salt packages. I hope you don't mind," she mumbled.

"Of course not. They're there for you." His nose continued exploring her neck, and when his hand caressed her arm, she rolled over to reach around him. The four or five hours of sleep had revived her spirits. Or maybe it was the touch of his hands. But her body came alive and was humming with new energy.

His exploring fingers reached the hem of her short nightgown and stroked the bare skin on her thighs. An electric jolt ran through her. Her body was thrumming in too-long neglected places.

She needed him. Now.

She pushed against his shoulder. Wanted to straddle him.

"Sorry, baby, I shouldn't have waked you up. Let me hold you," he said, rolling onto his back but keeping an arm around Stella and pulling her against his side.

Instead of saying anything, Stella reached inside his boxer shorts. He groaned and she felt him shiver. When she applied more pressure and moved her hand up and down, he said in a raspy voice, "You might want to stop touching me now, love, or it'll be a while before I let you go back to sleep."

Stella shook her head. She didn't want to sleep, and she didn't want to talk. She needed to feel him inside her. She squeezed a little harder and circled his moist head with the pad of her thumb.

"Baby, I'm serious. You're poking the dragon." His voice was low and breathless.

"Why, don't you want me?" Stella asked innocently and stretched up to kiss him. Her firm breasts, covered only by her silky nightgown, rubbed against the side of his body.

She pressed herself closer to him and began to circle her hips in slow moves.

"I believe...you're holding...the answer...in...your hand."

With one hand, he pulled the nightgown up and over her head and reached for his boxers, but she maintained her firm grip on his erection. With every move he made in his struggle to shed his boxers, he slid up and down inside her fist.

Stella let go of him and reached for her panties.

"Oh, no, let me..." he whispered and pushed them down, then shed his own underwear. He flipped her on her back and settled between her legs. "Baby, I wanted to take this slow, but I can't wait. We'll play more next time."

"Stop talking and do it." She was trembling all over and was about to come simply thinking about him, but it wasn't what she wanted.

His erection nudged her opening, seeking entrance, and she reached for him when he abruptly stopped.

He held himself up on one forearm and muttered, "Shit, I can't believe it."

Panting hard, hovering no more than an inch over her body, he dropped his forehead to hers.

"What's wrong?" she whispered.

"Condoms..." he gritted through clenched teeth.

"I'm still on the pill. And you said there was no one." She slid one leg around his waist and urged him on. "Please, I need you now."

"Baby, you're killing me." He entered her with one deep thrust, pushing in farther until he was fully buried. Then he withdrew, so slow it was agonizing, before sliding into her again. Stella clenched around him, arched her back, and whimpered, "David! Please!"

He pulled out again, letting his swollen tip rest against her throbbing entrance. With one hand he lifted her toward him, thrust in hard again, and started to move faster. In and out, in and out. Stella groped for a pillow to smother the sounds she was making. She wasn't a screamer, but she rewarded his lovemaking with a multitude of sexy noises.

"Don't hide from me, baby. Look at me when you're coming," he commanded and massaged her swollen spot. "Come for me—now." He added pressure.

She dropped the pillow and, with her eyes fastened on his, came with his next thrust. Her body shook and trembled, and her powerful, vise-like tightening around him pushed him over the top, too.

They kissed and cried while they rode out their climaxes, still connected in the most intimate way. Her arms circled around his neck, pulling him close, and she wrapped her other leg around his waist.

"Oh, baby, what are doing to me?" He kissed her some more. With each stroke of his tongue, he created new pleasures inside her. She could feel him staying hard, and it didn't take long until he began to move again, taking his time entering and withdrawing, teasing and touching her until they both climaxed for the second time.

"I think I need another bath," she said, after her breathing returned to normal.

"I'll join you. Even if you want to use lavender salts." He brushed a strand of sweaty hair off her face.

"No, I saw there's also a rose-scented bubble bath," Stella giggled.

When she relaxed in the bathtub, David walked in with a bottle of champagne and two glasses. "I couldn't drink before the show, but I think now is a good time to pop the cork. Would you like some?"

"Yes, please. You're spoiling me, love. Roses, bubble bath, champagne..."

"You deserve it, baby, all this, and so much more." He sat across from her in the large tub and touched his glass to hers. "To you, my angel."

"I never stopped loving you, David. Not for one single minute." She turned around and leaned against his chest, closed her eyes, and relaxed while he stroked her hair and kissed her head. Before the water turned cool, they dried off and took the bottle and glasses back into the bedroom, where they sat in bed and snuggled together. No words were needed. They were both sated and happy.

Stella knew she could never love another man.

CHAPTER 39

STELLA—SEPTEMBER 2018

On Thursday evening, Stella and David walked hand in hand through the streets of London until he stopped in front of the Theatre Royal Haymarket. It was directly across the street from Her Majesty's Theater, where he was onstage five days a week.

She had joined him on Sunday evening and watched him as The Phantom. No matter how many times she attended a show, she'd never tire of the music. On Monday, his day off, they visited Oxford, where they toured the Old Bodleian Library and had fish and chips for lunch at Turf Tavern. On Tuesday and Wednesday, they spent time sightseeing in London before his evening performances, and on Thursday he had an afternoon performance. David came home with barely enough time to eat a simple dinner of sandwiches and salads before they left for the evening show.

"We'll be able to sit in the theater like other people and relax. What are we going to see? You've been mum about it all week." She looked up at the facade of the theater.

"I don't know if I can behave once we're in the auditorium. I'm used to being on the other side of the curtain. What if I feel frisky in the middle of the play?" He raised his eyebrows and melted her heart with his mischievous grin.

"Then you'll behave like a good boy. You can't complain about a lack of...umm...activity this week," she said and blushed. Their need to be intimate and to pleasure each other was almost as strong as their need to talk or laugh together.

"I can't promise not to touch you, baby."

"You can hold my hand. But only if I get a glass of champagne during intermission."

"If I get you one before the show starts, and one during intermission, what's my reward?"

"Find out." She winked at him. "Let's go in. Now tell me, what are they playing?"

"Look for yourself." He turned her around—and she cracked up.

"*Breakfast at Tiffany's*? Seriously? I love it. Growing up, I watched the movie all the time and wanted to be like Audrey Hepburn. I can't believe I haven't noticed this before."

"Maybe because you only had eyes for me?" he teased her. "Why did you want to be like her?"

"Because she seemed to be genuinely nice, and a good person. And she was cute."

"Then your wish came true, because I don't know anyone who's nicer or more caring than you." He kissed her tenderly. "Or any cuter."

"You're biased, you're my boyfriend." She rolled her eyes, but grinned.

"I sure am your boyfriend, and I know what a lucky man I am." He kissed her again and pulled on her hand. "Let's get you your first glass of champagne."

After the show, while they slowly walked back to the apartment, Stella chuckled. "Seeing Holly Golightly and the cat made me think of Paris. On our second day, we saw so many newlywed couples posing for photos, and Naomi and I joked about how we should move in together with a house full of cats because there were no husbands on the horizon for either of us."

As soon as the words were out of her mouth, she wished to take them back. She didn't want to sound whiny. David squeezed her hand but didn't say anything.

Back at the apartment, he opened a bottle of wine and they sat in front of the windows. The door to the balcony was open, and mild September air drifted inside. Even at this late hour, the sounds of big city traffic intermingled with various voices from the street below.

He pulled her feet closer and massaged them. "What do you want to do tomorrow?"

"Can we visit Canterbury Cathedral and the White Cliffs of Dover? It's too late to book a guided tour from London, and they take up the whole day anyway. If we do it on our own, we can skip a few stops and plan the day the way we want it."

"It sounds like fun. I haven't been to either place." He typed something on his phone. "The first train leaves London at five, but I'd prefer one a little bit later. We can try to catch the one at 7:30, which will take only an hour to take us to Dover."

"Perfect. We'd better not stay up till the wee hours, then. But I want to finish this glass of wine."

"You could finish it in bed..." he suggested. "We don't need to sleep right away, do we?"

"I guess we can talk for a few more minutes. Wanna share ghost stories?" She batted her eyelashes at him.

"Sure. Have you heard about the one-eyed monster who comes out at night and feasts on cat ladies?" he said, wiggling his eyebrows.

"You are bad, Mr. Danvers, truly naughty. What am I going to do with you?" She pretended to think, tapping her finger on her chin. "Hmm. Maybe the cat lady needs to sleep in the other bedroom?"

"The cat lady can't hide from the monster. It's a very determined monster. And maybe the monster and the cat lady will fall in love and live happily ever after."

"I guess we'll find out," she nodded. "I'm going to bed. Feel free to bring the wine, love. And the one-eyed monster."

Strolling along the narrow chalky path atop the steep white cliffs, Stella watched the waves rolling onto the beach far below her. They are more ripples than waves, she thought. How would the scenery change in a fast-approaching winter storm when the waves were high and battered the famous rock formation?

The past few days had been the happiest of her life. Like the grass covering the top of the cliffs moved in the breeze, she just went with the flow around David's schedule.

But she also got a glimpse of a life which wasn't real—with him coming home to her, day after day. She could feel tears sting her eyelids and tried to blink them away.

She turned her face into the mild breeze. Maybe she could pretend the wind made her eyes water. It would be nine weeks until he was finished in London and came to Philadelphia.

Nine long weeks.

Sixty-three days without him.

And then he would leave again to visit his family in Chicago before spending most of December and part of January in Philadelphia. Then Paris. But what would come after France? Would he be farther away than ever?

His stint in Europe had broken them once. In his letter last year, he mentioned the possibility of going to Australia. If he went there, she'd have no way of seeing him at all.

Every time he visited her from some distant location, her delight was tempered by knowing he'd be leaving again. She knew what time his plane was departing before the plane bringing him to her had landed. The goodbyes had gotten more and more difficult for her.

And here she was now...

Knowing the next goodbye was inevitable was becoming unbearable.

The tears she tried so hard to hold back started rolling down her cheeks. She bit down on her lower lip. She couldn't do it. There was no other way, no matter how happy they were at this moment.

This wasn't working. She had to let David go.

It was time to say goodbye.

She couldn't imagine life without him. But after a week full of passion and closeness, a few minutes on FaceTime would never again be enough. She'd break his heart, and hers along with his, but there was no other way.

"Stella, what's going on? Why are you crying, love?" He sat down on a bench overlooking the English Channel and pulled her with him.

The sun smiled down from a deep blue sky and only a handful of clouds were visible on the horizon.

But appearances were deceptive. Deep inside her, a storm was brewing. She hid her face in her hands and sobbed.

"Baby, what's the matter?" His mouth was close to her ear.

Stella looked at him through a veil of tears. She couldn't say a word.

"You're scaring me. Talk to me! Please." Panic replaced confusion on his face, and it killed her to see him in such pain.

Is this how he felt last year? Is this what he was going through when he wrote his letter? *Did he hate himself as much as I'm hating myself right now? Did he feel as helpless as I do?*

"David, I don't know how to say this." She took a deep breath. "What we have is so special to me. But I can't..."

"No!" he cried. He didn't let her finish, wrapping his arms around her and stifling her words with a branding kiss. It was rough and left no doubt about his sincerity. "Don't even think about it!"

"What do you mean?" she asked while wiping her tears away. "You don't know what I was going to say."

"Oh, yes, I do. Because I recognize the look on your face. I know uncertainty when I see it. You're struggling with your emotions, and you're afraid. Don't let your doubts win. Your head is misleading you. You think you can lessen the pain if you inflict it yourself. But it hurts as much, if not more—believe me. Listen to your heart. Don't make the same mistake I made."

Deep inside, she knew he was right. And she knew she loved him more than anything in this world. So why had her fears reared their ugly heads now? Was this the culmination of the events in Paris and this week? Did she have more insecurities than she realized? Stella's mind was spinning.

She got up and walked a few steps back and forth, trying to take a few deep breaths to ground herself. It didn't work. Her tears began to roll down her face again, and this time she didn't stop them. Maybe they'd cleanse her from the inside out.

She turned to face him. "But how are we going to make this work? We didn't manage it the first time. What if the same thing happens again? I can't go through it another time."

"Listen to me, love. I want to tell you something. This week..." He took her hand and guided her onto the bench again, then wiped away her tears.

"This week was wonderful. It was beyond amazing," she said and tried to smile at him, but it didn't reach her eyes and her lips trembled.

Then she continued in a shaky voice, "But I want more than only a few scattered days. Maybe I'm selfish, but I want you all the time, David. I'm an ordinary girl hoping to live the old-fashioned American dream." She wrapped her arms around her middle. "And I want to have your babies..."

There, she said it. She confessed one of her most secret wishes.

He untangled her arms and took her hands in his. "Baby, you didn't let me finish. What I was going to say is, this week showed me that I can't continue this life on the road. I want what you want. With you! I want the white picket fence and children. A dog and a minivan." He chuckled. "Well, maybe I'll draw the line at the minivan."

He reached into the pocket of his jacket and pulled out a slim velvet box.

"I had this made before you arrived in London." He showed the open box to her. "I call it the Little Dipper pendant. Each diamond represents one of the seven stars in the constellation. You've been my North Star since we met, and you always will be. Please, Stella, believe in us. Don't give up on us."

He pulled the delicate white-gold chain out and presented it to her. "Will you wear it and think of me?"

"But...what..." she stammered.

"It's a promise to you, my love. I'll fulfill my obligations here and in Paris in the spring. But trust me. When I meet with Aaron in November, we will come up with a strategy for my future career path without all this traveling. Right now I don't know what comes next, but I want you to be part of it—if you want to be with me."

His eyes begged her not to turn him down and his mouth quivered. "We'll find a way to make this work together."

A middle-aged couple passed them, and the man asked, "What did she say, son?"

Without taking his eyes off Stella he replied, "Nothing yet."

"I love it. Thank you so much." She cried and laughed at the same time. A weight fell off her shoulders. She believed him.

After watching the couple walk away, she looked back at David and said, "I lost you once. I'm not losing you again."

A few hours later, while strolling through the cobblestone streets of Canterbury toward the old Cathedral, Stella said, "Baby, are—" she cleared her throat. "Are you mad at me because I decided to break it off with you?"

He stopped walking and wrapped his arms around her. "How can I be mad at you, love? Your worries are natural. But we need to talk about these things with each other. You know, I had an interesting thought the other day.

"We wear so many different masks throughout our lives, it's easy to hide behind them. We disguise our fears with anger. We fake laughter when we want to cry. But worst is the shield of ambition. In our yearning for success, we're often denying ourselves the one thing we really want. Don't get me wrong. You know I love my work, but it means nothing without you. From now on, I'm fighting for what I want. And I want you, Stella, because without you, my life is empty."

She nodded. "I love you so much, it sometimes hurts so much it scares me. I was scared today. But I promise you I'll be strong and won't doubt my own feelings again—or yours."

"Before I go to Paris, we'll have a plan in place—one that works for both of us. We're in this together, my angel."

That night, their lovemaking was more intense than it had ever been. It wasn't a race to reach climax. They showered each other with love. It was sensual and raw, seeking and reassuring, full of emotions and promises.

Much later, safe in David's arms, Stella remembered her vision of walking on a beach in France with David and their children. She allowed herself to imagine baseball practices and dance recitals. A house full of laughter and love.

She touched her pendant. Like Naomi, she would never take hers off.

Could she truly allow herself to dream this precious dream, to open herself fully to their possible future?

CHAPTER 40

DAVID—OCTOBER 2018

D avid turned on some jazz and poured himself a glass of wine. He had a few bottles left from Stella's visit, and it wasn't worth shipping them home. While he sipped, he imagined her here with him. The combination of earthy aromas of wet leaves and faint floral smell of roses made him smile.

Stella sometimes tried to pick out certain taste notes in a wine, but had a rather unique way of describing them. "I smell horse barn," was his favorite.

He stood in front of the cold fireplace, scanning the living room. It was finally time to pack up and prepare for his return to the States, to Stella. Just as in every other city before, he hadn't accumulated a lot of personal items. Long ago, he learned to travel light.

Since Stella returned home, he had often replayed their day in Dover in his mind. She had been on the brink of breaking up with him. Had almost turned the tables on him. He admired her for having the guts to do it in person, while looking him in the eyes.

When he realized what she was about to do, he couldn't breathe. His heart had skipped a few beats before it picked up again at record speed. He wasn't surprised at all that she had doubts and fears. It wouldn't have been normal if she didn't question what happened between them.

Every time when he made love to her, he saw her trust and her love for him in her eyes. And her silent plea that she was enough for him. She didn't seem to realize the question ought to be whether *he* was enough for *her*. Would he be able to give her what she needed?

What she didn't know was, she had shared some of her terrors with him almost every night, when deeply rooted fears took hold of her. She often whimpered his name, her mumbled "W*hy*?" and "W*here are you*?" shaking him to the core. And all he had been able to do was hold her, and slowly guide her out of the nightmares. Their middle of the night lovemaking was when they bared their souls and became one, until the world around them didn't exist.

His gaze fell on the object on the table. The book was identical to the one he gave Stella three years ago. But inside his were two other items: a photograph of them, and a copy of his damned letter. A letter not even written by hand, but typed on his computer like a routine cancellation notice for a boring magazine subscription.

Why did he save a copy of it? To remind himself of his own stupidity!

He didn't need to unfold the letter.

He remembered...Every. Single. Devastating. Word.

Dearest Stella,

I've been in Budapest for a few weeks now. Aaron is telling me already about other offers and gigs all over Europe, and he even talked about going to Sydney. It is thrilling—and humbling—to think about singing at the biggest and oldest opera houses. But it also makes me think about us. Where do you and I fit into this life?

We've been together for two years now, and under different circumstances, this could be the time to take our relationship to the next level. Yet I don't know what my future holds, where I will be next, and I can't offer you any stability or certainty.

When I left America, you said you'd wait for me. We thought I'd be gone for six months. When I visited you in May, and told you about going to Budapest, you took it in stride that I would stay here for at least another six months, maybe longer. But, Stella, I can't make any promises anymore.

I don't have the right to ask you to wait for me any longer, because it isn't fair to you. I'll have to let you go.

Take your love for me and give it to another man, one who can be there for you and give you everything you deserve.

Maybe our paths will cross again one day, and we'll meet as friends.

Yours, David

He crumpled up the letter and tossed it in the empty fireplace. What devil had ridden him to tell Stella to give the love she felt for him to another man? Talk about adding insult to injury! No wonder she never tried to contact him afterward.

Her willingness to talk to him in Paris was more than he deserved.

He reached for a match and lit the letter. The flames devoured the paper, and he wished they could also turn the painful memories into ashes and destroy the twin letter in her possession.

Because he would never take her love for granted and would prove it to her every single day for the rest of his life.

Stella was a romantic at heart. She didn't expect expensive gifts or extravagant vacations, had never once asked anything of him. All she wanted was to be loved wholeheartedly for who she was, to be treated with respect, and to be accepted as an independent woman.

He would not ask her to give up her work and her family to be with him. She had made too many sacrifices already. Never would he make her choose between him and her job.

David reached for his phone. He knew what he needed to do, and it was time to set his plan in motion. He had two messages to write.

The first would go to Aaron.

The second recipient would make him eat dirt.

CHAPTER 41

STELLA—NOVEMBER 2018

"You want *what*?" Stella plopped down in front of the spick-and-span fireplace, held the cell phone away from her ear and stared at it.

She should've let the call go to voice mail. But who was she kidding? There were a handful of people who could call her at any time, and she'd pick up.

"I need you to meet me in an hour," Naomi said.

"Why?"

"There's this guy I meet when I take out the dogs. I only wish Bozo would stop humping poor Scarlett every time he sees her."

"Who is Bozo?" Stella interrupted.

"He's Frank's German Shepherd, super cute. But..."

"And Frank is...?" she asked toneless.

"The owner of Bozo, of course. Anyhow, Frank is a history geek, and I may have let it slip how much I like it, too."

Stella wiped her hand over the hearth. "Since when? And what do I have to do with it?"

"He asked me to go with him to a special exhibit at the Museum of the American Revolution and to an early dinner afterward. You know me. I don't mind the dinner, but who wants to go to a museum?"

"So, tell him you fibbed. Or just go."

"But...umm...what if he asks me something about history and I have no clue what to say?"

"Wait a minute... Did you think I'd agree to come with you just to prompt the right answers?" Naomi was unbelievable. She knew Stella didn't have time for this kind of nonsense today.

"Sort of...maybe."

"You know, normally I would love to help you out, but maybe you forgot David is arriving tomorrow? I still have a bunch of things to finish before he gets here," Stella said, and once again ran through her mental to-do list.

She had changed the bed linens, cleaned the bathroom, and emptied out space in the closet for him to hang up some of his clothes, but squeezing in a museum visit wasn't on her agenda.

"Pleeeeaaaase...... I neeever ask you for aaanythingggg," Naomi whined.

"I know, but I have a pedi scheduled for later."

"You had one two weeks ago, and I'm sure the Troubadour is going to forgive you if your feet are not baby-ass soft tomorrow. Just make sure you shave your legs in the morning."

"Being rude doesn't help your case." She really didn't want to go, but she also didn't want to leave her friend hanging. "What time do you need me?"

"You weren't listening. We meet in an hour. At the park behind Carpenter's Hall. You don't have to dress up, it's only the museum."

"I really don't know, Nam…" Stella hesitated. "Why today of all days?"

"You still owe me one. Since I never set up a blind date for you, I'll let it slide if you help me out today."

"Blackmailing me isn't fair." She'd just about had enough and couldn't believe Naomi had the nerve to bring this up. "I'm with David again, which makes the need for a blind date obsolete. As you fully well know!"

"Don't use those big words with me. And a promise is a promise. In an hour! At the park! Your bench! Don't be late!"

Stella didn't get the chance to agree or refuse. The line was already dead.

When she arrived at the park, she spotted Naomi sitting between two men. They all had their backs to her. One had his arm draped over the back of the bench, tapping her shoulders. He wore a leather jacket and baseball hat. The other one had the hood of his sweatshirt pulled up.

What was up with a second guy being there? If Naomi had set her up after all, she'd be totally pissed. And she'd let her know it.

"Hey, I'm here," she called.

Hood guy's head swung around.

Stella gasped a lungful of air.

"Surpriii-iiise!" Naomi sang and clapped her hands.

David jumped up, rounded the bench, scooped her into his arms and spun her around, kissing her and laughing and holding her tight.

"I thought this moment would never come, my love," he said between kisses.

"What? Why?" Stella didn't know what to say, or what to do with her hands. "I thought you were arriving tomorrow?" She couldn't tear her eyes away, even after he put her down again and wrapped her arms around him.

Naomi stood, too, and grinned. "Yeah, well, it's a long story."

"You knew this? Since when?"

"Doesn't matter, missy. Maybe your boyfriend can tell you later."

"I still can't believe you're here, baby. Are you real?" Stella pinched her arm. "No. I'm not dreaming!"

Then she looked at Naomi and said, "I guess I don't have time to go to the museum right now." She held out her hand to the other man, "I'm Stella. You must be Frank?"

He shook her hand and said, "Yup. When Naomi told me about her little scheme, I couldn't refuse. It was nice to meet you and David, and now this lady and I are off to the museum."

"Are you sure we have to go?" Naomi whined. "Why don't we get the dogs and take them for a long walk down by the river?"

"Oh, no, I told you if I play along, you're coming to the museum with me," Frank took Naomi's hand and waved to Stella and David. "See ya later."

Stella didn't see any luggage or bags. "Where's all your stuff?"

"In a hotel across the street. I came in a few hours ago and wanted to take a quick shower. It was the hardest thing not to come to you right away, knowing you're only fifteen minutes away. But it was Naomi's first condition for helping me. Can you forgive me?" He kissed her.

"Of course, but now let's get your things and go home."

"There's another condition," he said as they started walking.

"Do I want to know?"

"She made reservations for dinner at seven o'clock tonight. She's bringing Frank. Do you mind?"

"I don't care if she's bringing Frank or Rumpelstiltskin. As long as you're with me. And yes, it's fine, because I don't have anything at home for dinner but a can of soup."

Stella had never eaten at City Tavern. In her opinion, it was reserved for tourists.

But as soon as she walked into the restaurant, she fell in love with the ambiance and was delighted to see the staff wearing eighteenth-century clothes. She knew the original building had been razed in the 1850s, but the tavern was rebuilt in the 1970s, and patrons dined in an accurate and astonishing replica of the historical building where many of the Founding Fathers were frequent guests.

"It's said this building is haunted by two ghosts. One is a waiter, and the other one a bride who died upstairs in a fire on her wedding day," she told David.

Naomi gave her a piercing look. "Listen, missy. Leave your ghost stories at the front door, if you don't mind. We're here to enjoy a nice meal, and we don't need any apparitions."

David kissed Stella. "You can tell me later. But I'm also looking forward to a quiet meal with friends. And with my love." He kissed her again.

"Is this how it's going to be from now on?" Naomi made kissy noises.

Frank turned her to face him and placed a kiss on her lips before he said, "Leave 'em alone."

"Thank you, Frank. I've heard she's difficult to shut up," David said and ducked when Naomi tried to smack him on the head.

"Don't worry, I'll take care of her. She'll be as quiet as a mouse."

"Are you out of your—" Naomi started...and was silenced again.

This'll be fun to watch. Has Naomi met her match?

While they chatted over appetizers and enjoyed a first round of drinks, Stella observed her friend closely. Frank wasn't the type of man Naomi usually dated. He was much more casual and seemed very easygoing. She'd have to quiz her later.

Putting down her menu, Stella said, "So, tell me, Nam, why was going out to dinner one of your requirements for helping David?"

"Well, I've never eaten here, and I figured your lover would want to celebrate with us. If I left you two to your own devices, you wouldn't leave your house for the whole weekend. What I did is called intervention."

"You're allowed to use his real name every now and then." It was annoying when Naomi referred to David as "Troubadour," and Stella didn't want "Lover" to become her latest nickname for him. "And I don't think we need any interventions. But...thank you for picking this restaurant. Why did we never come here?"

"Too much history oozing out of the walls and floors in this place"—Naomi grinned at Frank—"but now I'm getting a totally new appreciation for it."

"After one visit to a history museum? Wow," Stella teased, and studied her menu again. "I don't know what to order. The veal cutlet looks good, the beef tips sound amazing, and the filet mignon, too."

"Order the veal cutlet, and I'll get the beef tips. Halfway through, we'll swap. Remember our dinner in Paris?" David suggested.

"How could I forget?" she grinned.

"David, dahhling! I saw you walk in. Oh, my God, to run into you here, of all places!"

A woman approached their table and leaned down to kiss his cheek. Her platinum blonde hair was styled in an asymmetrical, chin-length bob. Dressed in slim-fitting black pants and a silver top, she was stylish, but the low-cut top, which offered a generous view of two of her clearly enhanced assets, ruined the first impression and gave her an overall unpleasant appearance.

If she was wearing eighteenth-century garb and wig, she would've been a convincing harlot. Yet even a high-end restaurant like this wouldn't go to such lengths for the sake of recreating past times.

The woman kept going, "It's hard to keep track of you these days. You're never long enough in one place to catch up with you." Her manicured fingers rested on David's shoulder and her calculating stare slid over Stella first, then over Naomi, until she stopped at Frank, where the look turned coquettish. "Oh, am I interrupting something? Davy, I don't think I've met your friends before."

"What are you doing here?" His skin had taken on a grayish-greenish shade, and his cold voice gave Stella chills. She was surprised he hadn't even said hello to their intruder.

A terrible sense of foreboding settled in Stella's stomach. No, this couldn't be...

The woman ignored his question and rattled on, "I've wanted to talk to you for several months. Your phone number doesn't work anymore, and I tried to get your new one from Aaron, but that man is as useless as ever. I even explained to him that I want to patch up our little misunderstanding."

The room temperature dropped at least twenty degrees. What had she just said?

"Adrienne, what do you want?" David said under his breath, again not replying to her complaints.

Stella's head snapped around. Adrienne? This was *the* Adrienne?

Okay, call her slow, but it was no wonder Stella didn't recognize her right away. The new hairdo...and additional enhancements...had changed her appearance dramatically compared to the photos Naomi found of her when she and Nam were on the plane. Too bad she hadn't paid much attention.

"I'm in town for a friend's concert tomorrow. Did you hear they're auditioning for *Love Never Dies* soon? I was thinking we could try to get in together. Just imagine the attention we'd create if we were an item again! Maybe onstage *and* offstage... Tell Aaron to get on it!" She patted his shoulder.

"I have no idea what you're talking about, but it's not happening. How dare you even try to get information about me from Aaron? And what the hell makes you think I'd ever want to be together with you again? How twisted is your mind?"

David seemed as surprised as everyone else at their table at Adrienne's appearance, but why didn't he just send her back to where she came from? Or get up and walk away from her? This wasn't some pushy fan who didn't respect his privacy. This was the woman responsible for his insecurities—and, indirectly, Stella's hellish twelve months.

She looked at Naomi for help, but her friend's eyes were glued to the scene at their table. She could almost see Naomi's wheels turning, and tried kicking her under the table to do something, but Frank's legs were in the way.

She had to get out before she did something she might regret later. Without looking at anybody, Stella got up and left.

Once outside, she paced the street in front of the restaurant. It was cold, but she didn't mind the bite in the air. It was nothing compared to the icy fingers holding her heart in a tight fist.

"What are you doing out here?" Naomi demanded, and handed her a warm scarf.

"What's going on in there?"

"You'll find out when you move your ass back in there. Don't you think David could use your support right now? You know he loves you."

"Then why are you out here and not him?" Stella cried out and wrapped the scarf around her shoulders.

"Like it or not, he's trying to avoid a big public showdown. People in there are starting to take photos. This will be all over the tabloids tomorrow."

"She said she wants to perform together with him again. Hasn't she done enough to hurt him? What if he has no say in who his counterpart in a show is?" she asked, but she also cringed to hear how lame she sounded.

"Bullshit! Do you know if it's even true?" Naomi threw her hands in the air. "You know he's a celebrity, and he'll have something to say about who's performing with him. But you better get used to the idea of people trying to claim him or frame him."

"What do you want me to do? I can't go in there and cause a scene."

"No, because wacko Adrienne took care of it all by herself. But you can put on your big-girl pants and stand up for him. Go send the floozy packing." Naomi nudged Stella toward the door. "In with you."

"But all those people..."

"Ignore them. Are you going to live with those people, or do you want to live with the man you love? You've got to step it up, missy. Go after what's yours."

Stella looked from the tavern to Naomi, squared her shoulders and said, "You're right. Enough is enough. He's mine!" She started walking, then stopped and hugged Naomi. "Thank you for helping me focus."

"Don't you worry, I'll be happy to hold the lantern to help you see better. And I'm right behind you if you need reinforcement." Naomi flexed a muscle.

Stella didn't pay attention to the other guests, most of whom were watching David and Adrienne. She ignored the flashes going off where people took photos of the spectacle.

Approaching their table with unflinching determination, she stopped behind David and placed both hands on his shoulders. Adding some venom to her voice she said, "We've never met, but this is enough. I want you to leave David alone."

"Who are you?" Adrienne snarled.

"His girlfriend." Out of the corner of her eye, she saw Naomi walking closer with a full wine glass in her hand.

"You? Are you serious? You're nothing," Adrienne spat out.

"You're wrong," David stood up and wrapped Stella in his arms. "*This* is the woman I love. She's my everything. Now do yourself a favor and go back to your table. This scene doesn't help you or me."

"But… After all we've…" she stuttered.

"Goodbye, Adrienne." He looked around the restaurant. "I apologize for this unexpected show. I'll gladly pay a round of drinks for all, but please finish your meals and enjoy your own company."

Then he turned to Stella. "You scared me when you walked out. I was afraid I'd lost you again."

She snuggled into his arm and replied, "I didn't mean to scare you, and I'm not going anywhere. I only needed to take a few deep breaths. And now I *am* hungry."

Naomi raised her wine and said, "Glad I didn't have to waste this incredibly good pinot noir on Fakerella. I almost tripped there on a loose floorboard…"

Frank laughed and said, "Sit down, woman. This isn't your battle to fight."

"Oh, you! And don't kiss me again. What's up with you men?" Naomi rolled her eyes while she sat down.

CHAPTER 42

David—November 2018

"What are you doing down here so early? It's not even five o'clock." Stella wandered down the stairs and joined David on the sofa. Her hair was tousled, and she wore one of his T-shirts. *What is it about seeing your woman in your shirt?*

"Must be the jet lag. I wanted to make myself a cup of tea, but then I made the mistake of sitting down. Did I wake you up when I left the bed?" He pulled her into his lap where she instantly snuggled against him. "I thought about starting a fire. Would you mind?"

"No, you didn't wake me up, and yes, I'd love a fire. We can have our tea and coffee here. Also, the deli had fresh cranberry-orange scones. I don't know if they taste like the ones you had in London, but they looked yummy."

"Sounds good, my love. Do you need help in the kitchen?"

"No, I've got it, thanks."

While Stella busied herself in the kitchen, he stacked logs and some kindling in the fireplace and lit the fire. His eyes fell on a little book and a framed photo on the side table.

"Wow, when did the book make it out of its banishment?" He raised his eyebrows and smiled at her.

"After London, I decided it was time to let the poor thing out. And the photo of us on the Montparnasse Tower has special meaning for me, too."

He swallowed hard and scratched the stubble on his chin. If he didn't shave soon, he'd give Stella a nasty case of beard-burn in places only he got close to. Just thinking about how she responded to his teasing tongue a few hours ago made him hard. It was almost embarrassing...but only almost.

He wondered how he should best phrase a question he'd been pondering awhile. Might as well grab the bull by the horns and come out with it! *Ugh, not the best phrasing, man...*

"Baby, do you still have the letter?" he asked and shifted his stance to hide the growing proof of his arousal.

"Yes, it's upstairs. It'll *never* see the light of day again."

"I kept a copy of it and burned it after you left London," he admitted. "Wait a minute..."

Taking two steps at a time, he went upstairs and came back with his book. He opened it and showed her the photo he kept in it. "When I bought your book, I also got one for myself. I kept this in mine."

"That was taken in 2015, when we first met." Her eyes got misty.

"Yes, it was. It's why I put it in the book."

She rubbed a hand over her eyes. "Now you wait here."

He heard her rummaging in the bedroom closet, then she returned with her letter. "I want to burn mine, too. Like you did. I want it gone." She tossed it in the fire, and together, they watched the flames engulf it before the remnants whirled around the fireplace one last time and settled in the grate.

David began to kiss the side of Stella's neck, and she responded by making the sexy little sounds he loved to hear. He slid his hand up under the T-shirt and cupped her breast, teasing her hardening nipple.

"Doesn't every fire ceremony need a show of gratitude?" His voice was hoarse.

"Then what are you waiting for?" she asked with a wicked smile—and pulled him to the sofa.

After a long shower and leisurely breakfast—the first one forgotten and grown cold—Stella filled the dishwasher and asked, "What do you want to do today?"

"Why don't we call your parents and ask if they want to meet us for lunch? I'd like to see them again."

She beamed at him. "I'm sure they'd love to. Where do you want to go?"

"I like any place you pick."

"My phone's still upstairs. I'll call Mom from there," she said and ran up the stairs.

He could hear her muffled voice but didn't listen to the conversation. While he watched the last embers cooling off in the fireplace, his mind went back to the nightmare at City Tavern.

Adrienne had almost managed to ruin one of the best days of his life when she ambushed him. He vowed years ago he would never share a stage with her again. If she ever wormed her way into a performance with him, he'd rather be sued for breach of contract than sing one number with her. He made a mental note to ask Aaron if she had indeed tried to contact him and was grateful to know his friend wouldn't fall for her tactics.

Then he thought about how Naomi followed Stella out of the restaurant. He knew the two friends always had each other's backs.

When he contacted Naomi two weeks ago from London, she requested to FaceTime with him. Instead of a polite greeting, she said, "Okay, buddy, I'm glad it's just you and me. And what I have to tell you I'd rather say face-to-face so there are no misunderstandings. You destroyed my best friend's life last year. Without giving her feelings a second thought." He'd never forget how she pointed a finger at him through the small screen.

He told her, "Naomi, you have every right to be mad at me. But you're wrong if you think I didn't give her a second thought. I explained to Stella why I panicked, and I'm sure she told you some, if not all of it. I've apologized to her and asked her to forgive me, and I hope you will, too."

Naomi shook her head and said, "Oh, no, David. I don't care about apologies. We live in a culture where one is expected to accept an apology without batting an eye and to say everything's fine and dandy. But it isn't always fine.

"Apologies are like marriage proposals. Not accepting them is almost impossible. To me, a believable explanation is more important. I have forgiven you, David, but I'm not forgetting what you did. You ended things with Stella in a horrible way, but you and I were also friends, and I don't take friendships lightly. Being adults, we can put the bad memories behind us and move on. You don't have to prove anything to me, but I sincerely hope you'll never let Stella down again. Because I can guarantee you there will not be another chance if you do."

They had talked for a long time, and Naomi was thrilled when he told her how he wanted to surprise Stella by arriving early, and how he needed her help getting Stella to the park where it all began.

He snorted.

"What's so funny?" Stella asked from the stairs. Her voice brought him back to the present. It was the loveliest sound in the world.

"I just recalled my conversation with Naomi when she first gave me an earful and then told me her conditions to help me." He reached for her hand and played with her charm bracelet.

"I hope she wasn't too brutal."

"She was her usual self, and I welcomed her honesty and bluntness."

His phone announced an incoming message. "It's Aaron. Man, social media is a bitch. He's telling me the photos from last night are all over the internet. People sure don't waste time bragging about what they witnessed."

"Did he attach some of the photos?"

"No. I learned long ago it's best to ignore it all. But, wow, listen to this. He wants me to meet with him in Baltimore next week."

"What's going on there? Anything special?"

"He wants us to go to the Hippodrome Theater. I only know it's an impressive theater with lots of history. I'll call him later to find out more." He thought for a moment. "Do you think you can take Friday off? We could stay through Sunday and maybe have dinner with Andrew and Sarah."

"I'll put in for the day as soon as I get to work tomorrow. Are you going to take Andrew up on his offer to tour the Center?"

"I'd like to. Let's call them later, too." David kissed her again. "Did you notice how we're making plans like any other old couple? I love it," he said and nibbled on her neck. "How much time do we have until we meet your parents?"

"Not enough," Stella laughed.

CHAPTER 43

STELLA—DECEMBER 2018

Stella listened while David did his voice exercises upstairs. After his arrival seven weeks ago, they set up the second bedroom as his study. Stella loved how they had fallen into a routine so easily, and didn't want to think about him leaving for France in less than a month.

A gusty wind howled outside, and the sky was full of dark clouds. Stella wondered if they'd get their first snow today.

But it was a lovely day to be decorating their Christmas tree with her collection of ornaments. David wanted to get a fresh tree, so they bought one at a nursery outside of town. She told him he was lucky they didn't live in an apartment, because Philadelphia's fire code prohibited natural cut trees in high-rise and multi-unit buildings.

The tree stood tall and proud in front of the French doors, only slightly crooked near the bottom, but—she thought—imperfections were part of life, and it would look magical when they lit the electric lights. The ornaments she chose were the white porcelain stars and bells she had collected for many years, ever since Naomi gave her the first set as a gift.

She reached for the tree topper and stretched to put it on top of the balsam fir.

"Let me help you, love, before you fall onto the poor tree." David put his hands on her hips and lifted her up. "Good thing you don't weigh much."

"Thanks, I guess," she laughed. "Do you like it?"

"I love it. As you know, my mom always decorates theirs the day after Thanksgiving. I saw it when I was there, and she's still using some of the ornaments Sabrina and I made as kids, but I like your idea of waiting until closer to Christmas."

"It's what my family always did when Luca and I were little, and I have no reason to change the tradition." She clapped her hands, "All set. Want some tea?"

"No thanks. I have to run out for an hour or two. Do you need me to pick up anything from the store?"

"No, we're all set. It'll be fun when everybody's here tonight for our Christmas Eve dinner."

"Is Frank coming? He and Naomi seem to be spending a lot of time together."

"She invited him but wasn't sure what his plans are. He's making a lot of spur-of-the-moment decisions, which she says suits her fine. I'll just include a place setting for him, and if he's not coming, we can take it away."

"Sounds good. Okay then, I'm off. Text me if you change your mind and need something. See you later, love you." He kissed her on her nose and grabbed his warm jacket.

After she carried the empty ornament boxes to the basement, she began to set the table and mused about her earlier comment regarding family traditions. It made her wonder what traditions she and David would create with their children one day.

She was longing to feel his baby growing inside her. But she needed to be patient. At least things were moving in the right direction. Their trip to Baltimore last month had been promising.

David and Aaron had talked to the Board of Directors of the Hippodrome Foundation and been told one of the Foundation's goals was to introduce touring Broadway artists to students, so the students could learn about career opportunities from professionals.

When they met Andrew later at the Center for Music and Medicine, David was equally impressed with their mission and opportunities. At dinner, the men discussed the different programs of the Center and the Hippodrome

Foundation, as well as the benefits and need for music therapy in rehabilitation and in education.

She and Sarah had spent time shopping and catching up over lunch. Sarah took the day off and showed her two of the most outstanding libraries Stella had ever seen. The Enoch Pratt Free Library was opened in 1886, and was one of the oldest free library systems in the United States.

And the George Peabody Library, also nicknamed "Baltimore's Cathedral of Books," was widely recognized as one of the most beautiful libraries in the world, and an essential space for teaching and research.

She'd been in book heaven at both places.

A few days later, David surprised her when he said, "I can't stop thinking about our trip, and want to find out more about job opportunities in Baltimore. If you think about it, either place would be a perfect fit. I'd still be surrounded by music, but I'd also be able to pass on my knowledge to the next generation, or help people who are ill."

"What a wonderful idea. But—won't you miss being onstage?"

He replied, "I admit it's a strange thought, since I've been doing it for so many years. But I'm also ready to try something different and new."

Stella inspected the table and made small adjustments here and there. She wanted everything to be perfect.

She went to the kitchen and made herself a cup of coffee. Then she sat down in front of the tree. Lighting up the tree at the twilight hour, when the daylight waned and nighttime tiptoed in, was one of her favorite things to do.

Nobody was at home. The house was quiet. She listened to Pentatonix Christmas songs and was happy. There was so much to be grateful for.

Frank leaned back in his chair. "Delicious. Thank you for inviting me, guys."

"Stella is turning into a sweet little housewife. But I agree, the beef filet was yummy. I might have to ask you for the recipe," Naomi said.

"I'd be happy to give it to you, but since when do you cook?"

"I don't, silly, but my mom does," Naomi said and reached for the plates to start the clean-up. When Frank offered his help, she gave him a quick peck on his cheek and said, "You stay right where you are and hang out with the guys. You can do plenty of cleaning up when we're in Colorado for New Year's."

Jo said, "You know, Nam, you might want to start thinking about cooking. One day, when you have your own family, they'll probably want to eat every now and then. And not just frozen microwave dinners."

"I don't eat microwave food. Mom cooks every day."

"Did you hear what you just said?" Jo grinned.

"Is anybody in the mood for a nice glass of whiskey?" Rev called as he headed to the bar.

403

While he poured the drinks, he asked, "Jo, what did you say about Nugget having a family? Did I miss something?"

"Not to my knowledge. But some of us are hearing the tick-tock louder than others."

Revan cupped his hand around his ear, "Nope, I don't hear anything."

"Well, it doesn't concern you anyway, Shutterbug, so drop it," Naomi called from the kitchen. "But who's ready to open gifts? I love, love, love gifts!"

Stella chuckled. "Really? Nobody knew!"

Naomi rubbed her hands and almost danced over to the tree, eyeing the spread-out presents. "Do we all open our gifts at the same time, or do we go around and open them one at a time? Who votes for at the same time?" Only her own hand went up. "You guys are mean. Okay, but can I go first?"

"Yes, please," six voices called out, and they all sat down between the fireplace and the Christmas tree.

They had long ago agreed to only buy small but meaning-ful gifts for each other, nothing expensive or extravagant, and it took a while for everyone to exchange and open them all.

"You know, Nugget, had I known about your budding domestic ambitions, I would've gotten you a cookbook. Something like *How to Cook a Rainbow for Hungry Little Mouths*," Revan said later, and raised his eyebrows.

"How very considerate of you, but you won't find me in the kitchen anytime soon. I'm very lucky because Frank likes to cook and doesn't mind the cleaning up, either," she smiled at Frank and snuggled closer to him. "You're the perfect man for me."

"We'll pick up right there later, baby doll," Frank said, and kissed her.

Stella was surprised to see Revan giving Frank a look resembling the dark clouds from this afternoon. But Frank seemed oblivious to the storm brewing over his head. She couldn't quite put her finger on it, but if she didn't know better, she'd say Revan was jealous. Which didn't make any sense.

David cleared his throat and said, "There's one more thing I want to do."

All three women exchanged looks and said a well-choreographed, "Ooh."

Revan mumbled, "Are we in a Hallmark movie?" Which earned him a slap over his head from Naomi and a snarky, "Stop being such a Grinch. Where's your holiday cheer?"

"Sorry, my love, but you're kind of sitting on it," David reached behind Stella and pulled something out from behind the sofa cushions.

"Neat hiding spot, man," Luca said.

"Well, here goes..." David held up two envelopes. "Two envelopes, but you only get one. Which one do you choose? Left hand or right hand?"

"Hmm... what's in the envelopes?" She eyed them, but both were plain as far as she could see.

"Pick one and find out. Only one, though."

She glared at Naomi. "Did you have something to do with this?"

"I didn't do a thing!"

Stella looked at everybody else now. It didn't seem as if any of the others knew what this was about. "Okay, the envelope in your left hand."

David handed it to her. She lifted the flap and peeked inside.

"Two tickets for a performance of *Don Giovanni?* Nice!"

"Yes. But look at the date."

"March 29, 2019."

"I was hoping you'd be there when I take my final bow, when the curtain closes in front of me for the very last time." David swallowed a few times. "Flights are included, of course. Naomi has my credit card details for two plane tickets."

"You said you had nothing to do with this. Liar!" Stella leaned over and gave her a friendly shove.

"Well," Naomi held up two crossed fingers. "I didn't know about the theater tickets. David only came to the office today about the flights. He said he'd explain the rest later."

David pulled Stella close and said, "And it means we'll get to spend a few days in Paris again. You were curious about seeing it in the spring."

Jo asked, "There's two tickets. Who's going with you?"

"Choose wisely, missy," Naomi called out and waved her hand.

"You, of course."

"Good answer!" Naomi beamed.

Stella pointed to the other envelope. "What would've been in the other envelope? Coal dust?"

"Nope, see for yourself," he handed it to her.

"Two more theater tickets?!"

"I didn't know which envelope you'd pick, so I had to prepare two. Maybe you'd like to ask two more people."

She hugged him and said, "Thank you for the wonderful surprise. But way too expensive. You can't pay for the plane tickets."

"It's non-negotiable. Besides, I have connections now." He gave Naomi a high five.

"You said your final bow and last curtain. Are you really giving up the stage?" Luca asked.

"Well, if my next visit to Baltimore goes well, I think relocating there in the spring is a good possibility. Both organizations I visited have interesting openings, and Andrew mentioned a nice neighborhood where Stella and I could rent a townhouse and be within walking distance to work."

"What about you?" Luca asked her.

"I'll go wherever David is."

"We're in this together and will discuss it all in due time, baby," David pulled her into his arms.

She had to work hard to keep the tears from trickling down her face. "Don't make me cry in front of everybody. But this was the best gift ever."

Could life get any better than this moment?

CHAPTER 44

STELLA—MARCH 2019

S he was back! At the Paris Opera House, in the gaudy red auditorium.

Stella reached for Naomi's hand and squeezed it as she entered the exact same private box where she caught a glimpse of David nine months ago. "I can't believe it…"

Julia and Alexander stood as soon as they saw them. "This is unbelievable. I don't know what strings David pulled, but there's champagne! Look." Julia pointed to a small table with two bottles in an oval stainless-steel bucket, and four empty glasses waiting to be filled.

Stella went to the balustrade and pointed to the stage. "When I stood right there in the auditorium last year, I wondered how it would feel to watch a performance from up here. I couldn't imagine I'd like it, but now I have to admit it feels pretty special."

"Yeah, your man is spoiling you. Business class flights, VIP treatment at the theater. What's next?" Naomi mused.

"Do you want me to open a bottle?" Alexander offered.

"Yes!" the women said at the same time.

"Let's hope the cork comes out without announcing to the whole theater we're up here imbibing," Stella added.

"I don't think anyone can hear a sound over the orchestra warming up. And I doubt it's the first time someone has enjoyed a drink here," he said.

"It's so strange to know David will never sing on a big stage again. Singing is his life. I kinda feel guilty for being the reason for these changes," she said after they toasted.

"Don't even go there," Julia said. "Life's about compromises and priorities. After he lost you, he realized what his were."

"I guess you're right. I only hope the transition into the non-performing world will not be too harsh for him."

"That's when he'll need your support the most. Be there for him," Julia said.

"What's he going to do now? Has he made a decision?" Alexander asked.

"Yes, he had a few interesting offers and negotiated a combined deal. He'll be working part-time with the Musical Director of the Opera Theater Program at the Peabody Conservatory in Baltimore. It's part of Johns Hopkins University, and they bring small opera performances to schools across Maryland. Andrew introduced him when we visited. I think he'll enjoy working with children and encouraging them to follow their dreams.

"In addition, he'll be teaching Master classes at the Hippodrome Theater. So I guess he's not completely turning his back on the world of theater and performance. He's only doing it on a smaller scale."

"It sounds amazing. And it won't bother him to be working two different jobs?" Julia asked.

"Not at all. He didn't want to commit to one organization because he likes both, and this allows him to be part of both teams. Andrew also asked him to do some consulting at the Center for Music and Medicine. If an interesting full-time position opens at either place in the future, he can rethink his preferences. And he'll still consider taking on guest roles in stage productions or maybe a movie, but only if it doesn't keep him away from home for too long."

"He should have plenty of opportunities between theaters in Philadelphia, Baltimore, and Washington," Julia said. "Just wait until directors find out he's settling there."

"And what are your plans?" Alexander asked.

"I accepted a part-time job at the Enoch Pratt Free Library. I can pretty much choose my own hours, which is ideal. If I want to go to Philly or travel with David, I can work three longer days and take the rest of the week off."

The orchestra quieted down and the lights in the auditorium were dimmed. For the next three hours, Stella followed the fictional playboy and seducer's story until the demons caught up with him and dragged him to hell.

When she saw David putting his hand up and blowing a kiss to her before he descended into the demons' realms, she laughed with tears in her eyes. Leave it to him to send her a personal message in a theater packed with almost two thousand patrons. Of course he knew exactly where she was sitting. He had planned it all to perfection.

After the finale, when the applause died down and the curtains remained closed, the door to their private box opened. A young woman came in and asked in accented English, "Miss Harrison?" She carried a long piece of cloth over her arm.

Stella stood and said, "How can I help you?"

"I'm Nadine. Come with me, please. I'm taking you to Monsieur Danvers." The woman beckoned for Stella to follow her.

Naomi made a shooing motion with both hands and Julia said, "Go! We'll take Naomi out for a little bit."

"Okay, then. I'll catch up with you all tomorrow." Looking over her shoulder one last time, she left with Nadine. "Where are we going?"

"Monsieur Danvers instructed me to pick you up and to bring you to his dressing room."

"Oh, no, into the lion's lair. How mysterious," Stella joked, but Nadine remained quiet.

When they reached David's private dressing room, Nadine knocked on the door, handed her the cloth bundle and walked away. David stepped out of his room, wearing dark jeans and a white dress shirt together with a half-mask and a long cape.

"Are we going to a masquerade ball? You should've told me," Stella wiggled her eyebrows. "I would've brought my sleep mask and fluffy slippers."

He touched a finger to her mouth, reached for the cloth in her hand, and hung it around her shoulders. It was a cape like his. Taking her hand, he signaled her to follow him.

She couldn't stop the giggles from escaping. "Not even a hello kiss? And oh, by the way, I noticed the kiss you sent me during your curtain call. Unless you ended each of your performances with one, don't you think the critics will comment on it tomorrow?"

David shrugged and continued to lead her to the end of the hallway, where he opened a metal door and descended with her into the abyss of the theater. They went deeper and deeper, through spaces cluttered with electrical equipment and generators, storage rooms and stage props, and it turned colder and colder.

"Baby, why aren't you talking to me? Where are we going?" she wasn't scared, but they were in a very eerie part of the theater, and she shivered in the underworldly atmosphere. Grateful for the cape, she used her free hand and pulled it closer around her.

He glanced at her but kept walking, a little faster now. Her hands where sweating and she wanted to rub them dry. When her fingers almost slipped out of his grip, he stopped walking, kissed her knuckles, then tightened his hold and pulled her down a set of rickety, creaky stairs, into a short tunnel.

They hadn't seen a living soul for a while. Where were all the stagehands? "David, can we please go back?"

Instead of an answer, David began to hum a melody and they stepped out of the dim tunnel into a large cave with a vaulted ceiling.

An underground lake was in front of them, with hundreds of floating candles illuminating the dark surface. Not a ripple disturbed the calm water. A white wooden rowboat with two oars laid across the bench waited at the water's edge.

"The... The lake is real," she whispered.

Again, he didn't answer with words, but led her to a table covered with a white tablecloth. Three fat ivory pillar candles in different sizes bathed the table in a warm yellow light. A bottle of champagne rested in a cooler and two glasses stood next to it, with a single white rose lying across the two flutes.

David pulled out a chair and signaled for Stella to sit down. He took off his mask and placed it next to the crystal flutes.

As soon as she sat, he bent one knee in front of her and pulled a teal-colored soft pouch out of his pocket.

She gasped and opened her mouth, but David put his finger on it.

He pointed around the cave and to the lake. "You never liked the ending of *The Phantom of the Opera*. Why don't we write our own?"

The glow of the candles reflected in his eyes. They were like two dark pools of water, calm on the surface, but deep and mysterious beneath.

David lifted a ring from its velvety cushion.

"My angel, you've listened to your heart and believed in us. For the rest of my life, I want to fall asleep with you in my arms, and I want to wake up with you next to me. I want to be there for you. I want to share our joys with you and ease your sorrows."

He reached for her hands.

"You gave me your heart not once, but twice. Will you entrust me with it for the rest of our lives? Will you marry me and let me love you until I take my last breath?"

She nodded.

She didn't know how she found her voice, but she said, "I love you so much. Yes, I will marry you."

With tears spilling over and trickling down his face, he slid a sparkling ring on her finger. "We belong together." His arms went around her. "I'll love you forever."

Before their lips touched, Stella whispered, "Forever."

THE END

AUTHOR NOTES

───────◇○◠◡◠○◇───────

L ike so many others, I had this dream of writing a novel
since my adolescence, but the inspiration to sit down
and bring something to paper didn't come until the summer
of 2019, when I found myself with nothing to read—which
is rare.

Sitting in the backyard, I thought about my favorite musical
and one of my favorite cities, Philadelphia. I wondered if
a book, or even one paragraph, can have a life-altering
impact on us. I believe the answer is yes.

Gaston Leroux's *Phantom of the Opera* provided me with
the perfect theme and framework for this book. I "saw"
a woman mulling over what the book meant to her. And
because I love the phantom as much as Stella does, I had

no choice but to send her on a journey to pay homage to the fictional character.

I saw the musical *The Phantom of the Opera* for the first time in 1992 in Hamburg, Germany, and many more times since then in different cities—just never on Broadway (yet).

This book could not have been written and published without the unfaltering support of my husband and son. We called in pizza for dinner more times than I like to admit when I was lost in the world of my characters...*just one more page*... Axel and Mika, you are my rock!

I owe big thanks to:

- Susan Blair and Lynn Rhodes for reading an early draft and providing me with encouraging feedback.

- Nancy Porter, owner of Fork in The Road Travel, for double-checking everything travel-related, and valuable overall feedback.

- My beta readers Joyce Greenfield, Kendra Wallace, Kathleen Weekes, and Kristy Murphy.

- My friend Kimberly for taking the time to discuss some of the nitty-gritty with me.

- My friends Carrie Frost and Teresa Johnson for general advice.

- The amazing community of authors and writers! The warm welcome and amazing support is overwhelming—and much appreciated. Each and every day I'm reminded that we're not competitors, but in this together. It takes a village...

Thank you for buying this book! Please consider leaving a review on Amazon or Goodreads.

I hope you enjoyed reading Stella and David's story as much as I loved writing it.

Annette G. Anders

REFERENCES AND ACKNOWLEDGMENTS

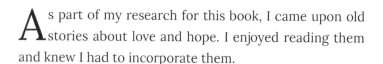

As part of my research for this book, I came upon old stories about love and hope. I enjoyed reading them and knew I had to incorporate them.

- *The Phantom of the Opera* by Gaston Leroux

- *The Death-Wedding of Honfleur* is a story originally told in *Excursions in Normandy, Ed. from the Journal of a Recent Traveller* [*Reise- Und Rasttage in Der Normandie, by Jacob Venedey*] by Frederic Shoberl (1838).

- *Laüstic* is a Breton lai by the medieval poet Marie de France. Her works have been dated to between ca. 1160 and 1215 and she is considered France's first female poet whose work influenced the development of the romance/heroic literature genre to this day.

- The story behind the *La Mère Poulard*, the restaurant on Mont Saint-Michel, is the real-life story of Anne "Annette" Boutiaut Poulard and Victor Poulard. I had the pleasure of visiting this mystic island a few years ago, and knew Stella and Naomi needed the experience of stepping back in time there.

Thank you to the following for helping me make this book shine:

- Editor: Faith Freewoman, www.demonfordetails.com

- Book cover design: Brandi Doane McCann, www.ebook-coverdesigns.com

- Interior design layout/Formatting: Nanette Littlestone, www.wordsofpassion.com

- Author photograph: Teresa Johnson, www.teresajohnson.com

If you like to listen to the songs mentioned in this book, check out my Spotify playlist.

ABOUT THE AUTHOR

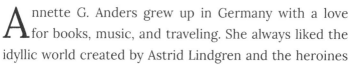

Annette G. Anders grew up in Germany with a love for books, music, and traveling. She always liked the idyllic world created by Astrid Lindgren and the heroines of Jane Austen, doesn't tire listening to ABBA, but also enjoys classical music. When she can't travel, Annette explores the world through the eyes of her favorite writers.

Annette has worked for many years as an Executive Assistant in international research and business consulting institutions in Germany and Switzerland. In 1998, she and her husband moved to the United States, where they raised their son. In 2018, she turned her love for books into a freelance editing career—and found the courage to write her first book in 2019.

Her favorite pastimes include reading, photography, and spending time with family and friends.

Annette looks forward to hearing from readers. Follow her on social media or join the mailing list through her website.

Website: www.AnnetteGAnders.com
Email: author@AnnetteGAnders.com
Facebook: www.facebook.com/AnnetteG.Anders/

THE FULL CIRCLE SERIES

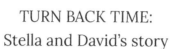

TURN BACK TIME:
Stella and David's story

IN DUE TIME (coming spring 2021):
Naomi and Revan's story

Made in the USA
Coppell, TX
31 March 2021

52769860R10236